VANCOUVER NOIR

EDITED BY SAM WIEBE

BROOKLYN, NEW YORK, USA
BALLYDEHOB, CO. CORK, IRELAND

Published by Akashic Books
©2018 Akashic Books

Series concept by Tim McLoughlin and Johnny Temple
Vancouver map by Sohrab Habibion

Paperback ISBN: 978-1-61775-659-7
Hardcover ISBN: 978-1-61775-683-2
Library of Congress Control Number: 2018931229

All rights reserved
First printing

Akashic Books
Brooklyn, New York, USA
Ballydehob, Co. Cork, Ireland
Twitter: @AkashicBooks
Facebook: AkashicBooks
E-mail: info@akashicbooks.com
Website: www.akashicbooks.com

To Chris and the staff at Pulp Fiction Books,
and Walter and Jill at Dead Write Books,
keeping the city well-stocked with darkness.

ALSO IN THE AKASHIC NOIR SERIES

BOWEN ISLAND
ECOLOGICAL
RESERVE

SALISH SEA

VANCOUVER

WEST VANCOUVER

I

STANLEY
PARK

WATERFRONT

ENGLISH BAY

FINANCIAL
DISTRICT   CRAB PARK

BRITANNIA

YALETOWN   STRATHCONA

COMMERCIAL
DRIVE

KITSILANO

GREEKTOWN

MOUNT PLEASANT

1A

SOUTH CAMBIE

99

VICTORIA-
FRASERVIEW

TABLE OF CONTENTS

PART III: NIGHT VISIONS

INTRODUCTION
Black Rain and Broken Glass

Noir is a messy term. Borrowed from the French and best-known in reference to film, noir has been applied to everything from *The Long Goodbye* to *The Dark Knight Returns*. Purists will only award the term to the work of half a dozen white guys who wrote in the early 1900s. Others throw it around as a loose synonym for *mystery*.

Dennis Lehane borrowed heavily from Arthur Miller when he called noir "working-class tragedy." I admire that definition, I think it's true, but it wanders slightly afield from the heart of the matter.

Noir is bad shit happening to people much like ourselves.

At its heart, noir is the ugly shadow of ourselves we always knew was there, but out of convenience chose to ignore.

You might wonder what shadows could exist in Vancouver, rain-spattered jewel of the Pacific Northwest. Nestled between the US border and the Coast Mountains, the city's postcard charms are familiar even to those who've never been here, thanks to the films and TV shows shot in Hollywood North: *The X-Files* and *Deadpool*, *Rumble in the Bronx* and *Jason Takes Manhattan*. Vancouver is the so-called City of Glass. A nice place, in any case, and much too nice for noir.

Looked at from afar, Vancouver may seem idyllic. But living here is different—cold and baffling and occasionally hostile. While outsiders focus on high-test BC bud, locals see a heroin crisis: Vancouver is home to the first legalized safe-injection site in North America, now heavily taxed by overdoses resulting from street drugs cut with fentanyl. It's ground zero for the National Inquiry into Missing and Murdered Indigenous Women and Girls, a nationwide catastrophe involving the deaths and disappearances of hundreds of marginalized women. Money and status trample culture and community.

If Vancouver is a city of glass, that glass is underneath our feet.

The stories in this collection come from very different writers, yet themes emerge linking them together. Land and violence, sex and community.

Vancouver is a colonial outpost on the unceded territory of three First Nations: the xʷməθkʷəy̓əm (Musqueam), Sḵwx̱wú7mesh (Squamish), and səlil̓wətaʔɬ (Tsleil-Waututh) peoples. Moreover, the city is one of North America's largest immigration hubs, and includes one of the oldest Chinatowns. Land speculation and a lack of low-income housing have created a real estate crisis: most of us nonmillionaires have either left, or cling tenuously to our homes. The cost of living here—the cost of *life*—is examined in Carleigh Baker's "The Midden" and Nathan Ripley's "The Landecker Party."

In the last thirty years or so, half a dozen serial killers have stalked Vancouver's streets. Most of them have targeted at-risk women: addicts, sex workers, those on low incomes, indigenous people, and people of color. Those whose voices struggle to be heard, to whom large parts of the culture remain indifferent. Gendered violence is a part of city life; the topic is tackled here in several forms, in depictions of the sex trade by Yasuko Thanh and Don English, as well as female perpetrators of violence, such as the protagonists of Linda L.

Richards's "Terminal City," Dietrich Kalteis's "Bottom Dollar," and Sheena Kamal's "Eight Game-Changing Tips on Public Speaking."

Neighborhood and community exist in Vancouver, though they are harder to define in a city caught in the throes of gentrification. Whether the elderly immigrants of S.G. Wong's "Survivors' Pension," the Lululemon-clad mothers in Robin Spano's "The Perfect Playgroup," or the aging mobsters trying to hold on to long-lost Greektown in Nick Mamatas's "The One Who Walks with a Limp," communities are made and refashioned by the people in them.

From Stanley Park to the Britannia shipyards, from Jericho Beach to the bohemian mess of Commercial Drive, *Vancouver Noir* offers readers a tour through the dark nooks of the city, from an expert group of guides. These stories knock holes in the City of Glass. They paint a picture of a city in flux, a city struggling to redefine itself. A city under siege by drugs, poverty, racism, colonialism, violence directed at women. In other words, a city like any other.

So welcome to Vancouver, the place where the west ends. And welcome to *Vancouver Noir*. It gets dark here. Know that going in.

Sam Wiebe
Vancouver, British Columbia
July 2018

PART I

Blood Money

TERMINAL CITY

BY LINDA L. RICHARDS

English Bay

I first hear about the assignment through a text, as is usual. The text never varies much in tone, though the number is always different.

Hey, sunshine! How's life treating you?

And my response is always pretty much the same: *I told you it was over. Stop bugging me or I'll block you.* Or, *I've moved on. Let's not do this anymore, okay?* Or something else that indicates there will be no further response. And that's how I know to go to e-mail.

The e-mail is untraceable. It comes from the deep web via a Tor browser and it stays on the server. There's nothing downloaded to my computer. I don't take any chances. And neither do they, even though I don't know who "they" are. Only that I get my instructions, execute the job (pardon the pun), then report back when it's done. Within twenty-four hours, there is a deposit to my Bitcoin account. By now I have more Bitcoins than I know what to do with. Not a lot of the things I desire can be bought. I keep doing the work anyway. At this stage, I wouldn't even know what else to do.

So I check my e-mail. And it is cryptic, but I know what it all means.

49.256094-123.132813 49.283847-123.093670 ASAP. AD.

And a name.

The first two numbers are the target's home. The second

two are the preferred location for the hit. And they want him taken out as soon as possible and it has to be an accident. *AD*. Accidental Death.

I plug the second set of coordinates into an app on my phone. It turns out to be an office building in downtown Vancouver. I book my travel and hotel then get an early night's sleep. Tomorrow will be a difficult day no matter how well it goes. Assignments always equal difficult days. Nature of the beast.

I decide to take my Bersa. Check a bag. I don't plan to use the gun, but I've done some research: license to carry means I can legally bring it along. I pop it into the compartment in my suitcase where I used to store my underwear while traveling. Most of the time I can't remember that person anymore.

There is nothing that binds me to my house. No man, no kids, not even a cat. Still, when I lock the door to go away even for a few days, I leave a little pang behind. Maybe missing something I don't have. Again. I try not to think about that.

There are no direct flights from my local airport to Vancouver. I have to go through Phoenix, an airport I know well, because it's a hub. I have a lunch in the airport so good it's ridiculous. Airport food is not supposed to be excellent, but I savor it. I'm heading to a foreign country. One I've never been to before. I'm not certain there will be anything good to eat. Maple syrup and beavers. Possibly cheese. I just can't imagine what Canadians might eat.

I sleep much of the way to Vancouver. There is nothing else to do. But once we land I have an awakening of the senses. It smells very green. As soon as the plane's stale conditioned air is released, I smell something rough and new. A bit of the mountains. A bit of the sea. My heart quickens with it in a way I don't understand.

In the terminal one must deal with customs.

What is the purpose of your visit?

Why, pleasure. Of course.

What else?

To see this jewel. This well-designed city perched charmingly on the sea.

How long will you be here?

A few days. Perhaps a week. There is so much to enjoy!

Have a great visit!

Oh yes. Yes. Of course. I shall.

The city itself is stunning. City of Glass. Of ocean. The Terminal City, I'd seen in my research. So called because it was the end of the line when they built the railroad. Or the beginning, depending on your perspective.

My hotel is on English Bay facing the ocean. A venerated hotel that has been here since the century before the one just past, I'd read. A long time.

"Do you know Errol Flynn's dick fell off at this hotel?" says one of the young women checking in right ahead of me. There are two of them.

"Who's Errol Flynn?" asks the other.

"Wasn't he with Pearl Jam for a while?" I offer, deadpan. The two girls look at each other, then give me a wide berth as they head for the elevator. I don't blame them. It's probably the right call.

I have arrived in the evening and it's raining. After spending not much time in my hotel room, I grab an umbrella from the concierge and head out the front door into a light and refreshing rain. I don't need time to think, but I've got time to kill and walking seems like the right call.

There is a seawall in Vancouver. It snakes around the edge

of the city, a pedestrian highway at the edge of the water. I walk this now. Not thinking about my destination or if I even really have one, just enjoying the city at night.

I am in a safe area, at least at first, populated by tourists and fashionable couples. I walk on the seawall toward the city, not the big park near the hotel. After a while I have an idea of where I am going. I let my feet take me there.

I walk along the seawall as far as I can, then up a few blocks to where tomorrow I plan to do what I've been sent to do. And when I get where I'm going, I stand there in the rain for a few minutes, looking at the building, thinking of what approach I will take on the following day. I am so focused, and maybe so tired, that I am startled when the front door opens and a man pops out. He is energetic and more youthful than the photo I'd been sent led me to think he would be, but I have no doubt it's he.

Though I am a few feet from the entrance, to my surprise my invisibility shield of middle-aged woman doesn't hold and he crosses to me in a few strong steps. He does it so quickly, I have no time to collect myself and scurry away.

"Is everything all right?" he says. He is concerned. It is possible this is not a neighborhood a woman can safely wander around in by herself at night. I hadn't known that.

"Well, sure," I reply reflexively. "I'm a bit of a tourist. Out for an evening walk. I guess I got turned around."

"I guess you did," he says, and I look at him quickly, but there is nothing but warmth in his voice, on his face. Honest concern. "What's *a bit of a tourist*, anyway? Never mind. You can tell me while we walk. I'm heading home now myself. Where are you staying?"

"I'm at the Sylvia."

He nods approvingly and starts guiding me west as we

walk. "In the West End. Good choice. Charming. Not osten-
tatious. And all the right ghosts."

"Errol Flynn?" I say, pushing myself to keep up with his
longer strides.

"Oh yeah. Him. Sure. But others. Some apparition sits on
the bed in one of the rooms on the sixth floor. Something I
read. You're not on the sixth floor, are you?"

I shake my head.

"You should be all right then."

"Well, *that's* a relief. Where are you walking me?"

"I live in Coal Harbour, which is quite close. I'm going to
see you home."

"Ah," I say, trying not to think about how complicated
this is getting. And then after a while, not minding. We enjoy
a companionable silence, and when we chat, words move easily between us. As we walk, he points out things of interest.
He does it easily and well, and I can tell he is used to being
treated like he has things worth saying. He asks what I do,
and something I'd read in the in-flight magazine provides the
answer. I tell him I'm a civic planner, sent to Vancouver to
evaluate local design.

"A lot of people are doing that now," he says. "I read that
somewhere. Apparently we have a lot of civic design worth
emulating. Who knew?"

I wonder if we'd read the same article, but don't say
anything.

"For various reasons," he says when we reach the hotel,
"I'm loath to go back to my lonely abode just yet. Will you join
me for a drink in the bar?"

We sit at a table by the window. As we sip and chat, a part
of me dips down to darker places. Who wants this man dead?
An ex-wife? A business partner? A competitor? I seldom won-

der. It's not part of my concern. And I seldom have reason to know or find out. I try to stop myself from wondering now.

"Are you married?" I give it thought before saying the words. It might even seem curious if I *don't* ask, that's what I tell myself.

"I was," he says. "I'm not now. What about you?" And this is another thing I find myself liking in him: his directness. Even his eyes meet mine as he asks. A pleasant slatey color. Like stone warmed by sun.

"Same," I hear myself say. "Just the same." And we smile as we sip, almost as though we've shared a joke, something like fire growing between us.

It is not inevitable that he should end up in my bed on the not-haunted third floor of the Sylvia Hotel. When it happens, though, I try not to think about consequences. I wonder at what I am feeling. As though I'd known it would happen from the moment he'd taken those few strong strides toward me as I stood outside his office building in the rain. Like nothing else had been possible. If I wasn't certain of that before, it had become clear in the elevator, the hard length of him pressed into me, his tongue exploring the delicate lines of my ear, my chin, my neck.

By the time our unclothed bodies join in the ancient bed, I know it solidly: this was meant to be. Human touch has become difficult for me. But not here now, with him. His warmth and laughter and the touch of his skin have melted whatever reserve there might have been.

We call for room service after a while. His exertions have made him hungry, he says. And he wants something to drink. He answers the door with a towel wrapped around him and I admire the way the muscles move under his skin.

He's ordered grilled squid and stuffed mushrooms, and a crab cake too big for its own good. We share the food and wine with the abandon and comfort of long lovers. Feeding each other and laughing together, giddy with something too precious to hold.

I like the strong, hot feel of him. And the way laughter storms his face. And the intensity with which he watches me when I speak, meeting my eyes. Watching for signs of things not said. Ever watchful.

There is a time when we sleep, feet touching, his hand cupped gently into the curve between my legs. I don't know when wakefulness falls away, but it comes to both of us all at once. After a while, though, I wake. I pull the covers over us and extinguish the lights and try not to think about what I need to do. As I've said: human connections don't come easily to me anymore. And yet I feel something easy growing more quickly than I would have thought possible. It leaves me a little breathless. Leaves me thinking about the possibility of a life that has more light.

I think about the Bersa, snug in the room safe. See myself, in my mind's eye, creeping toward him, holding the gun to the soft, flat spot just behind his left ear. Letting in the bullet that will find its way home.

His eyes fly open and he regards me levelly. I feel my color rise.

"What are you thinking about?"

"I was thinking about how beautiful you are," I say without missing a beat. "When you sleep, I mean. You looked so very peaceful."

He smiles then. A real smile. His teeth are white and even. A movie star's smile.

"You're lying," he says cheerfully. "But that's okay." I start to protest but he stops me. And he is right. It is okay. My thoughts are my own.

In the morning, he leaves early with the air of a man who has places to go. He drops a kiss on my forehead before he bustles out the door. I realize we haven't made any plans and I find I don't mind. I have my own plans to consider. My own future. Because, at the moment, his doesn't look bright. I feel a pang at the place where comfort and satisfaction should be.

I stay in bed for a while, luxuriating in the feel of crisp hotel sheets and my own postcoital glow. I am outwardly calm but my brain is seething with all of these new permutations. I am processing.

I have a job to do. If I decline, he'll end up just as dead. It might delay things by a week or so, maybe not even that. I'm not the only hired gun around.

Thinking that makes me realize something: they've brought me a long way and from another country to do this hit. There is a reason for that. I think further. Who *is* this guy?

Some simple googling brings results right away, but none that answer the question. He'd designed a Sterling engine that purifies water based on a proprietary system that uses graphene. A byproduct of the purification system had been a graphene-based fuel cell that is thinner and lighter than any other. That had been a decade ago. He now heads a company that develops and implements new solutions for both of those things: water purification and alternate fuel sources. The company has been successful enough that he is also at the head of a large nonprofit doing good work in third world countries cleaning water and providing power. He is a good guy with a social conscience and the success to do something with his gifts. Nothing I read about him makes me like him less.

And someone wants him dead.

I see no one obvious who might be responsible. He heads

a private company, so a takeover move seems unlikely. No visible enemies. But experience has shown me that you can never tell what it looks like inside someone else's life.

I give thought to sending a text, beginning a sequence, to find out who bought the hit, but I know it is a useless avenue. A network like the one I am part of didn't get and stay successful by easily giving up sensitive information. It strikes me that even asking about it might put both him and my livelihood in jeopardy. Maybe even my life.

I consider my options. I can do the job I have come to do. If I do, I will know it was tidy and he didn't suffer. Or I could feasibly *not* do the job without too much loss of face or reputation if I did it quickly and like a professional. "Something's come up." He'd certainly end up just as dead, but it would not be by my hand.

I don't love either of these options, so I toy briefly with the idea of telling him the truth, or something close to it. That there is danger here. For everyone concerned. But I know his knowledge won't protect him. Possibly nothing can.

I go for another walk. The seawall is a different place on a sunny midday than it was at night in the rain—large ocean-going vessels at anchor in the protected water of the bay, while sailboats bob around them like ponies playing in a field.

The seawall itself is packed with jovial traffic. Mothers and nannies pushing strollers. Kids on skateboards gearing up to make injuries they'll regret in a couple of decades. Hairy youths followed by clouds of marijuana smoke flouting a law that is imprecise. All manner of humanity out to enjoy Vancouver in the sunshine. I soak it in, enjoying the feeling of sun on my skin and the warmth that kisses the top of my head. I lift my face to it and my phone rings.

"What does your day look like?" he asks.

"Looks like sunshine," I say in truth. "What a gorgeous city."

"How would you like to see beyond it? I have to run up to Squamish to see a man about a dog. Wanna come? I figure after we could go to Whistler for dinner. How does that sound?"

None of the place names have any meaning to me. It doesn't matter.

"Do you really have to see a man about a dog?"

"I do not. It's an expression. It's a meeting. Won't take long."

"Sure. Okay. If it's not an *actual* dog, that changes everything. I'm maybe half an hour from my hotel. So any time after that?"

"Perfect." I can hear the smile. "I'll pick you up in an hour."

By the time he pulls up in a sleek, long car, I've checked out of the hotel and am sitting on a bench out front, enjoying the sunshine. Waiting.

We follow a ribbon of highway out of town—raw young mountains, snow-kissed peaks, an ocean that laps at the edges of our journey at various points. I am lulled. The feeling of being out of control, like a little kid, and the grown-ups are taking you on vacation. That is how I feel. It's not terrible.

At Squamish, he has his meeting while I find a café nearby and do more research, trying the dark web this time. Still nothing. He truly seems to be a straight-up, straight-shooting, well-liked guy. If there are skeletons, I can't see them.

"You looked *so* intense," he observes when he joins me. "As though what you were contemplating was life and death."

"I was googling you."

"Me? Why?"

"I just wondered if we had . . . I dunno? The right *stuff*."

He drops down into the chair opposite mine. "Right for what?" he asks with an air of innocence.

"Exactly," I say, deliberately obtuse.

"What did you conclude?"

"No conclusion," I say tartly. "And here we both are."

"Exactly," he says. And the smile he gives me goes right to his eyes. "And what would I find if I were to google you?"

"Nothing," I say. "I am an enigma."

One eyebrow shoots up, but he doesn't say anything.

"A cipher," I add. "Maybe I don't exist at all."

"A cipher. An enigma. Those are interesting ways to describe oneself. And if that is the case, how is it that this cipheric—"

"I don't think that's a word."

"—enigmatic woman should come into my life? What message does that bring?"

"That would be an arrogant way to frame things," I say, smiling brightly and hoping he doesn't see how close to the mark he's come.

To my relief, he laughs. "It would, wouldn't it? Of course. Everything is about *me!*"

"But all our worlds are, aren't they?"

"I guess they are. Never mind. Let's get back on the road. We've still got nearly an hour before dinner."

The big car slips along the highway soundlessly for a while before I chance the question I've been formulating. It seems a risk worth taking. And we've got a long drive.

"If someone were going to kill you, who would it be?" I say, as conversationally as I can manage.

He looks at me quickly before pulling his eyes back to the road. "That's a weird question."

"Right?"

He laughs. I'm not sure if I hear an uneasy note, though I listen closely for it.

"Okay," he says. "You first."

"Me?" He's taken me by surprise. He does that a lot. "Well . . . I'd have to think."

"That's what I'm doing. My turning it around was a stall tactic."

"Ah."

"But that doesn't mean I'm not interested. Go ahead and answer."

"Well . . . there might be too many to count," I say truthfully. "But they wouldn't know my name."

"Well, it would seem you are safe then."

"Yes, that's right."

"So no one in particular? Your ex?"

"No. He's dead."

"I'm sorry," he says quickly.

"It's okay," my response is automatic. In this moment almost not remembering the man who had been my husband. I put it from my mind. "Sometimes I barely remember myself."

"Children?"

"No," I say, turning my head quickly. I watch the darkening scenery. We are powering through a forest. The trees going by so fast, they are a solid blur of brown and green.

We are quiet for a while. When he speaks it's like there has been no interruption.

"I don't think there's anyone who would want me dead. I don't know if that means I've lived an exemplary life or if I'm just too vanilla."

"Maybe neither," I say. "Maybe something entirely different is true."

"I think most people go through their whole lives without anyone ever trying to kill them," he says, as though he's given it some thought.

"You say that based on what?"

He laughs. "I don't know. The number of people running around not dead?"

"So not your ex-wife?"

"We're still on the kill-me thing?"

I grunt.

"Okay then," he says. "But not my ex. No. We get along and our arrangement suits us both. And she's well compensated. It's possible she'd get less money if someone offed me."

"Well that's good. No one wants to sit around wondering if his ex is thinking about putting a knife in his back."

"Exactly. So do I pass?"

"Pass what?"

"Well, I don't know. It felt like some kind of courtship test. I wonder how I did."

"Anyone ever tell you you're too competitive?"

"All the time." He pats the steering wheel. "How else do you think I ended up with a Tesla?"

"You play to win." It's not a question.

"Always."

He is slowing, pulling into the village. We are months from ski season, but at a glance, the sort of Alpine-village-meets-Rodeo-Drive motif seems to have something for everyone year round.

Walking around the village, I see it is even more charming and unreal than I'd first suspected. Disney does a ski village. Quaint little shops, trendy bars and eateries block after block. See and be seen. He leads me into one of these.

The food is exceptional yet somehow not memorable,

though conversation between us is as engaging as ever. It's easy to talk with him. No uncertain pauses or painful holes. I am easy with him. I surprise myself.

After dinner, we walk through the village hand-in-hand, sharing jokes and effortless conversation. In that walk, a shaft of pure happiness comes to me. Just this moment filled with nothing but what is right here, in front of me. For the first time in my recollection, everything I have is enough. And maybe I am enough too.

Maybe.

Other thoughts try to crowd in, but somehow I keep them at bay. *Just a little longer,* I plead with no one at all. *Just let me feel this a bit longer. I'll figure things out later, but right now let me have this.*

"So what now?" he says when we're heading back toward the city.

"I don't have a plan."

"You checked out of your hotel." It wasn't a question.

"Yes," I say.

"How long are you in town?"

"I'm not sure."

"You'll come and stay with me."

"All right."

His place is exactly what I'd expected. The top floor of a glass high-rise with views of the city all around and whispers of ocean and far mountains beyond.

"Do Vancouver views get any better than this?" I ask.

"Not much," he admits. "That's how I ended up here."

"It's all about the view?"

"Sure. And the jetted tubs. Check it out."

He leads me to three bathrooms, each one more exquisite than the last.

"Multiple bedrooms too," he says with a theatrical leer. "You can take your pick."

"I'll want one close to where you are," I quip back, a line he finds uproariously funny.

He opens a beautiful bottle of wine and we sit on high stools at the counter in the kitchen. The view of the city is stunning. It takes my breath away.

"So beautiful you could die."

He looks at me sharply. "What is it with you and dying all the time?" I can't read his voice.

"I . . . I don't know. I've . . . I've lost people. I guess that's what it is. It brings it closer. Makes it more real."

"Your husband," he says.

"Yes. Him . . . and others. Listen, I'm enjoying myself so much with you. I don't really want to talk about this now, okay?"

"Some other time, maybe?"

"Yes. Okay. Some other time. Maybe."

We both know it is a lie.

In the morning, he gets up to go to the office. Before he leaves he drops a kiss on my forehead and a set of keys on the bed.

"Make yourself at home. And if you're into it this eve-ning, there's a new restaurant I've been wanting to check out. You're a good excuse."

"Again with the excuses. I don't know how I feel about that."

"Dork," he accuses.

"And the keys," I say. "Aren't you afraid I'll rob you blind?"

"Not particularly. As far as I can see, there's nothing more precious than you in this apartment."

I just look at him, my heart in a cloud. I don't know what

to say and part of me feels dangerously close to tears. I put it down to hormones and move on.

Without him in the space to warm it, the apartment is even more massive. I drink the coffee he left for me and nibble on some fruit, then roam around the space dwarfed by his bathrobe, looking at his stuff.

In the sports-themed media room I turn on the television, then spend a quarter-hour figuring out how to make the channels work, remembering for a moment a time when there was only on and off.

When I finally locate the channels, they are filled with news. A serial killer is under discussion. Everything is heinous. There are hushed tones. The thought comes to me that there are those who would view me as a serial killer. I sink into the plush sofa behind me, pushed by the weight of this thought.

They would not be wrong, those people. I have killed serially. One after the other, I have taken lives. I don't know how many now.

I wonder if I have not considered it that way before because of the money. There is no emotion for me with any of these killings. It's a job. These are not random, violent acts. I am a professional. I put thought into what I do, never emotion. And the deaths are always humane. Many of my targets go from living to death completely without awareness. I've watched their faces at times, so I know.

I look again at the sketch of the unknown serial killer on the screen.

I think again of my lover, my host.

I close my eyes tightly. Push back the flood that threatens. I've held it off this long. It has been years now. I know I can do it again. I turn my attention back to the screen. The clipped Canadian accent now describing the killer's heinous act. She's mixing gun control into the conversation baldly. And she is matter-of-fact. There are statistics that all add up to the fact that people kill people with guns. The numbers are so horrendous they seem to make no sense. So deeply do I immerse myself in these thoughts that when my phone rings I jump, startled, and feel my heart begin to pound.

"What are you doing?" His voice, firm and warm. I suddenly want him here. To feel the firm, real length of him. To feel his strength. His warmth. And, yes, his desire and humanity.

"I'm watching television, if you can believe it."

"Good! You figured it out. Bright girl. I often have trouble with it myself."

"Why are you calling? Did you want to check to see what I stole?"

His laugh is deep. I could listen to it all day.

"Not at all. But if you *do* steal something, can you please take the sculpture in the foyer? My decorator said I paid a lot for it, but I don't care for it much."

We chat a bit more. To me we sound like normal people and that wrenches at my heart. I had not thought I'd sound or feel like normal people again.

And yet, of course, we aren't like normal people at all. The reality of that washes over me again in a wave.

"You ever think about running away to a desert island?" The thought comes from nowhere and I just blurt it out.

"Let's do it. I'll peel grapes and fan you with coconut leaves."

"What sort of desert island has grapes?" I ask.

And so on. Because it is right there and because we can.

We agree: I'll meet him at the restaurant at six and then we'll come "home" together. The way that makes me feel confuses me so deeply I can't look at it.

I spend the rest of the morning performing a methodical search of the premises. I don't know what I'm looking for but I need to do something to dispel the restless energy. Plus I have questions. And I feel some of the answers might be hidden here.

So I toss the place. Searching deeply and carefully without leaving a trace. I don't know what I'm looking for but when I find it—deep in a bathroom cabinet—everything falls into place.

It is a stash of drugs. Prescription medications. Zytiga. Rasburicase. CAPOX. Lenalidomide. Dexamethasone. Elotuzumab. Neupogen. And more still. I have no idea what I'm looking at, but all of the prescriptions have been filled within the last year. And they are all in his name.

I photograph the bottles, then replace them before heading to my laptop to hunker down and do some more googling. I easily determine they are all drugs used in the treatment of cancer and, coordinating the dates, it doesn't take an oncologist to guess that the prognosis is not good.

I don't remember the rest of the day. There was waking in his arms. Then my discovery. And there was his potential explanation. And there was nothing I could put between that would have the balance of the day make sense for me.

The restaurant proves to be the kind Vancouver does very well. Elegance so understated it appears causal, until you glance at the prices and see a different story. In this one, everything seems like traditional comfort food, but with some exotic twist. And so hamburgers, but instead of bacon, the menu advertises the addition of lardon. And coleslaw isn't just chopped cabbage, it's a creamy ginger slaw with jicama and organic heritage carrots. It all seems a bit much.

"Isn't this place fun?" he says when he joins me.

I smile. He appears happy to be pleasing me, so I leave it be but find myself watching him closely, a new layer between us now. Are his hands stable? Does he look at all wan? How do his clothes fit his frame? But I only know this version of him; no *before* to hold against the *after* in front of me.

I find I can't focus enough on the menu and ask him to order for me. He lifts an eyebrow in my direction, but doesn't say anything, ordering vegetables that have been variously roasted and then put together with strong flavors—beets with harissa, cauliflower with chimichurri, and a chicken that has apparently been flame-broiled under a brick, which seems senseless, but I hold my tongue as I sip the cocktail he ordered us in advance of the meal.

"You're quiet tonight. Is everything okay?"

"Not really," I say. "There's something I want to talk to you about. I don't know where to begin."

"Sounds ominous."

Another sip. "It is."

"You want to talk about it now or leave it until after dinner?"

"Are you sick?"

"So we're opting for now."

"I think it's possible you are unwell."

The levity falls off him and he looks at me, exposed. There's a sudden haggard cast to his features.

"Sorry?" And it seems to me he says it in such a Canadian way.

"Yes," I say.

He dips his eyes to his lap. Then raises them to a point just above and to the left of my face. He is searching for a reply, for something to say. But he can't meet my eyes.

"How could you tell?" he asks at length.

"I couldn't. I didn't. I found your stash."

"It wasn't out."

"I dug."

"Ah." He drops his eyes again. I can't imagine what he is thinking about.

"How bad?" I ask when neither of us has said anything for a while. The remnants of cocktails are whisked away. Wine brought and approved and poured. We are sipping that, largely ignoring the appetizers that arrive at the same time.

I see him consider my question then appear to decide to give up and give in. I have the feeling that whatever he tells me at this point will be the truth.

"As bad as you can imagine," he says. It's not what I want to hear.

"You don't look sick." The words escape before I can stop myself.

He laughs. A brittle sound. "I even say that to myself. To my mirror self. It's foolish, right? *Perfect health.*"

"And yet . . ."

"Exactly. I'm assured it won't last."

"The appearance of health?"

"Right. I'm told from here it will get ugly."

"When?" I ask, but I don't think I really want to know.

"Weeks. Possibly months. Certainly no longer."

"And so you ordered a hit." My voice is quiet. Still. I can feel tears standing in my eyes, but I will myself not to cry.

He looks at me sharply. Is he surprised? Or not surprised at all? I can't tell.

"That's right. It seemed the most humane thing for all concerned."

"Under the circumstances."

"Yes."

"What were the specifications?" I ask, though I think I know the answer. "How did you imagine it would be?"

"Well, obviously, I want it to be fast. Other than that, I'd rather not know."

"That makes sense."

The waiter arrives with our entrees. We sip some more at the wine and push the food around on our plates.

"I really am very sorry to learn all of this." I hesitate. Add, "I can't even tell you how sorry I am."

"Thanks. And I guess I know."

"I guess you do." I hesitate again. And then, "So . . . now?"

"I don't want to know. Don't want to see it coming."

"But now is too soon," I protest, keeping my voice calm. And my heart.

"I don't want to be one of those who goes out flailing." He says this calmly. Matter-of-fact. "I can't be."

"But you're so far from that. Look at you! It could be years."

He shakes his head. "Not years, no. Do you think I would do this lightly? I've given it a lot of thought. All of the angles, keeping in mind my kids, my insurance, the business, everything. This is the best time."

And suddenly I understand. "Things go better if you don't die of the disease."

"Yes."

We put it away for the time being. We have our dinner. It is delicious in addition to being pretentious. Afterward we walk hand-in-hand down Robson Street, stopping to watch street performers. He asks if I want my fortune told by an old woman who is reading tarot cards at a table she has set up outside Muji. I decline. I understand that there is nothing in the future that I need or want to know.

That night we make love with a new ferocity. We are clinging to something that can't be held, that's how it feels.

I wake to strong sunlight and the call of seagulls. I get up before he does and pull the pieces of myself together. Then I pack my things. It doesn't take long.

He wakes as I head for the door.

"Will I see you again?" he calls, his voice sounding suddenly weaker. Not from illness, I'm sure of that. But from something that wrenches my heart.

I don't answer, as I leave his key on the sideboard next to the sculpture in the hall. What is there really to say?

I go to the airport. Get a rental. I only need it for a few hours. I park it safely, my stuff neatly in the trunk. I head out on foot to find what I need. It doesn't take long. The car is long and old and perfect for my needs. It is solid, like a tree, and the ignition is broken easily.

From the time I sight the car to when I start it with a screwdriver is under five minutes and then I'm gliding around in a full-sized piece of Detroit steel that was old enough to vote before I was.

I don't wait long outside his office. I know I've timed things well. We haven't known each other long, but I have a handle on his routine and so I idle the big car down the block. Lying in wait.

When he emerges from the building, I try not to analyze the firmness of his step or the jut of his chin, the tilt of his head. I try not to think about how he is feeling. Is this a good day for him or bad? Is he in pain? Has he said all his goodbyes?

I follow him for three blocks before I see the right moment to approach. I wonder if he feels the shadow or the ghost of me, but I discard the thought. It is fanciful, and I have no place for that here.

I begin to accelerate as his feet leave the curb. I admire again the spring in his step, the length of his stride.

He is in the middle of the intersection as I reach him. It happens very fast.

SATURNA ISLAND

BY TIMOTHY TAYLOR

Kitsilano

1

Friendship. *You know it's real when it ends in blood.*
Harris wasn't sure who said that. Maybe nobody. But
as he typed the sentence—fingers to the keys of his
computer, hands shaking—it had the ring of truth.

Fifteen years gone. They were stupid kids not to see it
back then. Harris typed that too: *Saturna Island, that whole
bohemian summer. We were stupid kids.*

Drinking and arguing and fucking. Harris remembered
rocky beaches, dense forests, steep cliffs, a TV tower, and an
auto graveyard in the deepest part of the forest where they
took morning hikes. He remembered the ferry from Vancouver every Friday afternoon they could get away, cutting the
steel-blue waves. Their shared ritual, seeking freedom from
jobs they hated. But didn't all such cleansing rituals conceal a
sacred violence in the end?

Harris typed: *Sacred violence.* He thought of Roen who
ran the B&B on Boot Cove where they'd all stayed. Sitting
at that big dining room table while the Szekszárdi and the
weed went around. Arguing about film and music and their
dreams for the future. Murch was going to quit lawyering,
go work at Habitat for Humanity. Purma wanted to counsel
teens. Harris was still a banker then, not yet having quit to
become a writer—three published crime novels featuring a

detective named Harvey Raven, a recently cratered marriage, broke and alone in a Kitsilano basement surrounded by empty pizza boxes and spent Tetra Paks of French Rabbit pinot noir, remembering.

Time to end this, Harris thought. Typing now: *Time to end this.*

Roen had been the leader: thin, handsome, Roman nose, dark hair flowing to his shoulder blades. A musician, he said, though plucking tunes for his girlfriend Calliope was the only performance anyone ever saw. The B&B was owned by a man named Jimmy. Biker, Roen said. Member of the Exiles.

Bullshit, Harris thought at the time, given the fact that things Roen said often were. But then it all turned out to be crucially true. Some boring Tuesday at the bank. Roen calls. He's in town hanging at the Railway Club waiting to meet the man. Wouldn't Harris like to join them? And Harris said yes, hating himself for his seeming vulnerability to whatever Roen might suggest.

No subtle clues required. Jimmy arrived wearing Exile colors complete with a *One Percenter* patch. And in the awkward fifteen minutes of small talk—before Jimmy downed two fingers of Maker's neat and made his departure—Harris was mostly successful in not staring at the tattooed tear leaking from the corner of Jimmy's right eye.

Roen of course had to spill everything soon as the guy was out the door. Jimmy popped down from Whistler every couple of weeks with a delivery, Roen said. Cash. Like twenty-five, thirty grand, dropped off in a briefcase similar to the one Roen then produced from under the table.

"Fuck sake," Harris said. "Don't show me that!"

But Roen knew he was curious. So here came all the details. The shrink-wrapping involved, the secret storage compartment in the old studio building at the bottom of the B&B orchard, the old key he then flourished on a key fob shaped like a guitar.

"All access, motherfuckers," Roen said, tossing the keys onto the bar while Harris recoiled. "What? This is material. I thought you wanted to be a *writer*."

Fucking Roen and Murch and their snickering about his pathetic ambitions. Roen the wannabe musician/crook. Murchma-fucking-Ghandi.

Harris at the table in his tiny kitchen, hands quivering over the keyboard. Of course he'd still been on the ferry that Friday, the whole gang as usual. Choppy seas on the voyage out, something changed in the air that he was not detecting. Purma and her friend Zach. Shanny, with whom Murch devoutly wanted to sleep. Her friend Jin, who Harris could still close his eyes and see, black hair shining in the dusty rays of sunshine coming in through a cracked window. How many crossings had been made by then? How many ritual cleansings to prepare them for that final night? On the ferry. Over dinner and all that wine and arguing and job talk that climaxed with an inebriated Shanny climbing onto a chair to announce that she could never be involved with a lawyer.

Harris took no pleasure remembering Murch's humiliation. Something had been launched in that moment. Something Harris saw now in the dark clouds rolling to the top of the inlet. Gray rain approaching. Shanny poised in memory, working it through. You couldn't trust lawyers, she'd finally announced, because lawyers were paid to lie. And thus was the entire law itself a lie.

Silence in the room. Pity for Murch who was red-faced and seething. Except Roen, who only twisted the blade: "Isn't that true, me droogie? A lawyer will rep a drug dealer that he knows is guilty. He'll rep a drug dealer who's stashed away money somewhere, his proceeds from crime, money that will later be used to pay the lawyer's own bills. Isn't that what Shanny is saying, what makes the entire law itself a lie?"

The evening unspooled. Shanny and Murch continued to argue. Calliope cried for no real reason. Roen disappeared upstairs only for Harris to numbly register that Jin had gone up the same stairs only moments prior.

Purma joined him on the deck, smoking Pall Malls and smirking. Harris realized he was host to murderous, omnidirectional thoughts. The futility of everything. The smell of blood.

Black rain on the window in Kitsilano, the storm unfurling. Harris hearing Purma as if she were in the room, speaking her precise and killing words. Jin was gay, anyway. They'd kissed earlier, no big thing. One other thing too. "You mind I say one other thing, Harris?"

Like he could stop her. Square face, dark-skinned. Punjabi, he remembered, daughter of a big-time area trucker. Purma didn't think he was destined to be a writer, she went on to say. And he remembered her words on the topic as if they were typed on the page in front of him, which he realized then that they were, his own type, letter by painful letter. *You're a banker dude and good at it. Ford Windstar, wife, kids, and dogs. Harris, cheer up. I predict you end up with a minivan and lots of money.*

Harris in agony then, and now. Harris with tears streaking his cheeks. The phone ringing. Four in the afternoon, rain hammering down. Harris had just cracked his second beer of the day that would end once again down in Chianti's bar over wine and more wine. He caught his face in reflection in the darkened window. The bandage applied late last night was leaching blood.

What had the man said on the beach where Harris had

been drunkenly wandering? Harris couldn't remember. Only what the man did. Three quick applications of what felt like a concrete fist.

Harris, broke and alone with a busted face. Fifteen years it had taken for the blood to flow, and it was flowing now.

His phone ringing and ringing. Harris typed the words before picking up. He just knew.

Fifteen years later, Murch calls.

2

Murch started in like no time had passed at all: "Writer dude. World's most coveted jobs, droogie. Up there with porn star."

Harris was holding a fresh beer to his face in his crappy apartment in Kits. The rain had stopped. No rainbows. Just the threat of more rain. "Murch," he croaked, "how goes building houses for poor people?"

Murch laughed and shifted his weight in what Harris imagined was an expensive leather chair. He was visualizing Murch's thirtieth-floor harbor views, mountains opposite, sailboats tracing lines in the water. Murch had quit lawyering and gone into real estate, where any idiot could score.

"Follow the money," Harris said.

"Or be poor," Murch said.

"The law taught you that."

"It did indeed, me droogs."

"But the law is a lie, Murch. Don't you remember that?"

Big laughs. Harris hated himself for being pleased.

"My God, Shanny," Murch said, "she sure had a rack. Saw her in Home Depot a couple years back. About the size of an eight-person tent. But listen."

So here it came, as quick as that. And the rain surged harder than before, charging up the slope of Larch Street toward him. Harris with his eyes closed, seeing that strewn dining table and empty room. It was about Roen. Harris knew it.

"Shit news, man," Murch said. "Roen's dead."

Harris leaned forward, elbows on his knees. Suicide. A week, maybe ten days prior.

"Jesus," Harris said, hand in his hair, scalp sweating.

Bullet to the head, Murch informed. "All fucked up at the end too. Living in the Downtown Eastside, drugs and scumbag friends. You know about this, me droogs?"

"No," Harris said. "Hadn't heard from him since way back."

So Murch filled him in. Seemed Roen had actually made an album that got some play. Then got ripped off by a manager, taken for everything. Tax bills. Rent arrears. Bankruptcy. Welfare. Escalating addiction problems. "A decade later he's broke like you never get unbroke."

"Fucking fuck," Harris said. "Meth?"

"Purma said dope," Murch replied. "I thought that was heroin but what the fuck do I know?"

So Purma was in the picture. Purma, who Harris would've been happy never to see again. "So they were in touch? Purma, Roen?"

She'd gone into addiction counseling and Roen had walked in her door. "Three months ago," Murch said. "He was at quit or die. So she helps him out. Six weeks clean. Then something happens."

Hard relapse. Worst thing for an addict, apparently. He disappeared and Purma finally had the cops bust down his door. "Grim scene," Murch continued. "The body liquefies after a week. Who knew? Here's the thing, though."

Not this, Harris thought. No fucking funeral for a friend. But it wasn't that. Ten times worse. There was a will. Purma had it and wanted them to take a look.

Harris's right ear was ringing. Amber pus was oozing from his cheek and came away on his fingers, sticky and odorous. The man had said something before punching, from the shadows of a black hood.

"You okay?" Murch asked.

"All good," Harris said. "All good."

Thinking hard here, calculating, weighing what new things the moment now made necessary.

"This one time," Harris said. "Totally forgot, me droogie. I saw him, I mean. I saw Roen."

3

Murch's office. Priceless art and beautiful real estate people rushing around. Murch in gleaming black wingtips, blue striped shirt, dark suit. Grinning, of course. Big hand outstretched. "Writer dude. Warning: I'm a star fucker."

"Let me just come clean," Harris said. "It was me. I killed Roen for fucking Jin that one time."

"You did too, didn't you? You psychopath. You fucking simmered for fifteen years then wasted him."

"Ask," Harris said, fingering the bandage. "But it's a boring story. I got jumped."

"Course you did," Murch said. "Purma's in my office. Drink? Perrier? Latte? You want booze but it's the twenty-first century, for fuck's sake, not *Mad Men*."

Thirtieth-floor views, boats in the harbor. Check, check. And with the whisper of a glass door breathing shut, they were together again. Purma, with the soil-y smell of patchouli about her. A courier bag over one shoulder and an envelope in her other hand. So Roen joined the reunion in his own way. No mistaking why old friends were gathered. *Do not bend, fold, or mutilate.*

Purma took Harris's hand in her iron grip. "Harris," she said, "I stand corrected."

"Meaning he got more beaten up last night than expected?" Murch said. "Careful, he's dripping."

"A few days ago," Harris said. "It's healing."

"I meant you becoming a writer. Harvey Raven. Serious props, man." Purma still had not released his hand.

"You seriously read one?" Murch asked. "I had to google that shit. Amazon ranking five million something. Right on."

"Ignore him," Purma said. "I read all three. Sorry for what I said on the island. That was me being jealous."

Harris was stunned. She projected such power. Chin high, proud to clear her personal air.

"Twelve-stepping," Murch said. "Hey, respect."

"Yeah, that's it," Purma said, finally releasing Harris's hand. "No more vodka and OJ for breakfast. Twelve years now and the best decision of my life. Harris, we good?"

"Sheesh, you coulda called him," Murch muttered, gesturing to the couches.

"It's fine," Harris said, sitting. "It really is."

So they turned to the envelope, Purma extracting a single sheet of paper and cutting right to it: there was no money, no bank accounts. Roen was on welfare by the end.

"You saying he didn't own that place on the island?" Murch with this hands spread.

Purma read on. The contents of his apartment were what remained. And Roen had left instructions for the dispersal of these: *Let any friend of mine take one thing, if any useful thing might be found.*

Poetic, Harris thought. And emotion surged, affection and regret.

"I already took a guitar with no strings," Purma said. "His

other so-called friends don't deserve shit. But you two have a look."

An awkward silence fell, but there was no refusing. So Harris took the key from Purma and she stood to leave. Almost, but not quite.

"Harris," she said, "you saw him near the end."

Yeah, he'd told Murch already. "A couple months back."

"Any chance it was three weeks?"

Harris squinted. "Don't remember. It was a random thing."

In Chinatown. Lunch with a friend. Harris turned a corner and there he was. Skinny as hell. Harris didn't recognize him at first, not until he swept the hair out of his eyes and held up a hand in greeting. The wheelchair was for his ankle, Roen explained. Twisted it falling out of a friend's truck.

"All right," Purma said, shouldering her bag, turning toward the door. But then not leaving. Harris waited, dread mounting.

"Either of you remember a guy named Jimmy?" she asked.

Not this, Harris thought, wondering how far Roen had spread his secret story. But he only shook his head and squinted again. Murch had stopped texting and was listening too.

"Guy who owned the B&B," Purma said. "Well, he's dead too. It was in the news."

"Missed that," Harris said. "What'd he die of?"

Of being burned alive in his Dodge Viper parked out behind the old grain terminal, Purma said. Hands tied to the wheel so cops weren't thinking fuel leak. "That was a month ago," she explained. "A couple weeks later, Roen. Is that weird?"

Murch picked up his phone again. Harris shrugged, made a face like, *Who knows?*

Purma with her hand on the door handle. But with one

more thing to say, Harris sensed. Purma and her dramatic last words. She turned to face him again.

"You didn't go drinking with him, did you, Harris? You couldn't have known. But he was six weeks clean. And best I can figure, he picks up a beer at the Union Tavern and a week later he's dead."

Harris frozen, hands spread. No, no. He never did. And with that Purma was out the door. Gone.

4

Murch had work still to do, so they made plans to meet at Roen's place. Harris walked down Hastings Street into the Downtown Eastside, buoyed in mood by the dereliction still to be found there. Spiffy restaurants on the 100 block, sure. CrossFit gyms and beardos with purse dogs. But east of that, it all skidded back to the gritty norm. Boarded-up buildings. Parks full of drifting figures in hoodies with gym bags full of whatever had been most recently stolen. Bad dental situations. Scabby arms. Harris couldn't deny the faint encouragement— now under the milky gaze of a hooker on Carroll Street—of realizing his own problems might be smaller.

Murch was late. Forty minutes. The light was failing and the air was cool. Harris hadn't dressed for standing around the Downtown Eastside. He was shivering and ill-tempered by the time he saw Murch clicking up the sidewalk on leather heels, communicating with hunched shoulders and a grunted first greeting that his own life had by far the greater concerns. Files. Clients. Kid dramas. A hot dinner waiting at home served up by a nanny from Manila.

"You could have started," Murch said. "Like I'm dying to get my hands on Roen's shit."

Six floors up, no working elevator. The woodwork squealing underfoot, every door leaking garbled voices, moaning, arguments. At Roen's apartment Harris fumbled the key into the lock, then pushed the door inward so they could process the two hundred square feet of squalor that had been Roen's final plot. Broken toilet, dangling sink, peeling walls. Clothes spilled out of garbage bags. Food wrappers covered the fraying carpet. There was a metal counter down one wall strewn with evidence of complex cookery: burnt spoons, a one-ring burner, dirty glassware. There was the sagging bed frame where Purma said the body had been found. No mattress. But a striped blanket with tattered edges, blackened blood spatters across the headboard and the wall.

Murch, surprisingly, did not recoil. He stepped past Harris, navigating through the garbage and crusty clothes to the center of the room where he stood still, taking it in. He seemed oddly at ease in the midst of the carnage, the evidence of crushing poverty and dire disease.

"He was good-looking, remember, me droogs?"

"Yeah," Harris said. "I do remember."

"Got to fuck whoever he wanted," Murch said, with no evident malice. Another pause, then an impatient gesture. "So we doing this or what?"

Finding a *useful thing* did not seem likely. But Murch started looking down that side counter, opening drawers. And Harris, feeling lost, moved across the room to the window, where he looked down onto West Cordova, to the ebb and flow of people there, shrunken shapes in the lengthening shadows. There was a plastic bag looped over the inside handle and left to dangle outside. DIY refrigeration. Harris cracked the window and pulled it in: moldy cheese, two black bananas, a pint of milk gone yellow and pungent. He found himself drifting, Roen's last groceries in his hand, thinking of his own place in Kits, the creaking couch, the beer and French Rabbit in the fridge, the bloody bandages in the garbage under the sink. How distant was he from the situation here? How many pints of sour milk away?

A car horn on the street below brought Harris back to the moment. He registered silence in the room. Murch had been behind him, working his way down the strewn counter, clattering and talking. Now nothing. A stillness, the air suspended.

Harris turned slowly, just until he picked up Murch in his peripheral vision. Back corner of the room. Murch with a ratty gym bag, groping inside. The sound of a zipper. Then this: the muted jangle of keys. And Harris could see them now too. In the very corner of his eye, a guitar-shaped fob. *All access, motherfuckers.*

A faint smile creeping across Murch's features, one of remembrance and calculation, as those keys slid into his jacket pocket without a word.

5

Maybe the keys were a memento. Maybe Murch was going to hang them from the rearview mirror of his black Mercedes parked opposite his firm's office in a reserved street spot that must have cost him ten grand a month. Maybe. But after four days staking out the car in question, Harris knew Murch had other ideas.

Harris in his Car2go. He watched Murch saunter out of his office at 5:30 p.m. sharp three days running and drive home to Point Grey. Day four, Friday, here came Murch two hours early in jeans and one of those oilskin hunting jackets, carrying an overnight bag and looking pressed for time.

Rushing to catch a ferry, Harris thought, sliding lower in his seat. There would be a flashlight in that overnight, a sweater, extra socks. A ring of keys. *You thieving bastard.*

Harris's gamble was the cost of a one-way chartered float plane that would get him onto Saturna ninety minutes ahead of the ferry. And once Murch had pulled out and headed southbound against his normal patterns, Harris wheeled his car around and sped to the seaplane terminal in the inner harbor.

The plane touched down in Plumper Sound in the late afternoon and taxied in to the marina. Harris found himself on the familiar quay, hefting his backpack as he had so many times before, heading up the road that wound around the cove to the place where it all began.

When he got to the B&B, Harris realized he hadn't even considered the possibility that the place might have been sold. But the leaf-strewn driveway and overgrown orchard told a different story. And approaching the front door he felt a penetrating familiarity, like nothing had changed for the ritual sustained at that dining room table he could see through the glass, at that porch railing there, where his hand had rested during Purma's judgment.

Harris, cheer up. I predict you end up with a minivan and lots of money.

The path to the studio was overgrown, but Harris picked his way down through the orchard. At the door he pulled on work gloves and punched through the glass pane above the knob. Harris inside, and sitting now in the shadows at the back of the room to wait. He could see where the ferry would come in, the slice of road where Murch would shortly appear. He closed his eyes and dozed, jolting awake when the ferry thrummed into view, growing in Harris's binoculars until it reached the wharf, disgorging cars, among them a single black Mercedes.

Harris watched as Murch's car pulled onto the road at

a confident speed. Murch charged up, filled with his plan. And there was a tight and lean feeling gripping Harris too just then, in his gut and his groin. *Bring it on.*

Five minutes later Murch was in the drive. Tires on gravel. Parking brake. Door slam. Murch took in the view and Harris imagined the same memories spilling: Shanny, Roen, Purma and her Pall Malls. But he didn't come directly down through the orchard. He went to the big house first, knocking tentatively, then louder. Then trying keys and entering. And staying for over an hour as the shadows stretched. Searching, Harris concluded from the glint of his flashlight beamed into the corners of rooms, floor by floor until it winked from the windows of the basement.

There followed silence, during which Harris imagined Murch taking a seat, running the numbers, wondering if Roen had lied or if Jimmy had long ago collected the money or if there was some other explanation entirely.

Murch looking up slowly, eyes drifting down the orchard.

The house lights went out. Harris heard the front door slam again, long strides coming down through the grass. Harris's heart was pounding in his chest. And there was Murch, looming outside the glass, his light on the door handle, on the broken glass, but not finding Harris who surged forward and flung open the door, beaming his own flashlight directly into Murch's eyes.

Complete surprise, achieved. A spectacular moment. Murch's arm rose in slow motion, his flashlight pirouetting into space. His mouth was open and contorted, no sound coming out. And all this while stumbling rearward toward the low porch rail which upended him into the long grass below.

Harris might have laughed had Murch not been up so quickly. Out of the grass and vaulting the stairs, arms flailing.

Harris was no fighter and had the injuries to prove it. But he kept away and finally landed a slapping punch to Murch's nose that made him bleed.

"Stop," Harris said. "Murch. Fuck."

And Murch did stop, hands to his face, blood coming through, breathing in and out in ragged gasps. "You fucking prick," he said. "You motherfucking cock-sucking prick. What are you doing here?"

"I'm not the one who lifted those keys."

"We were supposed to take something, moron."

"And come right here?"

Murch raised himself to his full height, face twisted, lips quivering. "Go fuck yourself! You came right here too!"

"Roen dying got me thinking," Harris said. "I wanted to say goodbye."

"Fucking liar."

Long pause. Then Murch pushed past Harris and went into the studio, grabbed a chair, and sat. Harris followed him slowly, did the same. And they sat for several minutes in the darkness, nothing but the sound of slowing breath.

"That last night here," Murch said, finally. "Shanny talking about lawyers. And Roen went off about a dealer hiding money somewhere."

"So you looked."

"You didn't?"

"Not in the house," Harris said.

Murch looked up sharply.

It took them five minutes, less. Crawling around on hands and knees. A recessed brass handle under the corner of a faded Persian carpet. An old key on a guitar-shaped fob. The door swung up to reveal a ladder down to a cellar just high enough to stand. Concrete walls. Evidence of industry. A low wooden bench with tools, a vacuum packer and bags. Felt markers and a logbook with entries. A slim brown briefcase with gold latches. Plastic storage tubs, neatly stacked.

"Holy shit," Murch said, after climbing down first. Harris sat on the ladder's lowest rung and watched him haul down a tub, which thumped hollow as it hit the ground. Empty. And the next one too. The next. Twelve in all. Not a single shrink-wrapped dollar to be found.

Harris slumped on the ladder, shoulders rounded, face slack. Murch was sweating from his labors, lips in a frustrated snarl, eyes flitting around the room and finding the briefcase. Locked. But he did not hesitate. He smashed the latches open with a hammer taken from among the tools. He flung it open on the bench. Inside: a pouch of weed, a wad of bills tied with an elastic band, a pistol which Murch took in his hand, opening and closing his fingers around the grip, eyes narrow.

"Roen, Roen," he whispered, leveling the pistol, then pivoting slowly until it pointed at Harris's chest.

There was a long pause during which Harris felt his pulse hammering in his ears.

"That summer," Murch said, at last. "Ask me if I fucked Shanny."

"Murch," Harris replied, sweat beading on his forehead and falling into his eyes.

"Ask me!"

"All right!" Harris said. "All right. Goddamn. Did you fuck Shanny?"

The moment stretched. Murch's arm was trembling. "Nah," he eventually said. "Roen did."

Then he lowered his arm and laughed. And Harris tried to join him but couldn't, thinking only of Roen's body on that bed, blood spatters, cold dead and laughing.

The bills were hundreds. Counted and divided, barely two grand each.

6

They didn't talk on the ferry the next morning. Murch disappeared into the Seawest Lounge without a word. At the terminal on arrival, Harris didn't join him on the car deck, just walked off and bussed into town. Same strewn apartment. Same brewing storm clouds. At his computer, he looked at those last paragraphs he'd typed, what seemed like months before.

You know it's real when it ends in blood.

Sacred violence.

Fifteen years and a gun leveled across an empty cellar. The two droogies invoked the third. And that had always been an unstable arrangement.

Harris held off until three p.m. before having a beer. He made it to five o'clock before heading over to Chianti's, measuring his mood and finding that despite all that had happened, he was feeling pretty good, a rare flame flickering within. Harris felt the onset of *writing*. And it cheered him. So he'd fucked up his marriage and was neither rich nor famous. But he was still a writer. *World's most coveted jobs . . . Up there with porn star.* So he had no memento from Roen's apartment. But he had a *story*. And the bar door opened just then, someone entering at that exact and auspicious moment.

First thought: *Roen*. Crazy. But something about the confident stride, bearing down on Harris out of a halo of light that only extinguished when the bar door finally closed. Not Roen. Of course not Roen, who was entirely dead.

Purma. In Harris's favorite bar in Kitsilano, an unlikelihood exceeded only by how happy he was to see her. He got off his barstool and opened his arms. And they hugged for several seconds while the regulars looked on and wondered.

"Is this okay?" Purma asked. "Me being here?"

More than okay, Harris thought. It was right somehow. People did this after a loss, sought each other out and took time to reflect. Murch wouldn't understand. But Purma did. So she pulled up a stool. And sipping wine and cranberry juice respectively, they talked. Harris heard about Purma becoming a counselor. He heard how she loved helping people. And Harris spoke about getting married and quitting the bank. About early successes and a later slow turning. A stupid affair, a messy divorce. A basement apartment in Kits, trouble with money, an uncertain future.

"But you have a new book!" Purma exclaimed.

True, Harris did.

"About what?" Purma asked.

Harris thought for a minute, then couldn't help himself. Well, it was *inspired* by real life, in fact.

Purma was intrigued.

Three friends. A musician, a writer, and a lawyer. Hung out on Saturna Island back in the day but drifted apart over the years. The musician had a drug dealer friend for whom he'd been hiding money. Years later the drug dealer dies. The musician dies separately. The two surviving friends learn about it and get to wondering. Competition ensues.

Purma was leaning forward, seemingly riveted. Harris plunged on. The mutual pursuit. The island confrontation and the disappointing results. Purma stood up next to her stool and applauded.

"Maybe hold off on that," Harris said. "I still need an ending."

"You got it already! The money's not there. Those two

jerks get what they deserve and it's exactly what the musician would have wanted," Purma said.

"It is?" Harris said.

"Yeah! To put those two jackasses back into competition, like revenge from the grave."

Harris sat back. "Revenge for what?"

"For trying to steal the money! That musician was smart. And good-looking, right? Probably slept with both the women the other two were after."

Harris laughed tightly. Purma with great gusto. Harris wondered if he was drunk but thought either way that what had been so happy when Purma arrived now felt distinctly darker in tone.

"But what about this?" Purma said. "An alternative ending."

"Nah, listen," Harris responded, fumbling for his wallet, "I better go. Let me get this."

But Purma would not be deterred. She turned to face Harris. And she told him another version of how things might have happened. The lawyer lied. He'd been in touch with the musician as soon as he heard that the drug dealer was dead. No random encounter. He'd gone and found his old friend.

"Why?" Harris asked.

"To get ahead of the writer!" Purma said, eyes bright. So the lawyer confirms with the musician that the drug dealer's money is still there. And he heads on over to the hiding place to preemptively loot the stash. "Some biker dealer getting whacked isn't exactly CNN news. The writer totally missed it."

Harris didn't remember mentioning any bike gang. But he couldn't stop her now. "Of course, the writer finds out eventually that the dealer is dead. Only the lawyer arranges for them to both go over and *discover together* that the money is gone."

Harris's drunkenness was moderating, replaced by unwelcome clarity.

"They go over. Nothing there. Too bad. Back to their lives, only the lawyer now has a couple million in cash stashed in the basement of his house in Point Grey."

Harris couldn't speak.

"Clever," Purma said.

"Yeah," Harris managed.

"Only also *really* stupid."

"And, um . . ." Harris stammered. "Why's that?"

"Because bikers have associates. And those associates would go looking for the dealer's stash after he died. First move: shake down the musician. Maybe they kill him. Maybe he kills himself. Either way, he talks. And that means second move: go find the lawyer."

Harris's mouth was so dry it felt welded shut. Purma watched him closely for several seconds, expression now very serious. Then she pushed her chair back and stood.

"Leaving you only one plot point remaining," she said. "You just gotta come up with a good way to kill the lawyer."

Which was a mental exercise Harris had invested time in already. Harris, who was in an alley by that point. In an alley lined with dumpsters, running home.

7

In his apartment, blinds drawn, lights out, trembling uncontrollably. The worst part of the cascading moment wasn't Purma proving the transparency of his plan. It was instead the sudden clarity with which he could now remember what the man on the beach had said before hitting him. Not a cruel voice exactly. Only deeply disconnected.

"Just say the word," the man had said. "Tell me where."

So Purma had only missed a single detail. It was the death of the writer that remained unwritten. And there was little doubt how that would unfold. *Say the word,* said the professional now waiting down there among the darkened, skeletal trees. Waiting for further conversation. Different tools this time. A pipe wrapped in cloth. A short blade or pliers. Harris weeping, feeling read to the bones.

Three weeks. Purma had been exactly right about the timing. Three weeks ago that Harris had gone looking for Roen, found him on Cordova in his wheelchair, skinny as hell. But still with the glossy hair and high cheekbones. A woman at his side, beautiful. Dark eyes, coffee skin.

Another lie to add to the many. It was Roen who didn't recognize Harris, struggling even after Harris tried to remind him. The girl kept tugging on his shoulder saying, "Roey?"

"Hey, come on," Harris pleaded. "We all partied at that B&B on Saturna Island."

"Saturna Island," Roen said, looking up through his shades. "You a friend of Jimmy's? Dude just died, man. Pretty sad."

Sad, sure. Only maybe not for the two of them if they cooperated, which was exactly what Harris wanted to talk to Roen about, though not right there on the goddamn street, which meant they had to get themselves into a bar, which meant Roen would have to remember who Harris was.

"Roey? Roey, let's go, baby."

"Jimmy was a fucking rock, man. Hey, I just remembered who you are!"

Harris smiled and nodded. Finally.

"You're the lawyer! Murch, man, put her there!" Roen thrust out a bony hand and Harris took it.

"I'm Harris," he tried again. "We hung out with Murch. The three droogies!"

Roen's expression was dreamy. "Murch," he mumbled, "knew a girl named Shanny."

"That's the one," Harris said, looking around for a bar.

"Roey? Roey, please."

"Get on down to the corner," he said to the girl. "Stay there till I come get you."

Roen back looking up at Harris. He'd taken off his sunglasses. "I remember this other girl from back then. Black hair. Shanny and that other girl and I did it all together once. What do they say—*manger a trois?*"

Harris swallowed and looked away. How pathetic was it that he couldn't even seize control of this degraded situation? Very.

"We need to talk," Harris said. "Let me buy you a drink."

Roen protested thinly about not drinking. But Harris knew that resolve was going to fail. They went into the Union Tavern. Found a table in a dark corner. Blue lights over the bar. People hunched over pitchers of terrible draft beer and shots of Jägermeister. In a nearby booth, a glowing pipe made the rounds.

"Who else did we hang with that summer?" Roen was asking.

"You, me, and Murch," Harris said. "Jin and Shanny you remember. Then Calliope and Zach and Purma."

"Purma," Roen said softly. "Purma I still see around."

Even if Harris had understood what that meant, he knew he wouldn't have done anything differently. He went to the bar. He brought back four beers and two large vodkas.

"Murchie, you devil," Roen said.

"Harris."

"Right," Roen said. And he tipped a vodka down his throat.

It wasn't hard to do, in the end, to slide back into those very old rhythms, altered only in a minor way by the years. They had four beers and two vodkas apiece inside an hour and Harris didn't even feel buzzed. But Roen was flying. He was laughing. He was making fun of Harris's clothes and his books, which Harris stupidly mentioned.

"Harvey Raven?" Roen said, eyes wide with mirth. "See, that's a problem, right there." Cultural appropriation, he explained. Raven sounded First Nations. And Harris himself was quite clearly not. Roen laughing. "My round?" he said. "Oh, no, wait, Murch here is buying."

Fuck, Harris thought. But he did not even bother correcting him. More beers. More vodka. At some point he realized that they were hunched in over the table, talking in urgent voices, Roen protesting, Harris stabbing the air with his finger. At some later point, Harris realized that they were sitting amidst that squalor of Roen's apartment and that Harris was holding a pipe from which he was about to take a hit.

He'd never used meth before. And as he stood trembling in his Kits apartment remembering all of this, he realized that he wouldn't be doing it again. So terrible and wonderful had been the experience. The rush visceral, physical, enormous. He surged out of himself. He rose to the ceiling. The high was like white water rafting, followed by a steep and sheering free fall, his belly aflame and taut. He would consume the world.

Harris holding a set of familiar keys in his hand which he'd just declared he was going to copy. Roen crying. "You can't do this to me, man," he was saying. His nose running and his eyes bloodred. "You cannot fucking do this. You have no idea who these people are. They will fucking find you."

But Harris would not be stopped. What he was taking, which didn't belong to Roen anyway, had a broader, rectifying power, a means by which his personal history might finally and truly be cleansed after all that earlier, pointless trying.

Time to end this. The ritual that ends in blood.

Absolute darkness. That's what such moments required. Harris saw it and left Roen where he sat, bawling in his wheelchair. His life didn't last long after that. By Harris's own best math, he was himself on Saturna Island when it happened, down in the orchard. A creak of a door to a hidden cellar opened, heavy plastic tubs thudded down to the floor, bales of cash into black garbage bags, loaded into a rusted minivan he'd bought for the purpose. Ford Windstar. What luck to discover one of those for sale, the exact vehicle envisioned for his future. It worked for the purpose, parked and waiting in the long weeds. The whole operation took an hour, at the climax of which Roen either pressed the gun to his own head or submitted to it being applied there by professionals in that trade. Either way, Harris felt the shot in that instant. He heard it in his heart. And it knocked him to his knees in the wet grass, where he stayed a long time sobbing, one hand on a rusted fender.

Alone in Kitsilano and trapped utterly. All that money, enough to dissolve the biggest problems, all useless to Harris now; he didn't dare show his face outside, much less spend a single bill. Defeated in his own crafty victory, while the rain gathered, and something circled possessively, some entity in the night drawing close.

He took to the window, pulled back the blinds. His breath was coming in ragged tears. There was only a single path open now, only a single decision possible in that blackest of moments.

He was on the street. He was in the park. He slipped through the trees and out onto the sand, running now, a shape moving behind him. Footsteps that were not there. Between the logs and to the water's edge, where the world tipped away from what it was into the airless blackness of a world that was not.

A whisper behind him: *Tell me where.* Nobody. But Harris still moved forward into the waves, up to his knees, his thighs.

Absolute darkness.

8

The body on Kits Beach made news. It was a bigger deal than a drug dealer dead in a burning Viper. He was a local writer, after all, if not that well known. And he'd drowned off one of Vancouver's most popular beaches, pulled onto the sand by a Portuguese water dog whose owner did not wish to be interviewed. Drunk swimming, they said. But who swam drunk in March at two in the morning?

No one. Not the lawyer either. Found dead in Crab Park. One shot to the back of the head.

The headlines screamed: "THEY KNEW EACH OTHER!"

Didn't matter. They were dead. They couldn't talk. Neither did anyone else who mattered.

Purma, for her part, went directly to the police. The three of them had met not long before the two men died. It had been a memorial for yet another friend who'd apparently committed suicide.

All this was very confusing. Lots of speculation. But she was clean. The cops liked her. She did good work in the Downtown Eastside and they left her alone. Last question she fielded from the detectives was if Harris owned a car.

No, Purma said. He used a car service, Car2go.

Which was curious, the cops thought, given they found a car key in his apartment but nothing registered in his name. What kind of car? They sent it out for identification and waited almost six weeks. The results did not inspire any kind of follow-up.

Purma went back to what she had been doing. Three old friends gone in a couple of months. It was the kind of thing you tried to forget if you had people dropping all around you, which she did, literally. The Downtown Eastside was not getting better. Her work wasn't getting any easier.

Three years passed.

And one day, it was time. A year per loss? Maybe. Purma on a ferry. Purma in the swell, in the rolling waves. Purma on an old road with a backpack, walking those two kilometers to the place where it all began, or where it had all stopped. Thinking back on it, she couldn't be sure.

Purma on a morning hike that they had themselves done so many times before. Up the ridgeline to the back road. Around to the lip of trees. Left into the auto graveyard. Purma had no reason to be there other than having been many times before, long ago. Rotting vehicles consumed by moss or sprouting trees. In some cases, the salt air had whittled the frames down to intricate carvings.

To the back. To a car in the middle of the last row wedged in tight against a Garry oak. Nothing special about this one. But she rubbed the moss clean off the grill to find the word: *Windstar*.

Frozen. Remembering. How awful had she been back then? And in an impulsive instant, she acted on the thought. She hefted a rock. And she heaved it through the windshield.

"Whoa." Said aloud as the glass dissolved. As it folded away. As the van's interior was torn open to view, revealing that it wasn't empty. That is was chock-full instead. Bales of something wrapped in black plastic, stacked to the roof.

She held some of it her hands, leafy, smelling of crime. She said aloud: "You fools."

EIGHT GAME-CHANGING TIPS ON PUBLIC SPEAKING

BY SHEENA KAMAL

Financial District

1. Smile, motherfucker.

I t relaxes you on stage. You will not need to take a Xanax and fall asleep on top of Bridget the night before your big presentation, the one that you are flying into Seattle from Vancouver specifically to give. She has put up with too much of that shit already and girlfriend deserves a break. If you play your cards right, she may be compelled to share her suspicions that someone has been stealing from you for the past year, but whether or not that will happen depends entirely on your willingness to search for the mythical clitoris—which, let me tell you, actually exists. I can find it blindfolded with my arms tied behind my back. It's right at the top of the—you know what? I'll draw you a diagram.

For someone who has written *astute* in his web profile, you have a lot to learn. Not just about the female anatomy either, although it does show a certain lack of respect for the women in your life. I'm talking about the little details. I'm talking about the drips of money that have become a nice, steady river into someone else's pocket.

We have worked together for two years now. Me in my Beyoncé-inspired wardrobe and you in your . . . how about we get to that later? For now, let me just say that the first day I walked into your corner office in the Financial District, overlooking Coal Harbour with the trees of Stanley Park edging the frame of your view, I knew something would give with this job. Or someone. I gave first.

Now it's your turn.

2. Use the stage, but don't pace.

It makes you look like an asshole when you do that. All those years you spent dodging the homeless and the addicts on Hastings has made you surprisingly agile for a man your age, but you don't need to advertise this during your speeches. Plus, your fashion sense can't hold up to that kind of scrutiny. It's amazing when people who have earned as much shady money as you have refuse to invest in a decent suit. Off the rack is not a good look on you.

People don't talk about the Panama Papers anymore, they really don't. But they should. It boggles my fertile, college-educated mind that the biggest white-collar corruption scandal of our day—with sexy highlights such as tax evasion, front companies, doctored communications, financial havens—seems to have disappeared like a puff of quality BC kush. Unsurprisingly, a haze of collective amnesia has set in. Nobody remembers that a company heavily involved in advising on these illegal havens for the yacht owners of this country was based in Vancouver. Your old company, in fact. You have stayed off social media and, because your family barely talks to you anymore, it was difficult for me to make the connections that I have recently made—but not impossible. Oh, the thrills of working for a tax planner!

Please don't think I'm judging, even though, according to my nan, this kind of behavior is clearly not beyond me. I have done my share of pacing, so I know it is a sign of a guilty conscience. But you really shouldn't reveal that much of yourself to a paying audience. They want the tips, not the guilt. That burden is for your battered soul alone.

3. Tone down the gesticulation.

Repeat after me: "My arms are not windmills." Keep them at your sides, bent at the elbows. This will allow you to highlight important points with a little flourish, but will prevent you from getting too worked up. Like the time you surprised me in the office with Juanita. We both knew that Juanita wasn't helping me find my contact lens while we were half-naked under your desk, but you didn't have to increase my workload by 30 percent because of your barely disguised homophobia.

What was I talking about?

Oh yeah, your arms. Keeping them at your side will also hide your pit stains. Honestly, I don't know what Bridget sees in you—except for piles of other people's money. She held the less-than-exalted position of being your executive assistant before leaving to work on her back. Make no mistake about it, it is work. I happened to see that nightmare video on your phone, which is not password protected for some ludicrous reason. How many times have I forwarded you those *HuffPo* articles about the security of your personal devices? I mean, people keep their entire lives on their phones these days. Terrible sex videos, appointments you haven't synched to your official schedule, logs of shady phone calls to contacts at what seem to be shell companies, screenshots of certain account balances . . . you haven't let go of your past yet, have you?

If Bridget has any sense, and obviously she does, she would have noticed the exact same discrepancies. Do you really think your phone sits untouched on your desk during your epic morning bathroom visits? It may seem that those bran muffins Bridget makes are your friend, but they truly are not. And, since we're talking about Bridget, is it weird that she hired a lesbian to replace her? So that nobody else would get any ideas about her cash cow?

Please. She didn't need to worry, bro, honestly. I wouldn't touch you with someone else's dusty vagina.

4. Rehearse, rehearse, rehearse.

I can write your speeches for you (like the good little executive assistant I am), but I can't make you good at giving them without a little effort on your part. Don't practice in front of a mirror, do it while you're puttering around the house—excuse me, golf course. Get the speech in your body and it will stay in your mind.

You know what stays in my mind?

The night you found me in your office with Juanita. That was when I first realized something was off. A late-night visit to the office isn't exactly your style. You hadn't forgotten anything—I made sure of that. And you haven't burned the midnight oil in years. You needed to clean up a mess, didn't you? Later I looked over your accounts.

It took me awhile to notice all that foreign money pouring into companies that you helped establish, before *poof!*, the money disappeared into the ether of various offshore accounts. You did an awesome job at hiding the paper trail, by the way. I have to give you some grudging respect for that, at least. I used to think you were a total idiot, but I was wrong. Your idiocy isn't all-encompassing. You've got your skills, man, you really do. Creating documents to cover up money transfers, contracts, and invoices. Slow applause from me for this. But there's very little you can hide from your executive assistant when she's got revenge on her mind.

I only had the time to do all this investigating and uncovering of trails, you understand, because Juanita broke up with me. She hasn't come out yet, but we'd been slowly getting there until your surprise visit spooked the hell out of her. I won't lie, this was a serious blow to my personal life. Do you know how hard it is for a lesbian to get laid in Vancouver?

The calls I made to her went unanswered. I got worried, because she'd taken to running the trails up by Pacific Spirit Park in the evenings after work, so I went by her place in Point Grey.

I waited for hours.

This is what love can do to a perfectly rational person when it slaps her upside the head. I was about to leave when I saw her walking down the road. She was just coming home from drinks, I assume, because I saw her on the sidewalk, wobbly on the high heels they made her wear at the perfume counter. There was a man holding her up by her elbow. She looked into his eyes and let him kiss her. Right in front of me.

I beat a hasty retreat right then and there but wasn't sure if she'd seen me until she texted me the next day.

I'm sorry, but it's over. I'm really sorry.

With the periods and everything! In a text!

The man she was with looked like your average married guy with an itch to scratch away from home. But he had money. I could tell from his suit, which was leagues above the quality of yours.

So she wanted money?

It's not so hard to get some of that, if you know what you're doing.

5. Know when to quit.
(See above about letting go of your past.)
Just because something worked before doesn't mean it's going

to work again. If you sense you're losing your audience, don't double down. Move on, man. Move on. For example, when I was at the University of British Columbia, I crammed myself into Intro to Economics along with a horde of other undergrads reeking of weed. We were all hoping for a career in investment banking so that we could go yachting with models. The others seemed to do okay, but I could not, to my shame, read a simple line chart to save my life. Numbers I can handle. Concepts I can rattle off with no trouble at all. But there was that god-awful midterm where it was all about the line graphs. Let me tell you, economics as a prerequisite class is not geared to the graphically disinclined.

When the Papers came out, naming your old firm as the center of a Canadian shitstorm of what could have been epic proportions, that should've been enough for a thinking person to walk away. Yet you maintained your connections to your past. You still advertise snow washing, because why not tempt fate?

If I had to draw a graph to explain what snow washing is, it would look like a pile of garbage. So I won't even bother. Plus, you already know, don't you? It was your specialty. Advertise Canada as a more lucrative tax haven for high-net-worth foreign individuals, set up a front company with no legal obligation to disclose the real owner, and bada-bing, bada-boom. Tax haven benefits without the money-laundering stench that now pervades the Caribbean. Which is still used, but not as often as it used to be. Speaking of . . .

6. Make eye contact.

But only hold each pair of eyes for a few seconds. You want to include the regular plebes in your presentation, but you don't want to be creepy. Save that for one of your island getaways when you send Bridget off to the spa and sit on the beach ogling women who are young enough to be your granddaughter.

Which reminds me, I sent a card to your granddaughter for her birthday last month. She said thank you for the personal note and the generous dollar amount on the check I signed on your behalf. You're lucky I know how to forge your signature so well. It keeps your personal life in order and everyone, including me, happy. Birthday cards, apology notes, memos, miscellaneous documents pertaining to your secret accounts . . . I sign them all.

Were the Cayman Islands nice? What about the Bahamas? Boss, you have no idea how happy I was to get that shitty little box of chocolates you brought for me from Switzerland. Airport chocolates from the Swiss are so much better than what you get here, am I right?

There's an interesting pattern that emerges when one is of the mind to look into the timing of your vacations with Bridget. It took me awhile to get the documents sorted, but when I did, *boom*. There it was. Secret accounts for your secret accounts, and vacay spots that line up perfectly.

7. Know your audience.

When I first moved to Vancouver from butt-fuck nowhere Ontario, I wanted to get laid. So obviously I signed up for all sorts of websites, run by people who were all too happy to take my money. They understood their demographic well. I wanted sex, and money for school—therefore I needed a sugar mama. Vancouver isn't a sugar-baby mecca for nothing, my friend.

The first "date" I had was with an older woman named Carla, in her fifties. She had no time for bullshit, kept multiple phones to keep her various lives separate, and would spend no more than one hour each week in my apartment, which she helped me pay for.

It was the most blissful hour of my week. Carla could have me naked and panting in three minutes flat, but usually made me wait. We lasted six years.

One afternoon—it was always afternoons—she came in looking rushed and overwhelmed. Something was clearly on her mind, and it was so pressing that she wouldn't even let me touch her first. I sensed it was the end, so I popped a bottle of champagne I kept in the fridge and poured two glasses. She didn't even smile when I handed one to her. We drank half the bottle before she took me to bed.

Afterward, she asked me who I worked for. I said it was you, of course. She nodded once, because she already knew, and said that she'd seen me at an event, holding your phone and whispering the names of VIPs into your ear like a goddamn idiot.

"You're better than that," she told me. "You're better than him. After what he's done . . ."

"What?" I said, even though I'd already started to suspect the worst about you. This was before the night in your office when you found me and Juanita.

"I hear there's an investigation going on," said Carla. She was a real estate agent who worked exclusively with wealthy international clients. She found them investment homes in the pricey Vancouver marketplace, then helped them figure out how to avoid paying hefty taxes on said mansions.

"There's massive corruption, and your boss is a part of it. A bunch of journalists around the world are working together to investigate a series of documents that show where and how the super-wealthy have been funneling money for years. They're calling them the Panama Papers. I'm warning you right now, if your boss goes down, so will you."

"Speaking of going down," I said, reaching for her.

She pushed me away and slipped back into her clothes. "I'm serious, Mags. You could get into a lot of trouble working for this guy. It's always the staff that gets scapegoated when this stuff comes out."

"You worried that I'm going to ruin your reputation? Nobody knows about us."

"It's not that." Her look was clear as day. When she made a decision, nothing in the world could turn her away from it. And it was obvious she had already decided about us. "We're going to have to stop, me and you. My wife just retired and she's spending more time at home—if she ever found out about us . . ."

"Is this about my boss or your wife?" I asked, watching her from the bed. She never talked about her wife with me.

She shook her head and leaned against the doorway. "Look. I just don't want to see you hurt because of your boss. It's tough enough for a woman in business, especially in the financial sector. You have to work twice as hard—and you already go above and beyond. Don't let this man ruin your career."

What career? I didn't have a career, as anyone who watched me settle your dry cleaning bill would know.

It's not the only thing she was wrong about. I wasn't going to be hurt because of you. She didn't know her audience, you see. Her warning me about you only sped up my timeline.

You know, everybody underestimates the sugar baby. You have a number of little companies of your own, and you know who has signing rights on them besides Bridget? Well, of course, the person who can forge your signature like a pro. Setting up my own company was simple. There's a reason why those rich foreigners do this. Canada, land of opportunity, makes it so damn easy.

8. Keep it short and sweet.

Closing remarks should be brief. For example: "I would like to thank you for all the years you have kept me employed doing your dirty work without once giving me a raise. My *career* is a dead end and my love life is in shambles, but all of this has taught me a very valuable lesson. In a city taken over by the wealthy, where white-collar crime is the norm, where everyone has a price, nobody blinks at a little cream being skimmed off the top. When it comes to the 'tax planners' of Vancouver, who are the lubricant of the astronomically priced real estate market, everyone does it. The thing about stashed money and the misrepresented funds of companies that are not required to disclose their real owners, also, is that anyone can steal from a thief without repercussions. Nobody in this shady business wants to bring on any extra scrutiny. So thank you for all of your help in padding my own shady accounts, and sayonara."

See? Easy as Bridget.

Hope your speech goes well tomorrow. I have booked you an economy seat on a flight that's always jam packed. Good luck on getting upgraded to business class this time, asshole. And if you're thinking of trying to get back at me somehow, remember that I've seen the pervy videos on your phone and, whoops, made a few copies.

If you're upset about suddenly joining the ranks of the lower classes, remember that your office window opens outward.

And by the way, I left that diagram on your desk. Happy hunting ☺

Editor's note: As an idealistic youth, Sheena Kamal underwent extensive public-speaking training by a guy who was allegedly trained by the guy who trained Bill Clinton. She feels as though she'd have been far more successful in life if she'd gotten Obama's guy's guy instead.

THE PERFECT PLAYGROUP

BY ROBIN SPANO

West Vancouver

S age is more fabulous dead than alive. West Vancouver's finest boutique mortician has selected jeans, summer heels, and a silk tank, for a look of understated elegance. The look she sported when I met her, when she lured me into her web of lies that ended with a vial of poison in my hand.

We're in Whole Foods with our daughters, both one and a half. Sage and her blond-ringleted Emmaline share a kale smoothie while I struggle to keep Hannah from smearing mac and cheese all over her face. Sage is dressed down today, in five-hundred-dollar riding boots and organic green leggings. I'm dressed up, in jeans and my polo shirt from Costco.

Our tables are adjacent. Her shopping cart is filled to the brim with organic goodness. Mine has the discounted family meal, the Wednesday special where your family can get fat for twenty dollars. I wouldn't normally talk to someone so perfect, but Hannah shouts, "Hi!" and Emmaline giggles, and soon we're chatting gaily as rain pounds the two-story windows.

"There's a fundraiser on Saturday." She fishes a flier from her Coach diaper bag. "My friends and I are hosting. Proceeds send underprivileged kids to camp."

"That sounds worthy." Does the rip in Hannah's raincoat make it obvious we'd qualify?

"The event's sold out but I have an extra seat at my table. No charge. If your husband doesn't mind watching Hannah for a night, it could be fun, right?"

Husband. Yeah. I'd have better luck asking the grumpy Polish lady who used to clean his parents' house. They fired her when we moved into their boathouse last month. Now it's my job to scrub their toilets in lieu of rent. The upside? We get to raise Hannah in a neighborhood where all her little friends will have weekly allowances bigger than her parents' net worth.

"Why me?" I say.

"Why not? You're a mom. You seem like a good one, which means you need a break. Have you had a night out since Hannah was born?"

I snort.

"But your husband has, right?"

"Of course."

"So this is fair. It's also free and fun. Say yes."

I search for excuses. "None of my dresses fit since pregnancy."

"Come raid my wardrobe." Sage toys with the hem of her shirt. "I gave up and bought all new clothes after Emmaline. Stroller fitness, mom and baby yoga, and thousands of dollars in pelvic floor physio won't budge my annoying potbelly."

I laugh. "It's a generous offer, but your entire body could fit into one leg of my jeans."

"Not true! But there's a designer in Dundarave who's been brilliant for my postpartum body. Emmaline and I could play with Hannah while you try on dresses."

"Hannah won't stay with a stranger."

"Sure she will." Sage smiles at Hannah's cheesy cheeks, holds her arms out like she wants a hug.

Hannah shocks me by reaching for Sage.

* * *

Skinny women in artistic dresses mingle under the *Happy Campers* banner, their men standing by in tailored dark suits with bold ties. I want to slink back to the bus stop, but retreating home won't make me feel more significant. When I asked Jake if I looked okay in the first dress I've worn in two years, he glanced briefly away from his keyboard and said, "You look fine." He's watching Hannah, at least. Meaning he's working on his novel while she empties every drawer in the boathouse.

I'm about to find a bathroom when Sage grips my arm.

"You look supremely hot in that dress."

I feel like an elephant among the gazelles, but I remind myself I'm only five pounds up from prepregnancy—it's just all distributed in a jiggly balloon around my stomach.

At the silent-auction table, she introduces me to Jenna and Misty.

"We're bidding things up," Jenna says.

"Only items we want. Like wine."

"And weekends at Whistler."

"And wine." Misty pirouettes to face me. "What are you going after?"

Sage slaps Misty's hand. "Let her swallow a drink before you reach for her wallet."

Ugh. Of course. I have to bid or I'll look like a freeloader. But I maxed out my MasterCard to buy the little red dress I'm wearing. The tag is tucked into my bra and it's going back on Monday.

I scribble my name on bid sheets. Lowballs only, items I'll never win because the night's still so young.

"So what do you do with your daughter around town?" Jenna asks. "I don't think I've seen you at music class or Playmania or anywhere."

"Um, we've done Mother Goose and Strong Start." The free stuff. "What do you guys do?"

I expect the answer to include aquarium memberships and ski passes at Cypress. But Misty says, "We're outside every day. We explore beaches, hike the mountains. Last week we did a collaborative art project at Lighthouse Park using mud, rocks, and sticks."

"We make up songs as we go," Jenna says. "And Sage does snacks like no mom I've ever seen."

Hannah would love that life. I feel guilty that I've been barely treading water, that most days we don't make it out of the house until it's too late for anything but rushed errands.

"Have you met Tommy?" Sage drags a man into the circle. His suit is probably worth three grand, but the stubble on his face says that doesn't make him special. "He's the hired help."

"Please." Tommy's laugh is so infectious that I find myself smiling along with him. "Sage wishes I was hired help. I'm playing sax in the orchestra, but I'm donating my time so she doesn't think she can order me around." He reaches a hand to shake mine, his grip firm and friendly. "She tells me we have lots in common."

I'm about to say she doesn't even know me, but I'll turn back into Cinderella soon enough, so I might as well enjoy the ball. I flash my most mysterious smile and we chat until his next set.

"You know who that was, right?" Jenna says when Tommy leaves. "Thomas Townsend. Owns half the North Shore, plus the hockey team."

My mouth falls open. "He's playing sax in the orchestra?"

"Sage's husband saved him a fortune in his divorce. Still had to pay his ex thirty mil."

"Ouch."

Jenna shrugs. "All that matters is he's single."

"Oh, I thought you were married."

The look she shoots me tells me that's the squarest thing I might have uttered but she finds it adorable. "It's you he likes."

Bidding closes. I'm alarmed to learn I've won a basket of organic dog treats. For sixty-five dollars. I don't own a dog. I could kick myself, because my credit card will be declined, and these women will think I'm a fraud and a mooch and a complete waste of time, and Hannah won't be invited on any of those cool adventure playdates.

In the cashier's line, Jenna and Misty trip over each other as they place one bag of wine after another onto their arms like bangle bracelets.

I pass my paddle to the cashier, prepare my best look of shock for when my credit card fails, but then Sage hands me an oversized bag and says, "My treat."

I peer inside and it's the dog treats.

"What? You didn't have to—"

"I wouldn't be so generous if you'd won the Alaskan cruise. Come on, let's go."

Wine from the fundraiser makes our mattress feel like a bouncy castle. I roll on top of Jake for the first time in forever, tease pleasure out of him as if he were still the edgy beat poet performing in the club where I bartended. I close my eyes and picture Tommy in his suit, our silly banter, the stupid grin we shared the whole ten minutes we talked. Jake responds with confused compliance, gets off, and goes back to sleep, but in the morning when I make his coffee, he replies with a full-body hug, an arm that lingers around my waist and tells me all is not dead between us.

Hannah and I ride the bus to John Lawson Park. Sage and her friends take a bar class nearby with childcare. They hit the playground after, rain or shine.

"I read this article," Sage says. "Kids who play outdoors in bad weather approach problem-solving with more confidence than if they're taught to avoid the elements."

Emmaline looks like she'd rather be inside playing princesses, but Hannah races to the climbing apparatus. She's the first to soak her jeans going down the slide.

"Is Hannah allowed chocolate?" Sage pats her pocket. "Chili-flavored, extra dark. I'm intent on Emmaline enjoying full flavors."

"Wow. You give parenting wicked flair," I say. "I've been too busy feeling overwhelmed."

"Because children are designed to break us." Sage laughs. "The sleepless nights, the freedom lost, the adoring husbands who turn into selfish jerks after childbirth. It's why mom friends are a lifeline, more essential than air some days."

I bite my lip. My friends and family are two thousand miles away. My only lifeline is Jake, and he'd rather talk to his fictional characters.

"The cool thing about being broken, though, is that when we rebuild ourselves, we can be as creative as we like. Join us at my house tomorrow. I've had fun designing Emmaline's playroom."

I'm like an orphan from a movie, my face pressed against the rain-streaked funeral home window. Inside, Misty and Jenna make frequent trips to the champagne table. Tommy stands stoically, nodding, not saying much. A man who I assume is Sage's husband shakes everyone's hand with an air of bereaved self-importance.

Hannah's in her stroller, talking to her bear while she

waits for our walk to continue. I've been letting her sleep with me since I was released on bail. She nestles in and makes me forget that it's all going to shit in a week or two, when the verdict comes in.

I could plea bargain if I admit to what I've done, serve fifteen years instead of twenty-five. But either way, I'll be in custody until Hannah is old enough to hate me. I'd rather let the trial linger, have more of these long nights with rain pounding the boathouse roof, her soft little body pressed into mine.

Sage's butler lets us in. Hannah and I drip muddy rainwater onto the pristine hardwood floor. We're shown to a bedroom where dry clothes are waiting. It breaks my heart how cherub-like Hannah looks in Emmaline's Desigual tunic. For me, there's Lululemon. For the first time since I returned that red dress, I like the way my body looks in clothes.

The butler raps softly and leads us to an enormous play-room overlooking the stormy whitecaps of the Georgia Strait.

"We built into the cliff," Sage says. "We carved grooves in the rock wall for Emmaline to climb. We've planed down jagged edges and the floor mat is padded so when she falls it's no big deal. A few bumps and scrapes are good, though. Teaches respect for the elements."

Hannah toddle-runs to join the other kids. After observing for maybe five seconds, she tries to scale the wall herself. Emmaline hangs back, mouth open. When Hannah successfully climbs three footholds, Emmaline claps with delight.

"She's never put a foot on it herself." Sage sighs. "Maybe Hannah can encourage her sense of adventure."

"Maybe Emmaline can temper Hannah's," I say with an awkward laugh. "Thanks for the dry clothes. I'll try to keep her from playing too rough in them."

"No way. Kids should play as rough as they like. Emmaline has too many clothes anyway. I can barely stuff her drawers shut." She sips matcha tea. "Funny how your kid is dark and mine is fair, huh? Yours bold, mine timid. It's like they were swapped at birth."

I say nothing, because Hannah suits me right down to her core.

"Tommy asked about you," she says.

"What did he want to know?"

"If you're available."

I try to stifle the flutter, but a stupid grin betrays me. "Well, I woke up to my husband's breakfast dishes in the sink, so if he calls today, I'm wide open."

Jenna and Misty laugh. Sage says, "Is that a yes or a no?"

"No. He's delicious, but I'm married."

The housekeeper arrives with a tray of Indian food. The kids sit around Emmaline's play table—including Hannah, who has never sat still to eat, ever—and the moms take turns putting curried dahl and butter chicken onto plastic plates. There's nothing Hannah will eat, but I select a couple innocuous-looking morsels for her. She examines a samosa with her tongue. Wrinkles her nose, takes a tiny bite. Chews thoughtfully. Takes another bite.

Sage beams. "Hunger is key. Run them around, they'll work up an appetite for anything."

"Especially for napping." Jenna reclines in her lounge chair. "A.k.a. spa rejuvenation for the afternoon shift. The instant my son goes down, I hit the Jacuzzi with wine and Netflix. What do you do when Hannah naps?"

I frown. I can't say I polish my in-laws' silver for dinners that don't include me. I didn't contradict Sage when she dropped me off after the fundraiser and assumed I lived in the big house. How much longer before they figure out I'm not qualified to play with them?

I think of Toronto, the three of us in the duplex, how I cherished Hannah's naps even with dirty laundry piled around me. "I read trashy best sellers, drink an endless mug of tea, and eat too much dark chocolate."

"What are you reading now?" Sage asks.

"*The Help*," I say, because it seems less of a lie if I'm living it.

Another night out. A house concert at Sage's neighbor's. It's a jazz trio from Montreal, I think they're almost famous. They work the tap-pelt-tap of the rain against the solarium into the rhythm of their songs.

In the intermission, we spill onto the covered patio with a bottle of wine. Tommy's cracking jokes with men in suits. I avoid eye contact. I don't want to presume familiarity after one conversation. Also my dress. It's passable, a Diane von Furstenberg I scored for twelve bucks at the Salvation Army, but I feel like the plain cousin of the princess he met at the ball.

A tap on my shoulder. "Win anything good at the fund-raiser?"

I spin to face Tommy, my shoulder on fire from his touch. "Dog treats," I say. "Would you like them? I don't have a dog."

"Sure. I won a yachting adventure. You like boats?"

"I love boats. But Hannah—" I instantly feel stupid. He wasn't inviting me, just asked if I like boats. I recover with, "We haven't taken her boating yet."

"Is your husband into boating?"

"Are you kidding? He can't spare the precious time from the characters inside his computer." I should shut up. I don't know why I'm being so blunt. "He's a writer."

"Anyone I've heard of?"

I mumble, "Jake Carruthers."

"The Giller winner? Does Sage know?"

"No."

"She'll go ape. When she read *Rebecca's Room*, it was all she could talk about for months."

He lights a joint and passes it to me. As our fingertips touch, electricity shoots through my arm and down to the place I didn't think had any electricity left. I take a puff and feel the beat of the rain against the gazebo roof. I haven't felt this free since summer camp.

A shout from inside tells us intermission is over.

The second set is better than the first. I can see notes from each instrument float through the air, the smooth double bass, the lively piano, the melancholy saxophone. Tommy's beside me on the couch. It's only his leg pressed into mine, but it's enough.

He walks us to Sage's door. The others go in for a night-cap and he says, "I'm not going to kiss you. I hate to wreck a home."

"Good," I say. Because all my impulses urge my lips toward his, but it would be the end of everything.

The bus driver makes an aggro face when I ask him to lower the ramp for Hannah's stroller. I'd like to ask why he's too important to perform the entire scope of his job description, but I'm breaking bail. I can't afford to be memorable.

We're going on a little trip, Hannah and I. A ferry to Nanaimo and then up, up, up the island until we find our remote haven, a town with bad cell service and a diner where I can work for cash, where Hannah can get dirt in her toenails and slurp popsicles and it can be the two of us against the world.

Except I won't raise her to be against the world. She will firmly own a place in it, as much as Emmaline.

"Tommy told me who your husband is." Sage winks as we arrive at Gleneagles for music class. Jake's parents sprung for the ten-week course, so I'm less bitter about dusting their ugly art collection. "You're so modest, I can't believe you haven't said a word."

I unbundle Hannah. I bought her an adorable Hatley raincoat secondhand. Five bucks. No rips. Bought myself some lightly used Lulu too, so we're a snazzy West Van duo.

"I've heard artists are impossible to live with. What's he working on?"

"He calls it a love story."

"Are you still in love with him?"

Hannah is busy chasing Jenna's son around the music room. I glance to make sure she's out of earshot. "I love who he was in Toronto. I loved bartending on Bloor Street and walking home to our duplex apartment in the Annex, his hair a sexy mess because he hadn't left his desk the whole time I'd been out."

"Why did you move west?"

I smooth my hand along the dirty carpet. I want the teacher to arrive, the hello song to start. "Jake's parents are here. We wanted Hannah to be close to her grandparents."

"You live with them?" She puts two and two together real quick.

"We're staying in their boathouse while we look for a place of our own."

Sage nods. "The boathouse. I like it. *Rebecca's Room.*"

"I'll tell him you loved his book. It will make his day."

"Can I tell him myself?" Her eyes sparkle. "Come for dinner on Saturday."

* * *

"My husband's in Tokyo," Sage says as the butler hangs our coats. "I asked Tommy to stand in."

Tommy grins from the couch, raises his beer in salute. The cheesiest smile plasters itself onto my face and won't leave.

Sage touches Jake's shoulder. "I want to show you the library."

We use the library for story time, the round white room, twenty feet high of reclaimed wood bookshelves with a dome skylight and sliding ladder. There's a mezzanine with bean-bag chairs where Sage reads *The Gruffalo* and *Corduroy* with dynamic dramatization. She was an actor before she had Em-maline. Not famous, but I remember a Tide commercial she was in.

Jake whistles. He suddenly doesn't seem so annoyed to be away from his computer tonight.

"See the desk? You can write there if you ever need a change of scenery."

"No shit?" Jake's eyebrows shoot up.

"I'd be honored. Jake Carruthers working between these walls."

I leave to put Hannah to sleep in the spare crib. As I sing her a lullaby, I try to forget that Jake finds brunettes sexier than blondes, that Sage has everything to offer and I have nothing left to give.

The Amber Alert comes while we're exploring the upper deck of the ferry. The photo: Hannah beaming from the top of Sage's rock wall. The message: *Hannah Carruthers, twenty months, possibly traveling with her mother, a murder suspect out on bail.* A description of us that includes what we're wearing right now.

I hurl my phone into the Georgia Strait. If they're tracking it, they'll know we boarded the boat.

Sage's wine cellar could be in a magazine. There's a long dinner table, a full-service bar, and a lounge with comfy seating. She opens the dumbwaiter and presents four plates with one scallop each.

"An amuse-bouche. Qualicum Beach scallops in a white wine marijuana butter sauce."

"I'll skip this course," I say. "I can't be a mess if Hannah needs me."

"Maria has the girls covered." Sage air-swats my concern. "She has bottles, books, she knows a million lullabies."

Jake squeezes my hand. "Let's get our life back."

He's right. I need to chill. I spear my scallop and let the butter melt on my tongue. It's more exquisite still for the pinot gris Sage pairs it with.

Jake eyes up Tommy. "So you're the man, hey?"

Tommy grins like he doesn't understand the question.

"The sports team, the car dealership, the high-rises. No one can touch you."

I stroke Jake's hand to help him loosen up, to not be insecure, to enjoy his meal and not spoil the friendship that has opened new worlds for Hannah.

Tommy shakes his head. "There's tons of richer guys than me. What no one can touch is your talent. I read *Rebecca's Room* last year. Your Manderley was even better than duMaurier's."

Jake's hand relaxes. I melt into him and the couch and it reminds me of the easy days when we drank beer and watched Netflix with takeout. Before Hannah entered screaming, forcing us to claw for our fair share of showers and sleep like rivals on a game show called *Who's Got the Time?* I watch Tommy in his club chair, a linebacker's body with a mind I'm dying to penetrate. I want to combine them into one perfect human, and I want them separately, naked, with all their flaws.

The dumbwaiter chimes. Sage unveils a tray of salmon skewers. "Haida Gwaii spring, seared rare." She pairs it with a BC pinot noir, and I don't remember my mouth ever feeling so satisfied.

"Who likes drinking games?" says Sage. "We'll start light. Never Have I Ever."

I roll my eyes. The game where everyone's thrilled to cop to every risqué thing they've done since they were twelve. Jake hates it more than I do, but he leans forward and says, "I love games."

Tame questions go around, things we easily drink to or laugh when someone doesn't. On Sage's fourth turn, she says, "Never have I ever had group sex."

Jake and I share a grin that remembers our old life, patios rolling into booze cans rolling into random apartments. We drink. So do Sage and Tommy.

"Well now. Time to amp up." Sage takes a sushi platter from the dumbwaiter and sets the salmon tray inside with our used plates. "Truth or Dare."

Tommy groans. "Are normal dinner parties even possible with you?"

"Only when my boring husband is in town." She pours sake into ceramic cups. "Just for asking, Tommy, you're first. Truth or dare?"

"Dare."

She dares him to kiss me.

I look at Jake, who shrugs. "I'm game if you are."

Tommy's lips don't linger, but the split-second they're on mine is electric.

"Quid pro quo," says Tommy. "I dare Sage to kiss Jake."

She sidles up to Jake and plants a full but quick kiss onto his lips. His eyebrows shoot up and I can tell he liked it. A lot.

In the morning, the housekeeper wakes Jake and me up with coffee and a pajama-clad Hannah. We cuddle Hannah in bed for ten full minutes, soaking our little family in.

"We needed this." Jake strokes my cheek and gives me a kiss that lasts until Hannah breaks it up.

When we see Tommy in the foyer, it's awkward but delicious, like in college after you sleep with a jock you might never go home with again, but you want to savor your wild side a few minutes longer before you return to the science lab.

Jake leaves to use the washroom and Tommy says, "Last night, I felt like we were tandem paragliding, you and me. I forgot there was anyone else in the room."

I zip Hannah into her raincoat.

"Can we do this again?" he whispers. "Just the two of us?"

I shake my head. "I'm married. Alone would be cheating."

"You like Sage," I say to Jake when Hannah goes down for her nap.

"She's hot."

"Are you going to work in her library?"

"Do you mind?"

I picture Sage popping in with midmorning snacks, twirling in micro shorts, asking if there's anything he needs. But we said we'd never be that couple, the petty jealous type who hold each other back. We even wrote, *If you love something, set it free,* into our marriage vows. So I say, "If you need a creative shift, go for it."

"You're the best. I'm getting stifled in the boathouse."

I run my finger along his cock, stroke it a while before taking it into my mouth, because if I'm going to set him free, I'd better give him reason to come home. His sighs mix with the thunder and I lap my tongue to the rhythm of the rain.

"This is paradise," he says, and my grip tightens because of course this is paradise for him. He gets to write all day and ignore his daughter, and his wife makes his lattes and gives him blow jobs and irons his father's shirts so he can have this writing space by the sea, and if that's not fucking good enough, he can write in the library of a hot mom nearby and fuck her if he wants to because everyone in his life is just so. Damn. Cool.

"That library is the bomb." Jake shakes out his umbrella at the boathouse door. "This week alone, I resolved three plot points that have been snagging me for months."

"Good." I stir the bolognese and pour him a glass of the cheap Italian red we both like. "I like when you're creatively satisfied."

He slips an arm around my waist. "When Emmaline goes to bed, I want to creatively satisfy you."

"Emmaline?" I say.

"Shit. I mean Hannah."

We have the Horseshoe Bay playground to ourselves. Just us and the crows.

Emmaline is fussing. She doesn't want to ride the wet swings, won't eat the cut veggies Sage packed.

Hannah taps our diaper bag and asks for an applesauce pouch. Before I realize what's happening, she marches it over to Emmaline.

"No, Hannah!" I shout as Emmaline slurps the whole pouch down.

"It's okay." Sage grabs the empty package and scans the ingredient list. "Hannah was being sweet. It's just, if Em gets a taste for processed food . . . and it's sweetened with apple juice, which is basically sugar . . ."

Jenna rummages through her snack bag. "I guess she won't want homemade hummus after fruit juice."

"Oh relax, you guys," Misty says with a laugh. "Look how happy Emmaline is now."

"Because of sugar. She'll crash soon." Sage shakes her head. "I'm not mad. It's just . . ."

A week or so later, Hannah and I have a chill day, so I pack a picnic and we walk to Whytecliff Park. She falls asleep in her stroller, which means I should go home and vacuum the drapes. But I'm feeling rebellious. Let Jake earn our rent for a change.

Sage's Tesla is in the parking lot. I glance in the window and it slams me all at once.

Sage and Jake. Necking like teenagers. I slink away before they see me.

I push Hannah toward home, the hour's walk made twice as long when she wakes up and demands release. She splashes along beside me, holds my hand and half-sings songs from music class. I pay enough attention to keep her safe from cars and headed generally forward, but the rest of my mind is stuck in the back of that Tesla.

I could leave Jake, get a job bartending, and try to find a crummy apartment with whatever money's left after child-care. Or I could make the best of this fucked-up situation, put in my two hours of housework for a free ride in what most people in the world would call paradise.

By the time I reach the boathouse, I've decided to say

nothing. Hannah's thriving with her new friends. Jake reads with her now, even took her to the park the other morning. Before I met Sage, I was trapped inside my own Cinderella story. She waved her wand and everything is better. So what if she wants to share my prince?

And there's another perk. I text Tommy: *Tandem paragliding?*

I drag Hannah to the ladies' room handicap stall. The ferry's rocking, but I manage to apply colored hairspray until her dark mop is blonder than Emmaline's. I spray mine gray to look like I'm her grandmother. A quick change of clothes and we're no longer the people in the Amber Alert.

I try to load her into the stroller but she clings to me, screams when I try to set her down.

We'll ditch the stroller. In case the bus driver remembers.

I clutch Hannah's hand and lead her to the gangplank.

The rain breaks, and Sage invites us for playgroup on her boat. Except when I arrive at the yacht club with Hannah, only Sage and Emmaline are waiting.

"Jenna and Misty couldn't make it. But we'll have a fun foursome with our daughters."

She skippers like a pro. Of course she has the perfect outfit, wide blue-and-white stripes and an adorable captain's hat.

She cuts the engine in a calm bay, puts the girls down for a nap below deck. She returns with a bottle of white and a thumbs-up.

After we've shared half the bottle, I say, "Jake's cheating on me."

"No!" Her eyes grow huge. "He seems so into you, and you give him all the freedom in the world. Why would he cheat?"

"It's fine." I'm sure my laugh sounds contrived. "Frees me up to play with Tommy."

"Oh my." Sage's eyebrows lift. "Have I created a monster?"

"I don't know. Did you create this?"

"I dragged you up from a life that was clearly no fun." Her smile gives way, showing a crack of a sneer underneath.

I refill our glasses, draining the bottle. "Why did you invite me out alone?"

"Because it's time," Sage says, no pretense left. "Time to give Jake up. He's mine. We've both known for a while."

"We can share him."

"I don't think so."

She shoves a vial into my hand. I frown and turn it over. There's no label, nothing to indicate what the ounce or so of liquid is.

"I learned everything about him after I read *Rebecca's Room*. It was clear on every page that he wrote it for me."

I push my wine away. "Most readers say that with fan mail."

"I wanted his daughter to play with mine. I wanted him to see what a good mother I am so I could replace you."

Replace me?

"I read about you being swinging singles back in the day, a regular Toronto Scott and Zelda. I knew that was my easiest way in."

I tap the vial. "What's in this?"

"You love Hannah so much, you should give her the life I'm offering. She can have the room next to Emmaline's. She can go to any school, any summer camp, any international exchange. She'll have the very best chance to be strong enough to take on this sad and crazy world."

"Are you telling me to kill myself?"

"Might be easier than watching your daughter grow up without you."

"Why would she grow up without me?"

"Read Jake's love story for the full answer."

"He never lets anyone read before his editor."

Sage cocks an eyebrow. "He let me."

"That's not . . ." I don't finish the sentence because it's impossible to accept that Jake let Sage read before me. "Jake can do what he likes, but Hannah stays with me."

"We'll let the courts decide, shall we? When Jake moves in with me, he'll have a fixed address. They'll award him initial custody. You'll have to fight to get her back, and I'll make sure that never happens."

"The court won't just *give* you my daughter."

"Courts can be bought like anything else. Plus, I have footage of you stoned and drunk and fucking Tommy."

"Jake d-doesn't know what Hannah eats for breakfast," I stammer. "He wouldn't want full custody."

"He wants me to be happy." Sage sighs, a contented cat with nothing left to wish for. "I've always wanted two daughters, but Emmaline's birth was atrocious and I can't have more. I told Jake he should spend more time with Hannah. Take her to the park, read books with her. I got a great photo of them together on the tire swing."

Of course. It was too good to be true, Jake wanting to be a better parent spontaneously.

"He agreed to let me tell you. He's a coward that way. Can't stand conflict."

It's true. Jake couldn't even fire his first agent. He sent me to their coffee meeting to do it for him.

"He's packing now," says Sage. "He'll be moved into my house by the time we're back to shore."

"What about your husband?"

"He'll keep our New York and Hong Kong apartments. He barely has any business in Vancouver anymore. Honestly, I think he's relieved." She stands up to go get us another bottle of wine.

I study the yacht's control panel. A steering wheel, a gear shift—forward, neutral, reverse. I might give it a few knocks while docking, but I could get the girls safely back to shore.

I picture Hannah growing up in that house. Jake, loving but distant. Sage, disturbed beyond belief.

When Sage turns away, I grab the wine bottle and crash it into the back of her head. She yelps and crumples to the floor. I lift her tiny body over the edge. The water is a thousand feet deep, according to the dashboard GPS. She'll drown before she comes to.

I'm nearly back at Eagle Harbour when a police boat pulls up beside me. Over the megaphone, they instruct me to cut my engine and allow them to board.

The female officer finds Sage's phone mounted to the dash. "Didn't know you were being broadcast?"

In my stomach, I know what's happened. She wanted to die. Jake might have fucked her senseless, he might have taken her advice to spend more time with Hannah, but he rejected her invitation to a brand-new life. I had what she wanted, what she truly thought was hers, and she needed to take me down with her.

"Our children—they're sleeping below deck." I realize with a thud that Sage put them down. If anything happened to Hannah—

I exhale with relief when the officers carry up a groggy Hannah, followed by an equally alive Emmaline.

"Mama?" Hannah reaches for a hug but my hands are cuffed behind me.

* * *

Police are waiting in Nanaimo, scrutinizing foot passengers as we enter the terminal.

A tap on my arm. "Could you and the girl step aside?"

The vial digs against my hip.

A few others are pulled aside. Moms mutter, annoyed for the delay. Kids are fussing. Hannah's enjoying the action, pointing out every dog, every baby, every boat.

They're checking ID. We could slip under the rope, but I wouldn't get far carrying Hannah. And without her, what's the point?

I slide two fingers into my pocket, roll the vial between them.

"You'll be okay." I stroke Hannah's hair, try to match her grin as she pokes my nose. "Your father will rise to the occasion, or close enough."

One cop won't take his eyes from me, speaks low into his radio.

I unscrew the cap, draw the vial to my nose. Bitter almond.

"Your grandparents will pay for an excellent education."

Three other cops circle, staring at Hannah and me.

It would be so easy to swallow, to erase twenty-five years of sporadic prison visits, erase the decades after release when she might meet me for the odd coffee but mostly make excuses for why she doesn't need me in her life. Or in her children's.

I brush hair out of her eyes. She'll need a cut soon. "You just have to stay confident, stay kind, make good friends, true friends who adore you for who you are."

I tip the vial back. She'll have to navigate her teen years without me.

But what if our prison visits go well, and I say even one thing that helps?

I'm about to dump the liquid on the floor when Hannah taps the vial, knocking the contents down my throat.

The circle tightens. An officer has handcuffs out.

I slump to the ground, clutching Hannah to protect her from the fall as I fade from consciousness. I whisper in her ear, "It's okay, munchkin. You'll be strong. You'll be loving. You'll be . . ."

PART II

*R*AGS *&* *B*ONES

THE MIDDEN

BY Carleigh Baker

South Cambie

Well, this is unexpected, but I guess no one ever expects dead bodies. Not in places that aren't morgues, or battlefields, or graveyards. I certainly didn't think there'd be one here, in the abandoned, boarded-up house next to my own home, on the corner of Cambie and King Ed. But here we are.

There are certainly *some* expectations when trespassing in a vacated home. It'll be quiet of course—a deep, engulfing quiet that only comes when the electricity is turned off for good, and the space has been empty long enough for the crackle of human existence to float off into the atmosphere. Energy never dies so it must go somewhere else. Maybe it goes to other neighborhoods, but what's left sinks to the earth like a deflated balloon. These leftovers—dust, moss, mold—are the biology of the dying home. Distasteful things that might make us feel better about the living, breathing biology of our own homes. South Cambie is a dead neighborhood slowly being ingested by condos, but I'll get to that later.

This body smells like someone threw steak in the compost. It's not overwhelming because the body isn't that old. It's dressed in a V-neck undershirt and a cardigan, pants cut awkwardly above the ankle, no socks. Skate shoes. Some people don't like this look—kind of normcore—but I do. Simple and youthful. There are no visible wounds, but rats have eaten its eyes. I assume it was rats, anyway. Maybe eyes are a rat delicacy, or maybe just a habitual first target, like when we get a chocolate Easter bunny and go straight for the ears.

Here's another unexpected thing, I knew this body when it housed a person. His name was Daniel, but he went by Diezl. I may have been the last one to see Diezl alive—around this time yesterday—and that brings a prickly feeling of responsibility to the situation. And so, standing here in this mausoleum, I try to remember what color Diezl's eyes were. And, obviously, wonder how the hell he ended up here.

It doesn't look like he was dragged—this would have left a trail of displaced junk, since the house is full of it: empty beer bottles, needles, piles of pink insulation. He must have died inside, but why would he come here? His territory is way down past 49th, in the neighborhood that's still mostly alive—for now. But Diezl's body appears to have just materialized here, the rotting sneakers and McDonald's bags around it untouched. He always had his skateboard and his bag of spray cans with him, but there's no sign of them. My flashlight flicks across his hands, curled into a rigor mortis grip. Diezl has huge hands, always stained with paint.

Through a busted window, I can see the dark outline of my own house. Ben will still be asleep.

I've been breaking into the abandoned places in South Cambie for a while now. A person needs to know the story of the land they live on, even if it's not pretty. Especially if it's not pretty. Some houses have been sitting empty since the push to redevelop the neighborhood started last year, while others are freshly vacated. Companies like Millennium and Bosa have bought up nearly everything, but not the place where Ben and I live, not yet. Ben's buddy owns it—he told us he's holding out for eight million, and if you think that's crazy, you don't know Vancouver. The last offer he got was four million, so for now we get to stay. He says that if the cops find us squatting, he'll deny knowing us. Ben hates that, but he puts up with it.

Most of the glass is long gone from the windowpane, but I still take my time crawling out. A couple of rats look up at my dangling feet, unafraid. There's been an influx of rats recently. A lot of them get hit by cars, their little mashed bodies rotting in the street. Yesterday, I opened a cupboard door and found a smallish one nibbling on Ben's cookies. It's not a great place to live, I'll admit. But it's practically free, and that feels like giving the finger to capitalism.

I'll also admit that when we moved here six months ago, the dying houses totally freaked me out. This one is in terrible shape: crumbled carport, roof caving, thick moss on the siding. Ample signs of the neighborhood taggers brighten things up a bit, but they worried me too at first. I thought they were gangs—Diezl had a good laugh about that. Fukit seems to be a pretty prolific artistic presence in this neighborhood; his tags are all over. There may be a turf war going on, though, since **Kitten** has been making a move, painting right over Fukit's old tags. Or maybe Fukit just got tired and fucked off. It wouldn't surprise me. Everyone in the city seems to have forgotten South Cambie exists. Weeks go by without anyone collecting our garbage or recycling. Most of the garbage in this backyard is ours, we just toss it when the bins fill up. This is supposed to be my last break-in, since it was the house I was the most intimidated by when we first moved to the neighborhood. Some kind of milestone, but I'm not sure for what any more. Diezl was disappointed that I wanted to do it alone.

Around the time things started to get a little rough with Ben, I started going for long walks in the neighborhood. The first time, I was getting out of the shower and he was pissed because I'd used all the hot water. This isn't hard to do, since the water heater has been leaking like crazy for ages. I told him if we just showered together it wouldn't be a problem, and for some reason he flew off the handle and started yelling, pushed me and I slipped on the wet floor and banged my face on the towel rack. I chipped a tooth and split my lip. Pretty dramatic, I guess, but Ben swore that hadn't been his intention—like, to actually injure me—and of course he was right. He's not a violent guy. Still, the last thing I wanted to do was crawl into bed next to him. I slipped out while he was screwing the towel rack back into the wall, looking miserable. He really did seem to feel guilty about it.

The place next door—creepy in the day and downright terrifying at night—looks right into our backyard, since someone ripped the plywood off the windows. Awful whether I pictured a human standing in the shadows watching, or the vacant stare of the house itself. I went out the front. We're on the southwest corner, surrounded by huge laurel hedges that hide the house completely. But we exist. There's an overgrown staircase that's easy to miss, almost like bushwhacking out of a magical secret garden, except totally not. I bushwhacked out of a giant, moldering house that was somebody's affordable palace in the seventies, but it's a dump now, because why would anyone take care of something with numbered days? Spongy walls, split hardwood floors, and high ceilings that cave in a little and dump plaster muck on the floor when it rains.

It was one in the morning, and there wasn't much open in Cambie Village. The presence of the Canada Line station across the street makes the neighborhood a fairly unsafe place to be at night, even though it's sandwiched between Shaughnessy to the west and Queen Elizabeth Park to the east. I decided to walk south, toward 49th. That's where I met Diezl.

He passed me on his skateboard, then stopped. "You should be careful, there's some guy in the neighborhood grabbing women at night."

"Grabbing them?" I looked at his hands and quickly back up at his face, hoping that hadn't made it seem like I was implicating him. Those humongous hands on such a small guy.

He didn't seem to notice. "Yeah, sorry to be creepy but . . ."

"That's not creepy—I mean, you telling me isn't creepy. Thanks."

"Okay." His eyes searched my face for a second and I felt a little thrill for some reason, like this was a movie and something amazing was about to happen. "Your chin."

I remembered my split lip, and rubbed the dried blood off my chin.

He nodded, and pushed off on his skateboard, looking back at me once before he disappeared out of the streetlights.

Three nights later, when Ben and I drank a lot of beers in the backyard, and he smacked me across the face for breaking his second-favorite pint glass, and then cried for nearly an hour, I took off again. This time it was closer to two a.m. Eyes peeled for any dudes who looked like they might want to grab me, I found myself smiling at the approaching sound of wheels clicking on the sidewalk cracks.

"You again," Diezl smirked. "Living dangerously."

"I'm looking for some action," I said, and then immediately worried that he might think I was hitting on him.

"You better come with me then." He picked up his skateboard and we walked down an alley, past several of those slightly-fancier-than-average Vancouver Specials. Special Vancouver Specials. From the sixties to the mideighties, these boxy beauties were filling up neighborhoods, until they were considered an eyesore. This isn't a very old neighborhood, at least from a colonial perspective. If you check Wikipedia, that's where the history starts—when the first colonizers arrived in the 1800s. Henry Cambie was an engineer for the Canadian Pacific Railway. The land was given to the CPR by the government, which is funny, because it wasn't theirs to give. It was xʷməθkʷəy̓əm territory. Forest and salmon streams. Some people call that untamed wilderness, and some people call it home. Diezl stopped in front of a boarded-up rancher. He put a finger to his lips and we snuck into the backyard through a space between the tall construction barriers.

"You're not a cop, right?" he whispered.

"Uh, SkyTrain police." My punch lines always come one second too late. He laughed anyway. That was nice. Ben only laughs at his own jokes.

This place must not have been empty too long—the backyard was clean, grass mowed. Developers are supposed to keep the acquired houses tidy, but they don't. Diezl put his backpack on the ground and pulled out some spray cans.

"Hey, you aren't Fukit, are you?" I asked. "Kitten, perhaps? With asterisks?"

"They're South Cam," he said with a sneer that suggested more of a friendly rivalry than any actual distaste. "This is Langara, baby." He deftly outlined a juicy-looking *Diezl* on the back wall, between two boarded-up windows. "I've never done this with somebody. You want to fill it in?"

"I'll fuck it up," I squeaked, and Diezl shushed me as a light went on next door.

We squeezed up next to the house and crouched low beside the bushes, my heart beating like crazy.

"Nah," he whispered, "go ahead."

We waited for the light to go out—"Probably just the bathroom," Diezl said—and he handed me a can. Purple, maybe—it was hard to tell in the dark. I held my breath and got to work while Diezl supervised.

"What room do you think is on the other side of this wall?" I asked.

"Bedroom, probs," he said.

"Ever go inside?" I cringed as a little paint dripped outside the lines.

"Nah. Hold the can farther away and it won't drip."

I wanted to tell him that I'd been planning to break into a dead house at the end of my block. Maybe invite him along. But I concentrated on spraying in the lines instead.

Afterward, Diezl offered to walk me home, but I wasn't sure he should know where I live. So we just walked around. Strange to see what affordable housing used to look like. Even the roads are sprawling, with big grassy boulevards. It's kind of obscene, all that space.

Our place is quiet when I let myself in, except for the hum of the fridge. I pull a bag of blueberries out of the freezer and dump them and some protein powder into a Magic Bullet and fire it up. This wakes Ben, and he waves groggily on his way to the bathroom.

Even a smoothie is hard to get down; I can't get the smell of that house out of my mind. Diezl's smell. What am I going to do with that kid? Call the cops, so they can return him to his dad? The first night we broke into an abandoned house together—a little hobbit house that I'd watched the family move out of three days before—he asked about my lip. Then he told me about his dad. Then we compared cuts and bruises.

"You've got a lot more than me," I said.

He shrugged. "Some of them are from skateboarding."

The hobbit house still had some life breath; it felt like any minute someone would come down the stairs and demand to know where all the furniture went. The carpet was still clean, though it smelled a little like cat piss. Wires poked out of the walls from where the fixtures had been.

Diezl dumped his spray cans on the floor. "Ready?"

I threw some devil horns, and then realized kids probably don't do that anymore. "Ready."

We propped up some flashlights and tagged the whole living room; I probably inhaled enough paint to take fifteen years off my life. I tried my hand at a tag, but it was kind of stupid. *#FatLip.* Who the fuck hashtags a tag? Maybe people do, who knows. It was all I could think of at the time, and it's what brought us together. We laughed a lot at that, and Diezl said it looked good. It felt nice to believe him, but he was probably full of shit. Anyway, I was glad it was inside, so nobody would see it except for us. I joked that maybe we should move into that place, and he looked around for a long time.

When we crawled out the window into the street, it was two a.m. A security guard from the building site next door walked by, holding a coffee. At the time, that high-density heaven was nothing more than a few stories of girders, but they sure do grow up fast. Streetlights threw its skeleton profile over the hobbit house, and that was the first time I really noticed how close the condos were getting. I went back by myself a few nights later to check out our work, but a demolition crew had already ripped the place apart and widened the construction site barriers around its memorial.

What am I going to do with this kid who showed me a fresh burn on his arm yesterday, when we met up to tag the back wall of Oakridge Mall? He told me that the cops had picked him up for skateboarding and insisted on driving him home, and then his dad held him down and drove a cigarette into him.

"Do you know what burning skin smells like?" he asked. Nobody wants to hear the answer to that question, so we walked in silence. I should have hugged him, or put my arm around him or something.

Well, something has to happen now, some kind of observance. I don't have any sage. There are a couple of tea lights and a piña colada–scented candle in the bedroom—that'll have to do. Line them up on the coffee table and light each one. Watch the candles flicker and try to think cleansing thoughts or whatever, but instead I think about a place past Diezl's neighborhood, deep into Marpole, called ċəsnaʔəm. That's hən̓q̓əmin̓əm̓ language. People who can't be bothered to learn the original place names given to this land call it the Great Marpole Midden. Midden means garbage pile.

This spot is an ancient xʷməθkʷəy̓əm village and burial site that's at least four thousand years old. The "midden" was uncovered in 1884, around the time the first settlers arrived in the area. It contained the ancestral remains and cultural artifacts of the Coast Salish peoples. The remains were removed by two white guys, who gave them to the Natural History Museum of New Westminster, which is funny, because this wasn't theirs to give. Another white guy found seventy-five more human skeletons in the midden, and gave them to the museum too. In 1898, these remains were destroyed in a fire. There's more to the story, but I'll get to that later.

Diezl and I never even got around to tagging the mall yesterday, and this was kind of a relief. I wanted to show him I was badass enough to do it, but that would have been undeniable vandalism, not like the dead spaces. A mall is a living organism—pushing shoppers through arteries like leukocytes. Of course, too many of those little white cells in the blood is a sign of disease. Not enough, and the whole system breaks down. Diezl said he wasn't into it. He said he'd rather just hang, so we went back toward South Cambie. He always seemed to want to be in my neighborhood.

This time we hung out in one of the new construction sites, after we watched the old security guy do his rounds and disappear back into the trailer. We climbed up onto the second floor and found a shadow to hide in, right in the belly of the beast. A beast with an insatiable appetite. In 2011, the xʷməθkʷəy̓əm learned that a 108-unit residential condo development was being planned for c̓əsnaʔəm. The following year, an intact burial of an adult ancestor was found at the site. Developers wanted to move it. Seven hundred burial sites had already been removed. The xʷməθkʷəy̓əm people fought hard to have the land honored as the national heritage site it was supposed to be. Eventually they won, which is funny, because it was always their unceded ancestral territory.

The condos are coming for us too. I wonder what will come next.

I'd bought us some beer, thinking I'd need the liquid courage to tag the mall, so we cracked them.

"Are you going to leave your boyfriend?" Diezl asked.

"Why?"

"Because he's a dick, and because you can."

"You want to run off together?" I asked, poking his leg with the toe of my shoe.

He looked at me then, and I felt awkward, like something intimate was happening. Not romance—more like we were brother and sister.

"I can't go anywhere," Diezl said. "You're lucky. You have options."

"You'll have options soon. After graduation?"

"No, I won't."

I tried to read his expression in the gloom. Everything always seems so dire to teenagers, but you're not supposed to tell them that. He didn't want to say goodbye, even when we walked back to my place, so we sat on the front steps for a few minutes before I got worried Ben might wake up and find us.

Oh shit, now I remember his eyes in the porch light. Green. And so sad.

A half hour later the tea lights are done; only the piña colada candle is burning. I'm just sitting, trying to get ahold of things. Ben comes out of the bathroom, dressed for a run. Maybe he's finally going to get his shit together. He kicks his runners toward the front door, opens it, and comes back.

"Where were you last night?" he says.

"Aren't you going for a run?"

Ben moves closer. "Any new hobbies?"

"Huh?"

"Skateboarding?"

"What?"

Ben narrows his eyes a little and motions toward the front door with his lips. "C'mere."

Diezl's backpack and skateboard are piled on the step.

"Weird," I croak, avoiding Ben's gaze, "I'll take them out to the garbage."

His grip tightens on the knob, and I realize how tuned in I've become to his every move. "Leave the board. Maybe *I'll* take up skateboarding."

"Okay, I'll get rid of the bag. Put some coffee on."

He just stands there and watches me. "Any new boyfriends?"

"Don't be stupid. Put some coffee on." I nod toward the kitchen, but he doesn't move.

Dead spaces look different in the daytime. Light filters in from cracks and holes I never would have noticed at night. The smell of Diezl's body is stronger now. I cover my mouth and take the bag over to him. Pull the zipper so hard it catches on the fabric and sticks, so I just yank on the thing until it rips open. Dump out the spray cans, let them roll across the floor.

At the bottom of the bag is Diezl's sketchbook. In the front pockets there are some smokes and a five-dollar bill, but nothing else. I open the sketchbook.

Diezl had shown me some of his art before: doodles and tattoo designs, and increasingly elaborate versions of his tag, incorporating stars or sometimes flames, depending on his mood. On the last page, *BURN AFTER READING* is drawn in an elaborate script. I close the book. Lay it on Diezl's chest.

"Okay, buddy."

Ben's standing in our backyard holding two mugs. "What were you doing?"

I don't have to answer him. Maybe I'll just drink the damn coffee and not say anything.

But he scoots in front of the door. His eyes are brown and wounded, but he turns everything to rage.

"You need to get out of the way," I say.

"Taryn!" he shouts after me. "Taryn, what the hell?"

A mug whizzes past me and hits a wall that's in such bad shape, it makes a sizable dent. But when I return fire, with a pitching arm that seems to belong to someone else, my mug smashes into the fridge.

"Whoa," Ben says. We look over each other's shoulders at the carnage. Coffee everywhere.

I open the cupboard over the sink, where we keep the booze. Sambuca definitely lights up pretty good; I've done a few flaming shots in my time. Oh, and Bacardi 151, that shit is high-test.

Ben keeps saying my name over and over, and I don't think he knows for sure whether he should be pissed off or scared. I rip a dry dishcloth in half and stuff the pieces in the bottles, leaving a little wick. There's duct tape in the cupboard under the sink. A lighter on the table.

"Taryn, Jesus fuck." Ben grabs both my arms with his death grip, nails dig in. "You're being crazy."

"Let go."

"Taryn, put those fucking bottles down."

"Let go."

"What were you doing in that house?" Ben's expression slides toward fear and his grip loosens a little. I try knocking my forehead against his nose. This definitely gets results, but it stuns me a little as well.

"Holy shit, I will kill you, you bitch!" Ben trails after me into the backyard, but he moves slowly, his nose bloody. He's not going to kill anyone—he's so full of shit.

I look around to make sure nobody's close by, and of course nobody is. Dead neighborhood is dead. I turn the Sambuca bottle upside down to wet the wick, and I light it. It flares up, but not as much as I'd expected.

I should say something good, but all I can think of is, "Bye, Diezl." Toss the bottle in the window, and do the same with the 151.

Ben stands beside me wiping his nose. "It's not going to work."

"Shut up."

We watch a little bit of smoke pool inside the window, then dissipate.

"Taryn, I don't know what you're trying to prove—"

"Lift me up."

"What?"

"Lift me up!"

Ben blinks, but offers a foothold and I take it, peering into the window. I'd expected an explosion, huge flames, something like a movie. The dead house seemed to absorb the fire; all I see is a scorch mark around a couple of paper bags. Diezl's body sucks energy from the light—reaches out and demands action.

Below me, Ben's voice is a bloody burble: "Alcohol's not flammable enough."

"Thanks for the tip."

Ben doesn't follow me back inside. He doesn't follow me into the basement, where the hot water heater has been leaking onto the cement floor for weeks, maybe months. All those cold showers. Half underground, it smells like sweet rot. There are layers of dust and dead spiders on the crap we've been storing down here, trying to make a living home in a dead neighborhood.

I pull back an old tarp where the jerrican should be, and see the legacy of the rat poison we left out in the winter—a nest of dead bodies peeking out of a hole in the concrete. Ben doesn't see this, but I do.

Shake that jerrican like it's an adversary—only half full. I'm going to need a lot more gasoline.

WONDERFUL LIFE

BY SAM WIEBE

Commercial Drive

> *The Drive is like a neighborhood in an older, more sophisti-*
> *cated city, where it's the poor people who are left wing and*
> *a certain particulate violence sort of hangs in the air.*

There's a lost name for every place in the city.

The man breaking into my apartment looked to be about seventy. He carried himself with a beat cop's bearing, his shoulders squared, but his clothes said assisted living—Velcro shoes, drawstring pants, polo shirt with the collar unbuttoned to display a thatch of white and silver hair. He was Asian, and he looked at me as if searching my face for a recognition that would jump-start his own. The man knocked the glass out of my patio door with a long-handled police flashlight, the same as my father had carried. He called me by my father's name.

"Matt," he said, "the hell aren't you in uniform? You forget we're on nights this week?"

Despite my credentials as a security consultant, I've never cared much about protecting my home. I live in East Van, on Broadway near Commercial Drive. I take it as a given that people will hop the fence, smoke dope on the patio, try the handle of the apartment door. If someone were to break in they'd probably swoon in disappointment—unless their dream haul is a half-decent Rega turntable, a few shelves of boxing books, and the dregs of a bottle of Bulleit.

The only possession with sentimental worth was my father's MagLite. After his death I'd had the bulb switched to a high-powered fluorescent. Now I pointed the beam in the trespasser's face.

The man squinted into the light. "Tonight's the night, Matt. Or did you forget?" I turned the beam away. His vision came back quickly. He said, "You're not Matt."

"He's been dead nine years," I said. "Hit and run. Who are you?"

"Me and Matt are s'posed to do something tonight," he said. "If you see him, say Joe stopped by."

"Joe Itami?"

I'd seen him at the funeral, and a few times during my very brief stint on the job. I'd gotten the sense that he and my father had once been close. Joe Itami had gone the command route, attaining the rank of inspector, while Matt Wakeland had persisted as a beat cop until the car crash that killed him.

Itami had always seemed poised, dignified. A comfortable leader. To see him now with his white hair askew, a piss stain spreading across his sweats, was disconcerting.

"I'll take you home," I said. "You still live on Nanaimo, right?" I put a hand on his shoulder. He shivered but didn't shake it off.

"David," he said.

"That's right. I used to hang out with your son, once upon a time. How's Katz doing? He's, what, a sergeant now?"

Itami looked back at the broken glass but I herded him through the apartment door, out onto the street where I'd parked my Cadillac. Joe shuffled as he walked. A crowd stood beneath the neon sign for the Rio Theatre, smoking and waiting for the midnight showing. They ignored us. At the car door, Joe blinked and peered around, then looked curiously at the flashlight in his hand. He snapped the light on, off, on, and off.

"David," he repeated. "Matt's son."

"That's right."

"You don't look much like him."

I unlocked the passenger's-side door and held it open for him. "Flattery gets you nowhere."

After a moment spent staring at me in what felt like evaluation, Joe Itami said, "There isn't one fucking shred of good in you, is there?"

Katz Itami finished putting his father to bed and joined me on the porch. He lit a cigarette, a Rooftop, and blew smoke toward Nanaimo Street. His father's house had a view of the distant North Shore mountains. Katz stared forlornly at the V-shaped strip of ski lights blinking atop Grouse.

"I got a woman coming in next week," he said, "make sure he takes his meds. Aricept, memantine. It's Alzheimer's, Dave. Dementia. Probably from all those years living alone."

"There been other incidents?" I asked.

"I've been on his couch less than a month. We have oatmeal together, then I go to work. He's usually asleep when I get back."

"Doesn't answer my question," I said.

Katz shrugged. "I mean, he gets names mixed up. When Barbara dropped my stuff off, he called her by her mom's name. But that's nothing new."

"Why me?"

"He was probably out walking, noticed your name on the buzzer."

"My name's not on the buzzer, Katz, but he knew it. Joe was looking for my father. Acting like he was still walking a beat."

"Christ." Katz flicked his smoke off the porch, into the trough of dead mulch that had once been a flower bed. Joe Itami's house had been standing for eighty years, and looked every day of it. The property alone would probably fetch three million.

Katsuyori was eleven years my senior, a sergeant with the VPD. He was taller than his father, slightly heavier, and had a genial, compassionate air that had netted him more than a few confessions. Katz also had the exhausted look of the recently divorced. I didn't judge him when he chained another smoke.

"Always thought my dad had it . . . not easier, but simpler," Katz said. "He was born the year my gramps came out of the internment camp. *Nisei*, second-gen. Him being a cop, and then on top of that marrying Mom, putting up with her WASP-ass family looking down on him—not a lot of guys could carry all that."

"No."

"But he always knew what to do. Work the job, raise a family, come home each shift in one piece. Difficult things, but straightforward, y'know? I admired that. Part of me moving back here, aside from getting my shit sorted, was to learn from him. How he kept it all together. 'Cept it's hard to ask him if he doesn't know me. Doesn't know himself."

I left him my card. "Anything comes up."

"'Preciate it, thanks." He put it on the guardrail and continued staring at the lights in the dark sky. I wondered if the card would end up among the crushed filters in the barren garden. Something else forgotten.

* * *

Katz must have kept the card, because at seven the next morning he phoned my cell.

"Joe's gone," he said. "Took my car, I don't know where, and Dave, fuck, he's got my uniform. He's got my gun."

I picked up Katz in my Cadillac and we drove across First Avenue to Commercial Drive. Traditionally the city's Italian and Portuguese enclave, the Drive was now also home to anarchists, activists, fashion casualties, and holdovers who viewed anyone under sixty with scorn. It was a spectacular mess—trattorias and mercados, German bakeries and African hair salons. And everywhere sushi and coffee, those two staples of East Vancouver life.

I tried to see the neighborhood the way Joe Itami circa 1974 would, when it was the center of his beat. What still remained after gentrification, real estate crises, countless waves of new arrivals? What would he look for?

Katz had the passenger's window all the way down, ignoring the light rain that soaked the sleeve of his shirt. He trailed smoke from his mouth. I'd asked him not to light up in the car, which he'd taken as an invitation to break out his vape pen. The car's interior filled with the smell of apricot and mint.

"The Drive was your dad's beat too," Katz said. "He ever talk about what he did, back in the day?"

"He didn't talk much period. Least not to me." I added, "I don't think he much wanted to be a parent."

"That's right, you were adopted or something."

"Or something, yeah."

We parked and knocked on the door of the Legion Hall. Built in the forties, the building had recently been painted bright blue and trimmed orange, the words *LEST WE FOR-*

GET printed above the entrance. Katz put away his pen. The door was opened by a white-haired woman holding a spray bottle of bright green liquid. She looked warily between us, sizing us up.

"Looking for my dad," Katz said. He held his hand flat at the height of his chin. "About yay tall, Japanese Canadian, seventy-two years old."

"The officer," she said.

Katz sent a nervous glance my way before nodding to the woman. "He say where he was going?"

"I told him we weren't open and he said he was looking for someone. Said he'd been waiting at the park all morning."

"Which park? Stanley?"

"I think he meant Clark Park." She pointed up the street in its direction. "He said he got tired of waiting and was going to find where this kid was hiding. Michael Something-or-Other, think he said."

Katz thanked her. Back in the car, we drove south, in the direction she'd pointed. It was a nothing park, a few hilly, grassy blocks, with a soccer field and softball diamond, playground and swing set. A deep diagonal rut across the western slope, hardened by bikes and the odd motorcycle. Joe Itami wasn't there.

We drove slow along the Drive, looking for anything unusual. I asked Katz if his dad had told him about his days walking the beat. Something significant might have happened to him then.

"It was a rough neighborhood, that time. We grew up three blocks from the prostie stroll, before that was all pushed down to the ports. I was in Pampers when he and your dad were busting heads."

"They do a lot of that, you think?"

"The seventies, Dave. East fucking Van. What do you think?"

Driving back up Venables, Katz pointed, "There," and told me to stop. On the pavement beside a Vietnamese sandwich shop, beneath a mural of blackbirds and First Nations orcas, was Joe Itami's MagLite. We noticed a commotion up the block, and headed in that direction.

A small group of elderly men sat and stood outside Abbruzzo Café. They were talking in English and French and Italian, and regarded us as intruders. I asked them what happened.

"Gook got Mikey," one of them said.

"Shut up, Mauro, you don't say that to someone's face." Mr. Voice-of-Reason smiled at Katz and said, by way of apology, "He's just nervous, got the jitters. Mauro's not s'posed to drink coffee no more."

"What happened to Mikey, exactly?" Katz said.

"We're just sitting here. Guy drives up in his Nissan. He's in uniform. Tells Mikey he wants to have a word. Mikey being Mikey, tells him what to do with that. Then the, uh, officer shows him his gun. Cuffs Mikey and drives off. Can hardly believe what I seen, y'know?"

"He looked Korean," one of the seated men offered.

"Like you'd know," Voice-of-Reason said. "You guys think he's really with the cops?"

"I am," Katz said. "And I appreciate your help. Anything else you can tell us?"

"Korean. I'm sure."

"His car's a piece of junk."

"Smelled like he might've gotten sick on the ride over."

"Or maybe Vietnamese."

I stopped the flood of wisdom to ask how Mikey had acted at seeing Joe Itami.

"Same as all of us," Mr. Voice-of-Reason said. "Came as a shock. We're just killing time till the Juventus game, not expecting nothing like this."

"Don't you remember?" Mauro said to him. "Mikey recognized him. Said, *Holy ess, it's you.*"

"Right, that's right," Voice said.

"What's Mikey's full name?" Katz asked.

"Michael." Chortles from the seated men.

"Rosato," Voice said. "Michael Rosato."

The group closed ranks as soon as we asked about Rosato's personal life. We went inside, bought espressos, and asked the barista, a thin woman with a hard smile and iron-colored hair. She hadn't seen the abduction, but she knew Mikey. He'd been coming there for years.

"Take him awhile," she said, "but he got himself back on track."

"From what?" I said.

She shrugged and took the money and slapped my change on the counter. "From drinking, and I don't know what else. He's okay now, Mikey, but back in the day . . ." She looked at the ceiling as if his misdeeds were written there. "Back then he run with a pretty rough group."

Another hour of searching produced nothing.

"You should call it in," I told Katz. "It's kidnapping."

"My dad you're talking about, Dave. He's old. Confused. He's no criminal."

"Didn't say he was."

"I'll call from the house, 'kay? Promise. By now he's probably wandered back."

But he wasn't at home, and he wasn't at Clark Park. Joe Itami had disappeared into East Vancouver, into 1974, into himself. Michael Rosato had been dragged along with him.

"Can you run Rosato through CPIC?" I asked. "Maybe Joe arrested him, back in the day."

Katz nodded. I left him at his house to make arrangements, call in what favors he could. I told him I'd keep looking, and meet back with him in two hours.

I cruised up Woodland, down Clark, over Venables, and back up the Drive. It felt futile, like looking for someone else's memories. Nick Cave played through the Cadillac's speakers. "Wonderful Life." For some of us, anyway.

My mother's house is on Laurel Street. She and her husband had built it in the midsixties, anticipating they'd raise a family there. That hadn't quite worked out. Instead, just as she reached the age and mind-set to give up on having kids, circumstances forced her to adopt her younger sister's son.

I say circumstances, but it was my birth parents' decision to leave me with the Wakelands. They'd been under the sway of a religious leader who preached that children (other than his own) were a spiritual drag. A tether to the flawed material world. Only much later did they recognize him as a fraud.

By then Beatrice and Matt Wakeland seemed to have the kid under control, so why complicate their own recently reclaimed lives? Easier to start over, to leave well enough alone.

I was luckier than most. And angrier than most. And tired of battling the past.

The woman I called my mother sat on the porch, smoking, looking slightly more frail than the last time I'd seen her, and just as defiant.

"What's the occasion?" she said, standing to embrace me.

She sat back in her rocking chair with a sigh, *Oooof*, which she covered for with an exaggerated yawn.

"Wanted to see how you're doing," I said.

"David."

"And," I said more truthfully, "I wanted to ask, do you remember Joe Itami?"

"Of course. Lovely man."

"What exactly did he and Matt—"

"Your father."

"Right, what did they do? How close were they?"

"Closer back in the day," my mother said. "They were partnered up for a while. Joe was a nice man. Handsome as all get-out. He wanted off the streets, order to be home more. That's why he got his promotion. Your father, well . . ." She shrugged. "He was who he was."

"Constable for Life," I said. I'd never quite escaped that mentality. "He or Joe ever mention a Michael Rosato?"

"I didn't ask about his business. Like I don't with you."

"What about Clark Park, anything happen there?"

She turned her pipe upside down and banged out the ash into a Kirkland coffee tin. The muscles of her face tightened. "Why?"

"Because Joe ran off this morning in his son's uniform, thinking it's forty years ago. Katz and I have to find him before he hurts this Rosato. Something happened in that park, didn't it?"

She tamped flakes of tobacco into the bowl and didn't look at me.

"Beatrice," I said. "Mom."

"It was different then," she said.

"Getting really fucking tired of hearing that."

"Well it was," she said. "You don't understand 'cause you

grew up in a safe place. Back then, the kids that hung out in that park were rotten to the core. A decent person couldn't even walk through there."

"Did Matt and Joe arrest Rosato there?"

My mother struck a kitchen match off the railing and bent low. I loomed over her, cupping my hands to provide a windscreen. She coughed and broke the match in two and tossed both pieces toward the can.

"Some things a cop's wife knows not to ask," she said. "Whatever your father did, I'm sure he felt he had to."

It was late afternoon, the sun screened by slate-colored clouds. I walked around Clark Park, trying to imagine a time when it felt ominous to do so. Instead I saw a troop of Catholic students occupying the fields, a pair of middle-aged women kissing on a park bench, a kid on a bike following his father in a circuit of the basketball court, legs pumping with more assurance as the motion became familiar to him. Joe Itami wasn't among us.

Katz phoned to say he'd looked up Michael Rosato, and found a record of drug offenses and property crimes going back to his twenties, probably further. Nothing in the last few years. Evidently he'd gotten clean.

"More a shit-disturber than a hard-ass," Katz said. "He would've been seventeen, eighteen back in the day. Part of the Clark Park Gang. I asked one of the old-timers about them. She said the park gangs used to be, quote, unquote, pretty rough customers."

"What I heard too."

"Rosato's known associates are mostly dead or moved away. The name that comes up the most is Holditch, Gordon, no middle initial. He did a stint for larceny back in the early eighties, but cleaned up and started a business. 'Member Gord the Stereo Guy, had the store on Alma and 10th?"

"Sure, with the commercials." A jovial fat man jumping over a whiskey keg to prove his customers had him over a barrel, but only for a limited time.

"Gord's dead, but his wife still lives at 30th and Main. She says a car went by her house this morning, a couple times, slow. Could've been a Nissan. Want to pick me up?"

I said I would.

The Holditch living room was a shrine to the late store as much as its late owner. Framed photos of Gord on opening day, full-page ads, an article in the *Georgia Straight*, all decorated the walls. On the floor behind a pair of recliners was the store's neon sign, unplugged, furry with dust, its cord wound loosely around the top of the G.

Nelly Holditch was a large pretty woman in a paisley blouse and dun-colored slacks. Her frizzy brown hair was loosely ponytailed, a few white roots showing. She had coffee ready, and while she poured, she told us about her husband's nightmares.

"Gord got sober the year we married. Never left the wagon after that. I know he'd had some bad times before me. Once, twice a year, he'd wake up with his side of the sheets soaked through. It'd take him hours to unwind. When I'd ask, he'd say he was thinking of old friends."

"Michael Rosato?" Katz asked.

"He mentioned a Mikey but I never met him. I guess Mikey's life hadn't turned out so well. He couldn't kick his problems the way Gord did. Poor guy."

"Something happened to them in Clark Park," I said.

"Lots. It's where they used to congregate. They were

kids—punks, I guess you'd call them. Lot of broken homes, abuse, parents who drank or did whatever. The park was where they'd get away from all that."

"The police bothered them?"

"Harassed them," she said. "Any time there was a fight or a break-in in the neighborhood, it was those evil kids in Clark Park. Some of the cops thought Gord was the ringleader, and really had it out for him."

"He ever mention a cop named Joe Itami?"

"No. There was one name . . ." She sighed. Her irises traveled in orbit as she tried to recall.

"Wakeland," Katz said.

Nelly's head made deep, emphatic nods. "Him, yeah. I remember 'cause we saw the name on a business ad somewhere, a couple years ago. Security company, I think. Gord tensed right up. That night he had one of his sweat spells."

I tried not to show any emotion. It was easy. Anger and shame and disbelief all roiled through me at once, canceling each other out. I didn't know what to feel. Joe Itami's words came back to me.

"People saw Gord as this happy, funny guy," Nelly said. "A real character. And for the most part he was. God, no one could make me laugh like him. But something happened back in the day, and once in a blue moon it would creep to the surface. I'd tell him to forget it, it was ages ago. Gord would say, *Easy for you, they didn't put you in the drink.*"

"You think his alcoholism resulted from whatever happened with the police?" Katz said.

"I do, yes. He fought it, and beat it, but it was always waiting to pounce."

We finished our coffee and left, making one last circuit of the

Drive. Rush hour slowed our progress. We peered at every building, down every side street, at every face no matter how unlike Joe Itami's. Katz smoked. The stereo hummed. Chris Cornell, "Preaching the End of the World."

Finally, Katz said, "It was their job."

"What was? Beating up teenagers? Or kidnapping—that part of the job?"

"Those gangs weren't just troubled kids," Katz said. "They caused riots. Hurt people. Scared an entire neighborhood. The word came down to clean up the parks, whatever it took. Joe and Matt were a part of that. The H-Squad, the Heavy Squad, they called it."

"Meaning they targeted the kids in Clark Park, Rosato and Holditch specifically."

"Not like my dad ever talked about it," Katz said. "I had to ask the old-timers on the job. No one speaks too much about what went on back then, who signed off. Black eye for the top brass and all that. But they went after those gangs hard."

"Son of a bitch," I said. I wasn't especially shocked by the revelation. I'd never doubted my father's capacity for violence. But the lack of specifics was frustrating. "Hard meaning what, exactly?"

"What I heard, they'd pick up a gang member at home, take him for a ride somewhere, and throw a scare into him."

"Take him fucking where, Katz? Scare him how?"

"I dunno, Dave, just that my dad must be reliving whatever it is they did. It's burned on his brain. Whatever it was drove one kid to drugs, another to the bottle."

"The drink," I said.

"Whatever. My point, we need to figure out—"

"Not *whatever*," I said. "Holditch told his wife, *Didn't put you in the drink*. Not *the bottle*, not *drinking*. You want to scare a kid in East Van, the kind that's not afraid of anything on the streets, where would you take them?"

Katz coughed, dropping his vaporizer as the answer came to him.

Joe had driven the Nissan across the uneven grass above the New Brighton Park beach, leaving the headlights on as he walked his captive out onto the narrow pier. It was almost dark, and he must have been waiting for nightfall to make his move.

The Cadillac bounced as it followed the tracks Joe had left in the grass. We parked alongside and raced across the sand toward the pier. The planks creaked and shuddered under our feet.

We heard the splash.

I was carrying my father's MagLite, and I aimed it at the water. A head bobbed above the black waves. We heard gasps and sputters, then the thundercrack of gunfire accompanied by a spout of flame from the pier's end.

Joe was aiming his son's pistol at the water. He turned and pointed the gun at me and smiled.

"'Bout time you got here, Matt."

Up close I could see the shirt of his uniform was unbuttoned, stained with something. A hole in the knee of one pant leg. He nodded his head toward the water.

"Smart-ass thought I wouldn't remember," he said. "We warned him, didn't we, about him and his pals hanging out in the park, bothering the nice people."

In the water, Michael Rosato thrashed. His hands broke the water, still manacled together in a pose of supplication. Katz knocked off his shoes.

"Think this one's just about got the message," Joe said.

"Either shape up or start swimming for Japan. You hear me, kid?" He fired again at the water, missing Rosato by several feet. Intentionally, I hoped. Rosato's scream was choked back by waves.

"What do you think, Matt, another couple shots?"

"Where's it stop?" I said.

"With the city safe for decent folks, and this hump in his place. Was your idea, Matt. You want a shot? You're up after me."

He turned and held the gun with both hands, sighted on Rosato. As I moved I thought of what he'd said to me the night before. He'd been right. Not even a fucking shred. I swung the flashlight as hard as I could and struck him across the temple.

The gun fell. Joe fell. Katz dived into the water.

And me, I collected the pistol, and stared down at a sick and bleeding man, and wondered for a second why I felt like I'd betrayed him.

Katz emerged from the water to the left of the dock, dragging Rosato onto the rock-studded beach. Rosato looked frail and ancient, his thin hair matted into dark gray tendrils. He crawled up to the sandbank and lay on his back, sobbing. Katz unlocked his cuffs and tended to him.

Joe Itami turned over and moaned softly. "Christ, my head."

I unloaded the gun, pocketed the clip. I helped Joe to his feet and led him toward his son's car. Joe glanced at the quivering figure of Michael Rosato with mild curiosity and zero recognition. He seated himself in the passenger's side of the Nissan. His eyes closed. Soon he was snoring.

"All forgotten," I said to Katz.

"Yeah. Lucky him."

I said I'd wait with Rosato for the ambulance. Katz thanked me and drove his father home. As the taillights of his Nissan bounced onto the pavement, I saw he'd left his cigarettes on my dashboard.

I hauled a Hudson's Bay blanket out of the trunk of my car and handed it to Rosato. He seemed shaken up but physically fine. He massaged his wrists, shivered, and refused the cigarette I offered him.

"Worst night of my life was when those cops threw me and Gord into the water," he said. "That man is sick, isn't he? His poor son. Lord have mercy on them both."

The ambulance approached, all lights and sirens. Rosato stood and walked across the grass to meet the EMTs.

Lighting a Rooftop, I leaned against the hood of the car and stared at the water for a while, thinking that there was a lost name for every place in the city. At one point I might have believed that if I could just learn enough of them, an entire secret history would reveal itself to me. The world as it was, or should have been. But it didn't work like that, and even if it did, there simply wasn't time. Not even enough to forget.

Author's note: Credit is due to Charles Demers for the quote at the beginning, taken from Vancouver Special, *and to Aaron Chapman for his article* "Gangs of Vancouver," *published on February 4, 2011, in the* Vancouver Courier, *later expanded into the book* The Last Gang in Town.

BOTTOM DOLLAR

BY DIETRICH KALTEIS

Strathcona

The way he did it, Lonzo D'Cruz pulled up out front, flicked on his four-ways, left the Benz running, and walked up to this French bistro. Some guy with a sandwich board walking back and forth out front got in his way.

Lonzo stepped right, the guy stepped the same way. Lonzo tried left, the guy doing it too, misstepping, smiling like it was funny. Taking it wrong, Lonzo gave him a shove. Awkward with the sign hanging on him, the guy went down and turned turtle. Not giving him another look, Lonzo moved past him and into the place. The maître d' looking horrified, asking if he had a reservation.

"I look like I'd eat here?" Lonzo weaved around the tables, up to the couple at the corner booth, nice romantic spot with white linens, candles, and a bottle of bubbly on ice. Cracking his knuckles to get their attention, he smiled and waved a finger at Carmen Roth, the guy who did the laundry, made dirty money clean. Lonzo smiled at the woman and asked if she'd like to dance.

"You hearin' music, Lonz? 'Cause if you do . . ." Carmen Roth looped a finger at his temple, grinning at the woman named Bobbi Lee. He picked up a cocktail shrimp, dipping it in sauce and sticking it in his mouth, now grinning up at Lonzo.

Clutching shirtfront, Lonzo sent a jab, accented by the big

ring he always wore. Carmen reeled, spitting bits of shellfish. The rocket that followed would have sent Carmen to the floor if Lonzo hadn't been holding onto his collar. Lonzo asking if Carmen heard the music now.

Coughing shrimp and blinking, Carmen put up a pudgy hand in surrender. Straightening his own jacket, Lonzo smiled again at Bobbi, held out the hand with the ring, asked, "How about that dance?"

"Jesus, gonna hit me if I say no?" Bobbi finished her drink.

"I'm a lover, not a fighter, you know that."

Sliding from the booth, she shrugged at Carmen, said thanks for dinner, slipped her hand on Lonzo's arm, and let him lead her past the tables, all eyes on them. The maître d' keeping his distance, snapping his fingers for a waiter to go clean up Carmen.

Stepping close, Lonzo pressed a hundred in the maître d's hand, saying his friend just had a bad shrimp. "Ought to be more careful what you serve in this joint." Leading Bobbi to the door, holding it for her.

"Mind me asking where we're going?" Bobbi said.

"Little place I know." Lonzo steered her around the guy with the sandwich board, the guy still trying to get up. Going to the passenger side, Lonzo opened the door, saying to her, "Feel like Italian?"

"You mean Umbertos?"

"Mean like my place."

"Thought we were going dancing."

"Yeah, after."

The guy with the sandwich board got his feet under him, the board cracked, bent, and ruined. Lonzo stepped over, tucking a twenty in the guy's shirt, telling him, "Get a real job, man. This is embarrassing."

* * *

It was raining when Ronnie Trane arrived at the Strathcona address. Some old factory near Venables and Clark, used to make sensible shoes. He'd heard some realtor on a talk show call this part of town gentrified. Lofts going in, an exotic car dealer with a Ferrari in the window, promises of Starbucks and yoga studios, ladies walking dogs that fit in a purse. Sure didn't look like that to Ronnie.

Counting a dozen heads in the outdoor line ahead of him, Ronnie guessed they were all applying for the same job. Some A-list entertainer needed a personal assistant. The Craigslist ad didn't say who it was, only that the successful applicant needed no experience, just a valid driver's license. Ronnie had to lie about that, not due to get his back for a few months.

The rain was light when the door opened, letting the next applicant in and closing again, the line inching forward. A couple of twentyish women under a black umbrella in front of Ronnie speculated who the star was. Too busy bandying celebrity names, they didn't notice him without an umbrella. Every man for himself. One hoping for Beyoncé, the other going for Bieber.

Flipping up his collar to the rain, Ronnie saw the guy across the street marching back and forth with the sandwich board, out front of some swank French bistro that just opened. Ronnie thinking, what kind of job was that, walking back and forth in the rain? Letting the world know soup, salad, and entrée was under twenty bucks.

The Mercedes pulling up out front of the place put on its four-ways. Recognizing the black S-Class, the same one Ronnie used to drive when he chauffeured Lonzo around, his name on the vanity plate. The psycho gangster got out and looked his way, but didn't recognize him. Lonzo fired Ronnie for losing his license to a DUI, told him he drove like an old bat anyway. Did it in front of Bobbi Lee and a few of his guys. All of them laughing except Bobbi.

With no job, Ronnie went back to his former livelihood, breaking into places, scraping up enough to pay the DUI fine. Tripping a silent alarm at this mansion in Altamont, he met two security guards as he came out, holding a pair of vases he thought were Ming. Noting the DUI on his sheet, the judge told Ronnie his grandkids played hockey in the street, then handed down twelve months, Ronnie getting out of Mission after serving six. Having to report to BC Corrections and show some guy named Maxwell a list of places where he'd applied for legit work every Friday. The system keeping him on a leash.

Standing in the rain, he watched Lonzo doing the two-step with the guy with the sandwich board, knocking him out of the way. Typical Lonzo. The women in front of him missed it, still tossing about celebrity names, one saying Ryan Gosling was dreamy.

"Asshole," Ronnie said, watching Lonzo walk past the guy on the sidewalk with the busted sandwich board. Both women turning on Ronnie, giving him a sour look, thinking he just dissed Gosling.

"You see that?" Ronnie pointed across the street, but Lonzo was already in the restaurant, the sandwich-board guy lost from view behind the S-Class. The women clicking their teeth and turning their backs, using the umbrella to block him out, talking in hushed tones. Ronnie shrugged into his jacket, feeling the rain coming through the denim. Watching Lonzo step from the restaurant a couple of minutes later with Bobbi Lee. Tall, blond, and fine. Lonzo escorted her around the sandwich-board guy. Opening her door, Lonzo got her inside, then played the big man and slipped the sandwich-board guy a tip and gave him some words of advice, like next time get out of the fuckin' way. Getting behind the wheel, Lonzo pulled away from the curb, the wipers swishing.

The job line moved some more, the rain picking up, water in Ronnie's shoes making a squishing sound. Thinking screw this, but he needed to show Maxwell his list on Friday—probably have pneumonia by then. Another ten minutes before the door opened again, the recruiter sticking her head out, looking surprised it was raining and saying sorry, that was it for today. Telling the rest of the applicants they'd have to come back early tomorrow, she wished them luck and closed the door. The star remained a mystery.

"Bitch," Ronnie said under his breath. The women ahead of him gave him another look and left.

When he got back to his flat, he stood under the shower's spray till the hot water tank ran cold, then he revived himself with a couple cans of Cutthroat, popped a thin-crust Delissio in the oven while he eyed the classifieds, still enough time to get to the library before it closed to check for any new online job postings. Looking out the window, seeing it was still raining, he decided to stay home.

Catching an early bus back to Strathcona the next morning, he was third in line, no rain and no sign of the two women, his hands wrapped around a Starbucks, still warm by the time it was his turn.

"Have a seat," the recruiter told him. Green-tinted hair, the ring skewering her lip looking inflamed and causing her to lisp. Reminded him of a pike he gaffed on a fishing trip back when he was a kid.

She eyed his CV. "You did time, huh?" Saying it like it was cool.

The recruiter asked the usual questions, explained the job was on-call, seven days a week. Asked if he was on any kind of medication. Told him it might involve travel. Finished up by saying, "The candidate we're seeking must be discrete, no loose lips."

"I'm not a snitch," Ronnie told her, smiling.

Turning the paper over like she was looking for something, asking about college or university. Ronnie said no, guessing you needed that to fetch stuff for entertainers. She mentioned he'd have to join the Association of Celebrity Personal Assistants, asked about his temperament and how he handled somebody else's. "Anyone ever throw anything at you, and if so, how did you resolve it?"

It sounded like these A-listers could get cranky. Ronnie thinking about it, getting a glimpse of Justin Bieber tossing something at him, a guy he could bench press.

"Mostly you just make pickups," she said, not waiting for an answer.

"You mean the stuff they throw at me?" Smiling at her.

"Like dry cleaning, takeout, stuff like that." Putting her clipboard down, she thanked him for coming, offered a handshake, her hand damp like she just licked her palm, saying they'd be in touch.

Going out the door, one of the two women from yesterday's lineup brushed roughly by him as she was heading in. The same guy with a new sandwich board that said they served breakfast was pacing across the street. Ronnie guessed there was a lineup for that job too.

It was six months in, and Bobbi couldn't do it anymore,

couldn't lie there listening to the hibernating brute that lived down Lonzo's throat, snoring like a chainsaw. The gasping and grunting thing with its wet sucking breath. Telling herself she was still in her prime, but starting to feel like she was creeping close to her best-before date.

Enough light shone through the window to show the man lying there with his head twisted to the side. Looking like somebody dropped him off a building. Bobbi thinking, God, close your mouth.

Lonzo had promised to get cleaned up the night he found her with Carmen Roth at the bistro, going pit bull on her date, then practically begging her for a second chance. To tell the truth, she kind of liked the way he just walked in and took what he wanted. Bobbi believed most men had short-man syndrome, no matter what their height. Lonzo just had it in spades, especially when he was wasted. But, true to his word, he stopped doing blow like Tony Montana. No more tapping a razor blade like it was Morse code. But the problem was, now that he was clean, Lonzo was dull and predictable. And while Little Lonzo didn't need the blue pills to rise to the occasion so much, sex had become routine. And the snoring was getting worse.

Making up her mind a couple days ago, she came up with the plan. She wasn't going to stick around and wait for Lonzo to fall victim to the usual hazards of his line of work. Like getting shot. Or pulling open his car door someday and *bam*. Chunks of Lonzo across the lawn and in the pool filter. And it could be her getting in the car, or catching one in a crossfire. Lonzo had plenty of enemies.

What really moved it along—Bobbi caught him crouching by his walk-in closet, taking out all his shoes, pulling out the bottom shelf, and lifting one of two Louis Vuitton cases hidden there. Working the combination lock, popping the latches, and grabbing a bundle of hundreds, slipping it inside his jacket. Didn't see her watching when he put the shelf and shoes back.

The next time Lonzo went off on business, she moved the shoes and the shelf, lifting the matching Louis Vuittons one at a time, shaking them, wondering how much cash was in them. Trying different lock combinations on the cases—his birthday, phone number, address—coming up with nothing. Driving herself crazy. Betting one was packed with American, the other with euros, Lonzo covering his ass either way, depending which way he had to run when the time came.

Dubbing the cases the twins, she set the shelf and shoes back the way they were. Then she started thinking how she'd do it, how she'd run off with the twins and live to spend the money.

Ronnie Trane had three rules for breaking into places. First rule: keep your edge, be smooth going in, and don't overthink it. Tighten up and you start screwing up. Rule two: no drugs, no more booze. A little weed maybe, a couple tokes to help keep it all smooth. Three: never go back. Forget about what you didn't get the first time. Greed spells prison.

That one time he got busted, Ronnie broke all three rules by the time the cuffs were on. Tripping a silent alarm in the same Altamont mansion he'd robbed the month before. He'd helped himself to a bottle of Cabo Wabo and drank most of it by the time he tried to make it over the back fence with the pair of vases in a sack.

Counting off his rules now as he drove along Chartwell, waiting up the street in the stolen Corolla until the lights in the house went off. Parking over by Vinson Creek, he walked back to the driveway, making it look natural, like Lonzo was expecting him to drop by, middle of the night.

Ronnie kept his eyes wide and ears sharp, ready for anything. Picking up a newspaper from the driveway, he headed around the back and slipped a hand in his pocket for the glass cutter—knowing the alarm-company stickers on the windows were fake, no surveillance cameras under the eaves. Lonzo used to brag when Ronnie was driving him around how he dared any asshole to break into his place. Being armed to the teeth was the only security a man needed.

Since Lonzo had fired him, Ronnie hadn't been able to find a straight job, not a decent one anyway. Nobody was willing to take a chance on an ex-con. It got him thinking a little payback was due.

He started staking out Lonzo's place, learning his routine and making sure the crook hadn't got a dog. He read in the *North Shore News* about some guy breaking into a place in Deep Cove last month, getting cornered by one of those German breeds. Had to lock himself in the upstairs can, the dog snarling and bashing against the door. The guy ended up making a 911 call on himself. Cops and canine control coming and finding the guy with a pillowcase stuffed with silverware next to the toilet. Never going to live that one down in any house of corrections.

Ronnie had followed them tonight, Lonzo and Bobbi coming out of Venue. Lonzo staggering, Bobbi having to drive. Perfect. Ronnie trailed the Mercedes across the Lion's Gate Bridge, giving himself a pep talk, convincing himself this guy had it coming.

Looking at the lights of the houses on the slope, thinking this part of town had been good to him. Broke into over a dozen places in what Ronnie liked to call Martini Hill. Scored over twenty-five grand in cash, jewelry, and easy stuff to fence. Ronnie feeling confident, thinking he knew these streets and the rich folks with their valuables and secrets, cars worth over a hundred grand in the driveways, usually more than one. Only got busted that one time. Ronnie blamed the booze.

First Bobbi got her hands on some club drug from a dealer in North Van, a guy Lonzo didn't know. The dealer promised this shit was the bomb, some name she couldn't pronounce, assured her it would last half the night.

Then she slipped enough in his drink at Venue to knock out a horse. Listening to his ragged snores now, she got out of the bed. Lonzo rolled her way, flopping his arm across her pillow. Bobbi waited till he settled, waited for the beast down his throat to start up again. Going barefoot past the windows that rose to the high ceiling, the panorama of the city lost in a bank of clouds, top of the British Properties. Great view when it wasn't raining. Going to the can, seeing the lit pool shimmering out back, the raindrops making little circles in the water. Lonzo always bragged about this place being worth ten million, easy.

Sitting on the toilet, she did some deep breathing and played it through one more time: take the Beretta he kept next to the bed, grab the twins, take his car keys, and get the hell out of there. Then pray there was enough cash to put an ocean between her and Lonzo, thinking maybe Paris would be nice.

Back in the bedroom, she was careful not to bump into things. Slipping into her panties, hooking her bra in back, she went to his nightstand and took the Beretta from the drawer. Lonzo out cold, the beast getting snagged between an inhale and exhale. That's when she heard it.

Bobbi's own breath caught. Standing, she held the Beretta ready, hearing it again, a slight rattle at the bedroom door. Grabbing her robe, she slung it on, moving to the door, sure she saw the knob turn. Bobbi wanted to shake Lonzo awake and press the gun in his hand, but he was drugged and useless.

The knob turned again, somebody on the other side of the door, working at the flimsy lock. Bobbi raised the pistol, feeling her heart and the wet under her arms, aiming just above the knob, her finger on the trigger.

Crawling in through the basement window had been easy. It took Ronnie two minutes to work his way through the house, stopping every few steps, listening, using the pen light to guide his way. The snores coming through the door sounded like a phlegmy musical with a chorus of wheezing. Getting past the flimsy lock on the bedroom door, Ronnie turned the knob, easing it open and peeking in, saw Lonzo splayed across the king bed. Thinking, man, how does that chick Bobbi sleep next to that? Guessing she was in one of the other bedrooms.

Keeping to the shadows along the wall, Ronnie moved to the nightstand, knowing Lonzo would have a gun in reach, the man bragging about all the firepower he kept stashed in the house. Easing open the drawer, finding nothing, he went to the dresser. Ronnie knew about Lonzo's getaway cash, Lonzo bragging about that too, saying it was to make a hasty exit in case the Mounties came banging at his door. All Ronnie had to do was find it, sure Lonzo kept it close to where he slept. He was helping himself to the Rolex and wallet on top of the dresser when he felt it—steel pressed to his ear. He froze, his heart jumping. The hairs on the back of his neck prickling, bladder nearly letting go.

Taking the pistol from his ear, Bobbi waited for him to

half turn, wagged for him to go to the can. One hand holding the pistol, the other snugging the dressing gown closed, she stepped behind him, easing the bathroom door closed.

"The hell you doing, Ronnie?" she whispered. Remembering the way he used to glance at her in the rearview, always pretending not to listen in on their conversations in the backseat while he played chauffeur.

"Hey, Bobbi." He shrugged, catching her scent.

"Here to get your old job back?"

"Funny." His eyes going to the pistol. "So, now what?"

"That's not the question." Thinking a moment, she reached behind her for the knob, keeping an eye on him, saying, "Give me a hand, and maybe you come out of this."

Not sure what she meant, but he nodded anyway.

Opening the door, she pointed to the walk-in closet, keeping the pistol on him. Whispering for him to move the shoes and lift out the lower shelf. Taking out the twins, one in each hand, he tiptoed behind her through the bedroom, Lonzo still out cold, snoring away like a freight train.

She stopped in the hall, whispered, "Wait here." Leaving him at the top of the stairs, she disappeared back into the room.

Ronnie thought of rushing down the stairs, knowing he was holding Lonzo's getaway cash. Still thinking about it when she returned, clothes draped over her arm, a pair of shoes in her hand, the pistol in the other. She motioned for him to walk ahead of her down the stairs. At the bottom, she told him to hang on, dropping the robe. Not too dark to make out the black bra and panties, Ronnie watched her slip into her clothes. One foot at a time going into the shoes.

Then she led him through the kitchen, to the garage. Ronnie acting like the chauffeur again, carrying the luggage, following her into the garage, glad to get out of there.

Pressing the fob, she unlocked the trunk of the Benz. Ronnie laying the twins in there and easing it shut.

Popping the door locks, Bobbi tossed him the keys, saying, "You drive." Getting in the passenger side, she pressed a button on the remote clipped to the visor, the garage door going up. Ronnie starting the car and backing down the driveway, driving the way he came, past the hot Toyota. Rolling down Chartwell, not fast enough to attract attention, the lights of the city like stars before them.

"How about putting that away," he said, glancing at the pistol. "You're making me nervous."

She ignored him.

"Man, that's some racket coming out of him," he said, going for some chitchat. "How you stand it?"

Bobbi told him about the club drug cocktail.

"Jesus."

"Wanted to be sure, you know. No surprises, like him waking up when I'm walking out with the twins."

Ronnie shook his head and laughed, saying, "Never pictured it, the two of you anyway."

"You going Dr. Laura on me now, Ronnie?"

"Sorry, really none of my business."

"Anyway, you telling me you don't snore?"

"Not like that."

"Yeah, well, guess we'll see."

Wondering what that meant, Ronnie coasted down the hill, seeing the flashing lights and barrier as they turned at the top of Taylor Way. His heart back in his throat, thinking it was the cops. Turned out to be a work crew in safety vests, one guy setting out orange cones, a couple others dealing with what looked like a burst water main. A flagger waved them down a single lane along the wide boulevard.

Ronnie got in the left lane, set to take the ramp and head east on the 1. Bobbi telling him to turn right instead, the pistol still aimed at him.

Powering up the ramp, sailing along. Didn't speak again till they were near Caulfield, then Ronnie said, "Could be he's got some tracking device in the cases. Should pull over, have a look. See how much we got."

"Just drive."

Staying in the outside lane, Ronnie kept an eye on his speed. No desire to get pulled over. They were quiet till they rolled past Horseshoe Bay, no lines for the ferries at this hour.

Then she asked, "Why'd you pick tonight?"

He told her he'd been watching and waiting. How he'd seen them that time, her and Lonzo at the bistro six months back, Ronnie standing in a job line across the street. Said it came to him soon after that. He figured Lonzo owed him.

She told him what happened inside the bistro, the way Lonzo just walked in and took her from Carmen Roth. "He owes you shit, by the way."

"Maybe so, but still, we got two bags of his money. One for you, one for me."

"That's how you see it, huh?"

"Think it's fair, yeah."

"Yeah, well, think again."

"You know how much's in there?"

"No."

Ronnie frowned, feeling his phone vibrate, reaching for it, doing it slow. Could be Maxwell, pissed off about the missed appointment, calling at a ridiculous hour to remind Ronnie he could send him back to the can—just like that. But it wasn't him.

Bobbi leaned close and looked at his screen.

"How d'you like that?" Reading the text, he told her it was the recruiter he saw all those months ago, how he'd long given up on it. "Says the last assistant didn't work out."

"What kind of employer texts at this time of night?"

"You got no idea what it's like out there." Reading the rest of it, Ronnie said he'd been short-listed to assist some big star.

"Like who?"

"Doesn't say."

"*Pffft.*"

Bobbi looked out at the scenery rushing past. The two of them talking about different jobs they'd had, people they both knew, most of them gangsters. Laughing as they passed a sign that read Squamish up ahead.

Ronnie thought of making a grab for the pistol, Bobbi acting like she forgot it was in her lap. He could take it all, leave her the Benz, and jack himself a fresh car in Squamish, drive back down, get his stuff from his flat, and split town. Maybe drive east. Saying, "You mind I turn on the radio?" Reaching for the knob, he turned it on.

Bobbi switched it off.

"You don't like country?"

"Turn at the light."

Putting on his flasher, getting in the left lane, guessing she was dropping him off at the McDonald's. Hopefully with some of the cash. Then she'd drive off and ditch him. Maybe he should be glad she hadn't shot him.

Showing him where to park, she told him to make hers black.

He reached for the keys.

"Uh-uhn." Giving him a smile, hand on the pistol. Ronnie noted her painted fingernails.

He got out and went into the restaurant, seeing himself

on the first bus back to the city, likely with none of the cash. Stuck following up with the recruiter with the pierced lip and green hair, then calling Maxwell, sucking up and telling him the good news, saying sorry for missing his appointment. Back to scraping the bottom.

He came out sipping a large. The Benz was parked where he left it. Bobbi in the passenger side, talking on her cell. Going back in the door that said *Welcome*, he ordered one for her. Going back to the car, he heard the country, some Willie Nelson number. Ronnie got in, handing her a cup, saying, "Thought maybe you'd be gone."

"Did cross my mind." She set the cup in the holder, stared straight ahead.

"So, how about it? We check the cases, see how much we got, see if they're wearing bugs."

"Was him on the phone."

"Lonzo?"

She nodded, trying to smile past the scared look. "Man sure is pissed. Wants it back, his million bucks."

Staring at her, Ronnie mouthed the amount.

"Yeah."

"Lemme see it." Ronnie held out his hand, meaning her phone.

A puzzled look, she handed it to him.

Opening his door, he dropped it out, crushing it under his heel.

Bobbi stared at him, the pistol pointing at him.

"Can track us by it. The car too. I say we jack another ride, maybe that one." Glancing at a plain van in the next row. "Figure this shit out."

"Not going anywhere in that." She sipped some coffee, saying, "I know this guy, he's got a chalet up near Whistler.

Spot with a fireplace and pool, real nice. He'll let us crash till we figure things out."

"He know Lonzo?"

"Carmen Roth, the guy from the bistro."

Ronnie looking at her, then they were laughing, sipping their coffee.

"Any chance he'd give us up?"

"None, 'specially after I tell him how I drugged Lonzo and ripped off his cash."

More nervous laughing. Ronnie finally saying, "Okay, so we drive up, wait till morning, then you call this Carmen, see what he says."

"I'd call him right now, but you just killed my phone."

Reaching in his jacket for his, handing it to her, looking at the pistol back on her lap. Saying, "You ever shoot one of those?"

"Not yet."

She punched in directory assistance, and he started the engine, knowing that lunatic Lonzo D'Cruz would be coming after them. The strange thing, Ronnie wasn't worried. In fact he was feeling pretty good about the way things were turning out. Ripping off a million bucks and running sure beat the hell out of picking up some A-lister's dry cleaning. Then he was thinking about the chalet and sleeping arrangements.

THE LANDECKER PARTY

BY NATHAN RIPLEY

Mount Pleasant

They'd opened another American Apparel on this side of the bridge, this one a fifteen-minute walk away from our place. Glass, plastic, primary colors, sex as branded by a Montreal megalomaniac pervert who'd drive his own business into the ground in just a few more years. I bought a gray T-shirt from a girl named Crissie who I'd seen last Tuesday at Rivko's doo-wop night at Shine, and around the city for the last few months, roughly since the start of the 2007 school year.

"You hear about the Landecker party?" I asked her while shaking my head no to the plastic bag she was offering.

"Who's Landecker?"

"It's a booze, not a very good one. It sells okay back east, and now they're trying to make an impact out here, I guess. Anyway, Landecker threw us a sponsorship—my friend Mark and I do shows—for a house party. Free drinks. It's our place, 16th and Oak-ish. I can write down the address if you want to come. Friends are cool too. Not many, but feel free."

"Cool," she said. Crissie was nineteen, tops, about four years between us. "Getting booze to sponsor your party is like, it's like—getting food to sponsor your dinner, or something. Sorry, that's lame."

"I've been trying to make the same kind of joke for the last week and I still can't get it to work."

* * *

Mark and Esther were still playing around when I got back, mixing some brutal new-country Tim McGraw shit with a pretty great house track, creating a sickening aural soup that made them giggle and made me want to pour a warm Coke onto Mark's PowerBook. We were on the lower floor of a shitty two-level, and Mark and Esther had the music cranked already, hours before anyone was due here.

The upstairs neighbor had been gone all week, his Jetta missing from its usual parking spot. Nice dude, a kid from Taiwan who near as we could tell was AWOL from his Sauder School of Business program and waiting for his parents to find out and haul him back home. We were surprised he was living in this place, one of the last true dumps on the block, instead of one of the endless condo buildings, only about half of which were tarped and scaffolded up for leaking roof repairs. He'd introduced himself to us when he moved in over a year ago, told us his name was Phil, waved off our occasional invitations to driveway beers, but clearly did some extremely committed partying of his own. In hangover he metamorphosed into a disapproving phantom, leaving us imploring Post-its about needing sleep. He'd knock on the door and run back upstairs, leaving notes on our door that said things like, *Pls turn down your Call of Duty.* But I'd seen Phil at an after-hours in the West End no less than three times in the past month, a booze-free and drug-heavy space where Mark and I netted five hundred dollars to split for playing from two to seven. A pretty shit deal, looking back on it, but we used each gig to get better at mixing, at reading a room. The more serious we were at clubs and parties, the more we could goof off at home.

Mark took mercy on me and switched from Ableton over to his iTunes, putting on a Hot Snakes record at low volume. There were twenty-four green bottles of Landecker around

the living room, kitchen, and bedroom, which we'd collab-
orated in cleaning up and turning into a secondary hanging
room for the party, carrying the couch over from my apartment on the next block and leaning the mattress against the
wall. It looked pretty good in there.

"You going to do the tent?" Mark asked. He was sitting on
this beautiful leather office chair with a circular base that his
dad had given him, a piece that looked alien on a carpet we'd
been staining into an accidental pattern and between the two
living room couches, both road salvage—this was before bedbugs
reared up big-time and made street furniture an idiotic risk.

"If I need to," I said.

Mark just looked at the ceiling, taking a pack of Belmonts
out of his pocket. He'd gatewayed into smoking last—after
booze, which we started with when we were fifteen and playing in a shockingly bad death metal band in Kamloops; weed,
which we'd dealt to pay for gas money for two summers of
touring cross-country in our slightly better prog-rock band;
and MDMA, which we both embraced eagerly when we sold our
Orange amps and Les Pauls for the laptops and decks we needed
to start making money in the clubs. We pirated all the software.

Esther, unwrapping a sleeve of red plastic cups in the corner, looked over at us. "What Mark means is, *Could you please
set up the tent, Raj, neither of us have the basic skills required.*"
She was three years older than Mark and me, about ten years
better at communicating, and Mark would collapse mentally
if she left him. Esther didn't need him at all, and all three of
us knew it, but she got something out of hanging out with the
two of us, watching us knock heads, develop, devolve. She
got paid double what we did for the same gigs and was worth
it. Rivko had her sub in for him when he couldn't do the doo-
wop night, and she'd gotten to open for Steve Aoki once,

Diplo twice. Guys we mocked endlessly and envied deeply.

I headed out back with the tent canvas, seeing through the kitchen window that the poles were already out there, probably from an earlier rage-filled attempt by Mark to get it up. It was a big one, tall enough to stand up in. I had it rigged in twenty minutes, and Esther and Mark carried a white table with folding legs out into it right as I finished up. We put three bottles of Landecker on it, and Esther took three steak knives out from where she'd tucked them into her belt.

"What are these for?" I asked.

"We need to ventilate the sides or it'll just become a hotbox for cigarette smoke, especially if it rains, which it's supposed to. I want to be able to tell people something nice if they try to smoke inside and complain that there's no covered porch."

"It's the point of the fucking tent," Mark said.

"Did we have some fight I don't know about, dude?" I said. Even with just the three of us in the tent, it was markedly hotter than it was outside.

"He's just stressed about the party," Esther said. "His hero Rivko's coming. So's Lana."

"Lana's Occasional Lana?"

"Yep." Lana took party pictures, good ones. Instant social capital for events, people who did parties, deejays. Enough notice for us, scored piecemeal through these pictures, through people talking about what we did for parties, could eventually mean regular higher-paying gigs, could mean avoiding getting a job. The point of all this shit.

I took a steak knife and started poking and slicing the sides of the tent my dad had given me when I moved out to go to college. I'd only gone camping once the whole time I was out here, anyway.

* * *

It was rammed by nine thirty, and had been pretty busy since eight, people stopping by to predrink our vile Landecker before properly going out for the night, then clocking that most of the people they wanted to see were in the room with them, the drinks were free, and Mike and Esther were doing pretty great on the music. So people stayed and the rooms filled up.

Landecker, I should say, truly is disgusting. I just tried some again at the Opus Hotel last night, where I was waiting for an LA commercial-director pal to turn up. First time I'd had any since the party, and I was wondering if it was just the memory of what we had to do later on that night that tainted its taste in my head. No. It tastes like Jägermeister with Scope and Palmolive notes.

At the party, we discovered that it tasted okay if you mixed it with Diet Coke. I sent Dave Proskich, an Emily Carr kid who badly wanted to be our friend, out to the Sunshine Market to get a half-dozen two-liter bottles. Later that night Dave got really wasted and took multiple pictures of his dick with the disposable camera that Lana always left at parties. He had a weird, trollish little thing, and hadn't realized that the limited-edition Vans he wore every day were visible in every shot. Lana told me a couple years after that that he'd paid her a hundred bucks to take the pictures off her site.

By the time Crissie turned up, it was beyond standing-room tight in the house. Mark's dad's office chair had two girls sitting in it and a guy on each arm—we'd discover the next day that the base was mangled and the chair permanently angled, useless. Mark started crying when he sat in it, but Esther and I just left him alone. He'd earned a decent cry, and if he wanted to attach it to the dead chair, that was fine.

"Is there any left?" Crissie asked. She wasn't wearing any AA, and looked almost businesslike compared to most of the other people in the room. A nice collared shirt with the sleeves rolled up, black jeans.

"Any what?"

"The free booze you promised was really gross."

"It's drained. There may be some in the tent, actually, come with me." I was drunk enough to take her by the hand and lead her through the party, Esther laughing in my face when I walked by the deejay setup.

It hadn't rained, so the tent had gone mostly unused, people choosing to smoke out front in the driveway or just scattered around the yard. There was an untouched bottle of Landecker on the table. I unscrewed the lid and Crissie and I swapped sips and revulsed expressions.

"That's really impressive in there. You guys throw parties all the time?"

"No, not really."

"You should charge."

"Would defeat the purpose. Plus, no one knows who the fuck we are. We want people to like us first, so we can get hired to play more stuff, rely on turnout. That's why this was important," I said. It was my longest conversation of the night so far—even Rivko, who I'd been meaning to corner, I'd only up-nodded to, him inclining a Pilsner bottle back at me. He was having a good time, which meant more than me talking to him.

"So I'm a statistical quantity?" Crissie asked.

"No, of course not. I wanted you to come. You, in particular." We looked at each other for a second and I was about to push my luck. Instead, I took another sip of the Landecker and passed the bottle over, then said we should go back inside.

Mark was waiting in the kitchen. "Neighbor's here, and it's weird," he said.

Crissie saw a friend, a narrow guy with unwashed Cobain

hair who worked at her same location, in the living room. She pointed to him and made a talking motion with her hand to me, and I nodded and smiled.

"What's the problem? Phil's fine. And he weighs like eleven pounds, he's not a problem."

"Yeah, but he turned up with like six randoms."

"Total randoms?"

"Mostly people I recognize. All okay. But one of them looks rough. And Phil looks fucking half-dead."

Rivko came into the kitchen behind Mark. Rivko, back then, was so handsome it made you look at your own shitty body in shame as soon as you saw him. I don't think he's that good-looking anymore, but maybe that's from spending every day of the last eight years in the office with him during the day and the clubs with him at night. When you spend enough time around it, beauty disappears the way a smell does.

"That guy's a heavy dealer," Rivko said.

"The big guy?" Mark asked.

"No, small Asian dude in the leather jacket. Big importer as of a few months ago. I think he got a few pounds of amazing MDMA muled to him from somewhere or another. Extremely delicious."

"That stuff we did last week?" Mark asked.

"Yep," Rivko said, drifting out of the kitchen. It was packed with people, incredibly warm, so many conversations happening that you could yell at the person in front of you without any fear of being overheard.

"You didn't tell me you got high with Rivko," I said.

"You're a jealous girlfriend now? I was trying to get us that Justice after-party, so we hung late, super late."

"Did it work?"

"No. Let's get these sketchy dealers out of our house, okay?"

Mark and I walked into the living room to find that the problem had vanished. Phil and the big guy, a random, were gone, leaving only the other five people behind. Mark and I walked out front to share a smoke and talk about Rivko. I think that's what we were going to talk about, anyway. We didn't get to it.

The door to Phil's unit was open, wide open, the light off in the stairwell leading up. There were some footsteps, and the guy Mark had been talking about came down. Big gut, massive beard, black T-shirt, sleeve tattoos. But he didn't have the friendly headbanger smile that usually went with that outfit. He was carrying four huge black backpacks, two in each hand, his biceps bulging and forearm veins popping from the weight of them. He walked past us, looking down, but he did say one thing, in a surprisingly friendly tone.

"Don't look at shit and don't say shit's my advice," he said, then walked across 16th and toward a silver car. The back passenger door popped open as he got there and he gently set the bags down, then slid into the front passenger seat. The car drove away, leaving its lights off until it got to Oak, flicking them on along with the right turn signal.

The noise of the party, which made the big cheap single-pane bay window in front of our living room seem nonexistent, must have made us feel safer than we should have felt, because Mark and I started walking up the stairs. Mark laughed halfway up, and I said, "Don't touch anything." We got to the apartment.

It had the same layout as downstairs, just with more, and nicer, furniture. And a black Samsonite full of unbound and crumpled money, and Phil lying facedown on the floor, except his face was looking three-quarters of the way back at us, on top of a broken spine.

We went downstairs and closed the door to Rick and Phil's suite, went back to our party. There was no consultation, just entering the room and going our separate ways, me finding Crissie and starting to ask her questions about what she did, what she wanted to do, how much her current job sucked, anything. Mark went over to Esther and tapped her out, taking over the music, looking straight down. He was getting really good, good enough that it was just a matter of months before he quit, same as he quit songwriting and the band.

Mark never started anything without knowing when he was going to quit, and he taught me how to do the same. Not some subtle, observed, by-example thing: it was a spoken strategy to avoid stagnation and to get onto the next thing, the next "arena of accomplishment," as he said. He would write great self-help entrepreneurial crap if he had the stomach for it. Finding Esther had been part of his next-thing plan: someone better than him, smarter than him, less weak where it counted. Halfway through a reliable Eric Prydz banger, Mark gestured Esther over and started whispering to her.

The party wound down at about four thiry, leaving us with one hour of darkness to pull off what we wanted to do. Not enough time, but we were drunk enough to think it was. Esther went out to the tent and made the precise cuts in the grass, rolling back the sod, while Mark and I headed upstairs. It hadn't rained after all.

Gloved up, but knowing we could excuse any DNA presence in the apartment as the residue of a friendly neighbor visit, we carried Phil, toes and lolling head facing the floor, down the stairs, checking to be sure no pedestrians were out there.

"It's hundreds of thousands," Mark said, pretending he wasn't out of breath as we carried the body around to the backyard. "Those were hundreds, down to the bottom, I swear. They're coming back for it."

"They're not," Esther said, as we arrived in the tent and set the body down. "They're sending a signal to other dealers that they don't care about the money. This is about the territory. Cops and the papers will report that the cash was just left there."

"That's some TV crap, Esther," I said.

"No, that's some my-father-is-a-lead-investigator-on-gang-related-crimes-in-the-Lower-Mainland crap," Esther replied. "Phil's car's not here, and if there's no cash and no drugs and no body in the apartment, then he's a missing person to the cops. It can work."

"If Rivko knew he was dealing, then other people know," I said.

"And that helps us," Esther countered, impatient. "Means that the same guys who took the drugs killed him and made him evaporate, and the cops will either look for him through those connections or just not bother. They won't look where we're going to put him."

Instead of steak knives this time, she had shovels, but just two. Mark and I dug, the booze sweating out of us and the tent getting incredibly hot, Phil facing away from us until we rolled him into the four-foot-deep hole and put the dirt back on. Esther came out to arrange the rolls of grass back over him: she was better with the precision stuff.

I had Crissie's number in my Razr, and I texted her when I got out of the shower. It was too quick to be doing that, desperate, but I wanted to do something normal and human.

hungover as fucc / glad you came

She didn't answer for another three hours, but it was nice when it came. Sincere. She even punctuated.

Me too.

When the cops came two days later, driven by desperate calls from Phil's parents, they barely bothered with us, it was so clear that this was unsavory drug gangster shit. I don't know the story they pieced together—Esther wasn't afraid of much, but she feared her dad's perceptiveness, even though she'd inherited it. She never asked him anything so we don't know what the official take was, just that they asked us about the party, took a look around and in the tent. (Esther had insisted we leave it up, said it made sense of any disturbance in the dirt they found. She was right, they barely looked.)

"What do we do with this money?" I asked Esther when the cops left.

"I told you, we buy this place with most of it, keep some to spend," she said.

"I mean now, what do we do with it? How can we spend it without—"

"We clean it through the after-hours, through Rivko," Mark said. "He barely claims any of his income, he knows this shit."

"Exactly," Esther said.

And that's what we did.

Rivko asked very few questions, just took a little cut and did the work for us. I asked my dad for the rest of the cash we'd need to buy out the landlord, which was less than we'd worried when we approached the old Sikh guy who owned the place but still drove a cab fifty-five hours a week. A vanishing-likely-drug-murder knocks a high five figures off any property value. And my dad was so proud to see me making a strong practical move that he signed the check the same day I asked.

The party worked too. The money I brought to Rivko plus the crowd we got out at the Landecker thing and the next few gigs gave him enough faith in me to ask for a trial run as VP of his new events company. Within six months I was barely deejaying at all—just booking Diplo, Aoki, Oizo, and taking a slice of profit, instead of trying to be them. Mark quit too, finishing his conversion into the housing game by taking his real estate licensing exam. It was Esther and Crissie who kept going, joining up to play shows, flying out to Europe on Phil's dime, eventually getting bigger in town and huge in Germany and Italy, packing out mega-clubs over there. Mark, Esther and I used a second mortgage on the place to buy and flip our first house, then our second, and just kept going.

Esther and Mark now live out on Saltspring, on some enormous compound they designed themselves. Crissie and I live in the place on 16th. We refurbished the shit out of the inside, of course, but I lied to Crissie about the yard.

"Permitting hell to relandscape. I've tried with the city a half-dozen times," I told her last year.

"We can't have a garden?"

"Two more hoops and we can."

So tonight, with Crissie playing a solo gig in Vegas, Esther and Mark came over. I'd bought a bottle of Landecker for the occasion, but wasn't sentimental enough to demand that we kill it. I already had the tent set up, exactly the way it was before, pulling it out of the storage shed in the yard.

Esther got there ahead of Mark, wearing a YSL sundress. She rolled her eyes when I looked at her questioningly.

"I've got a tracksuit in my bag."

"Should have known, sorry."

Mark got there a second after her—he'd been nostalgia-eating a slice from Zaccary's. We just sat there in the living room for a second, and right before I was going to make a joke about the Landecker, Mark spoke up.

"Is he bones yet? He must be by now."

"Yeah," I said. He must be.

BURNED

BY YASUKO THANH

Yaletown

Paula's always been a hard case. She's got those eyes. A.C. is her pimp and she makes bank even though there's something dead about her: like I said, those eyes, and her laugh is cold and hollow. A meanness hides beneath her top layer of pretty, fragile as a porcelain doll.

Paula's features are so perfect they look painted on. Deb, my best friend, is beautiful in every way that Paula is not. Deb's shorter than me and has hair in different shades of blond that spikes in all directions, and apple-red cheeks even when she hasn't been outside. Paula's body is willowy and Deb's body is warm and soft, the kind of body that makes you think she'd be a great mom someday.

Paula's been A.C.'s woman for years. Deb got with him just a few months ago.

I'll confess, when A.C. bumped Deb, I started hanging out with her just to get under Paula's skin. I was tired of how the other girls fawned over her. She reminded me of all the girls I'd hated in high school. I'd been an honor roll student, and the popular girls who'd once been my friends had stopped hanging out with me when I started smoking, stealing, and getting arrested. Paula reminds me of my old life too, but not in the same way Deb does. Paula reminds me of the bad parts. The parts I wanted to leave behind when I quit school three weeks into the tenth grade and ran away from home, a town house in the slums of the city on a street with no trees.

So I looked right at Deb, and asked her how she was getting along with her wife-in-law.

She looked at me, stunned, and then decided what to do. She snorted. The kind of over-the-shoulder snort that works best when you toss your hair at the same time.

Later I discovered I really liked Deb. I told her I used to be a gymnast and she said, "I used to do gymnastics too," and she said it so quiet, with a bit of a smile, it was like she was telling me a secret.

We worked the high track bounded by Nelson, Seymour, Helmcken, and Richards. We shared the block with a pub where people threw their peanut shells on the floor; a strip club with the oldest, most washed-up dancers you'd ever seen; a corner store that sold single condoms, cigarettes, KY lube, and scratch-and-wins; a nightclub for yuppies; and a pretty wooden two-story house. A little old man lived inside. Outside are birdhouses. Tons of them. He'd built them to look like little people houses, human bungalows and ranchers and country inns, this man with thick hands and a headful of white hair. His hand-painted sign read, *I'd rather be happy in my crazy world than to be sane and sad.*

I live in a condo on West 14th and Oak by the Jewish market where you can buy the best perogies in the city. I own a mountain bike. Drive a Beemer. Deb lives down the street. When she laughs too hard she sprays beer out of her mouth. Because I've started hanging out with her wife-in-law, Paula looks at me through that thin veneer of prettiness, and smiles at me in that I'd-stab-you-if-I-could way.

But I'm smart, I make money. Girls wonder how I do it.

Paula doesn't say nasty things to me. She knows better. I

get my respect. I knew Paula was fucked up. I never knew how much until the night in the Korner Kitchen when she was hissing in my ear, telling me about the robbery.

The streetlamp shines down on Deb and me and the corner store. All the action for us starts in the Helmcken Street parking lot, because if a trick won't pull over and take a cab from there, that's it for the date before it even begins.

I like working on Helmcken. From here we can see the Korner Kitchen, the window sill littered with a line of Styrofoam takeout cups, can see who's going in, who's coming out, who's spending more time taking coffee breaks than working.

A.C. told Deb right in the middle of their having sex, while A.C. was pumping it in and out, just like that he said to Deb, "Paula doesn't make love like a woman."

Deb tells me this in the cold, under a streetlamp, flicking her cigarette into traffic. Girls stand around the block, their elbows touching like paper dolls, two of us on one side of the alley, three or four girls on the other.

Deb puts on bedroom eyes and imitates a man's voice. She says, "*Now* you *make love like a woman*. And then he gave me the ring."

Paula doesn't make love like a woman. What does she make love like then? An alien? A zombie? I've seen her on doubles, when two girls take one guy ("One starts at your nose, one starts at your toes, and we meet in the middle"), or when two girls do a date with two guys in the same hotel room. But, naturally, there's no comparing what a working girl is like with a trick and what she's like with her man. You have to call both "sex" because there's no other word to use. But "sex" with tricks is about as interesting and erotic as peeling potatoes, especially since we mostly do fake lays. As in, there's no penetration. As in, we make the trick fuck our hand and they can't tell the difference, because they're wearing two condoms and there's so much KY slathered everywhere.

Now you *make love like a woman.*

Does Deb moan as she stares into his eyes, no shame in her own pleasure? Gazes locked as she comes, her eyes not letting go of his?

I imagine Deb on her back, looking at A.C., the roundness of her potbelly, the soft rolling hills of her breasts. He grabs her ass, fingers digging into her flesh. What does it feel like to make a man lose control like that? The sun rising through the curtains. The room smelling like sex. Maybe it makes you feel grateful. To know you're part of something bigger than yourself.

The two-carat diamond, rose-cut, catches the streetlight. They say you can't teach an old dog new tricks. Maybe if you turn out late—the difference between turning out at fifteen and turning out at twenty-five—you'll just always do stupid things on the track by accident. You've already lived too much square life to not have bad habits. Like carrying a wallet or wearing a diamond ring to work. But I put aside Deb's stupidity and try to take pleasure in her excitement. I nod politely and give her a big grin.

Paula bought A.C. the Mercedes he drives. A.C. has a reputation for having his shit together; he doesn't smoke crack, saves his money. Jesse Diamond, my people, is not together. But at least he never hits me with a closed fist, always an open hand.

Pimps sell you love, and considered from a mathematical angle it's a tidy arrangement, considering we get money from the tricks we turn for something a lot of them want to pretend is love too.

When I first came to Vancouver on a PCL bus and a ferry,

to work the streets in a new city, I wanted to see if the high track stories I'd heard were true, that girls, for instance, regularly made a g-note a night.

I wanted to see what the high track was like and keep all my money. Not pay some man to tell me I looked "fine" over dinner in the new ho clothes he'd bought me so I could earn him bank on the track. I'd dabbled with pimps in Victoria, but I'd always worked as a renegade.

So I lied on the high track when the girls asked, *Who's your people?* I made one up. It felt like a game.

But the high track's not a place to lie and get away with it, so when things became nasty, I chose Jesse, to save my ass. I've been with him ever since. Jesse Diamond isn't all bad. Tracksuit, long Jheri curls, and a Morris Day mustache. The night we met I had the feeling that anything could happen. The air seemed as full and rich as a piece of cake, and I wanted to swallow it whole or at least slip a piece into my pocket. I'd met better-looking guys, but he could talk, and he made me feel beautiful.

A.C. has given Deb—his tip—a diamond ring.

"She already hated me," Deb says. "I wonder what she'll do now."

Ever since Deb came along, Paula seems more hollow than she used to be, and colder. Her head like a porcelain doll's seems more like a glass flask about to explode. I watch her, waiting for it.

She's changing. There's a current of nervous energy underneath, high-voltage. Everyone can see that A.C. has a soft spot for Deb. For real. And Paula's humiliated.

Deb can't keep to herself what's making her happy, and soon everyone knows about the ring.

* * *

Paula's regular has a wardrobe full of fetish gear: leather cuffs, spreader bars, x-frames, sleepsacks, nipple clamps, gags, and whips. He's into bondage and obedience training. Paula orders him, at twice the normal hourly rate, to lick cabernet spills off his kitchen floor tiles with his tongue, and then punishes him for his defiance if he takes more than a second or two to get down on all fours. Typically she flogs his ass, making him pay her for the privilege. Paula keeps his beatings below the neck, so no one at his law firm knows.

There's nothing wrong with spanking a guy or whipping him for money. I've done it myself. Kinky *starts* at two hundred dollars and goes up from there. Though I usually feel like laughing halfway through. I just can't take myself seriously when I say, "Crawl across that floor, slave, and call me mistress." I have one regular who gives me over a thousand dollars when he smokes crack. I just think up nasty things for him to do and stash the cash—until he runs out of money or coke. The last time, I hurt him more than he wanted; it was an accident. I hadn't realized the buckle was whipping around and hitting him where it shouldn't have been, in the ribs. His bruises were so swollen they were wet-looking.

Most of my regulars are salt-of-the-earth types. One talks to me about Akira Kurosawa films and shows me photos of the commune where he grew up. Another gave me an electric guitar, another a Günter Grass book as a present. I have regulars who are loggers, or fishermen, who tell me about all the places they've been and all the places they'd still like to see.

Paula. She's different. But you already know that. Paula passes the pictures around in the Korner Kitchen.

We're in the last booth. She's squashed herself in next to Deb. Andrea sits with her ankle-length black sable across

from us, and I'm thinking, *Why us? Why now?* But it's because
the diner is full of girls and designer purses and compacts
brought out over the scarred tables to fix lipstick and powder
noses, and there's nowhere else to sit. Everyone came in like
bees in a hive, and now I'm stuck in a booth with Paula and
Andrea, when all I wanted to do was sink into the softness of
the red vinyl seat and massage my toes.

On any given night in this cheap diner on the track, a girl
might be crying on the pay phone, another girl in the bathroom might be pissing blood from a beating she got the night
before, another girl sitting in one of the horseshoe-shaped
booths at the front might be adjusting her waist-length hair to
hide the crisscrossing of stitches on her head from a bad date's
crowbar, and groups of women with brand-new breasts might
be discussing the pros and cons of enlargement surgery with
those who haven't yet had the procedure, saying things like,
Yeah, now I got no feeling in my nipples. But, you know, whatever.
Discussing the merits of different brands of hairspray, laughing
at anyone gauche enough to use one bought at a drugstore,
or rolling in the aisles like professional wrestlers, one woman
vice-gripping another in her long, lean, tanning-salon-perfect
thighs, before grabbing a sugar canister and bringing it down
on the other girl's head, knocking over a gashed stool that's
been repaired with yellow police tape.

Squashed in like this, I can't move my elbows. This gives
me an excuse not to reach for the picture Paula tries to pass
me, but it makes no difference to her. She lays it faceup on the
table for everyone to see.

I notice burns around his nipples. Angry red circles outlined with black, charred flesh in the center. More on his inner thighs, his balls. They look like smallpox, the pictures I've
seen in books of dying people. She passes me another one of

them pouring gross stuff on him like ketchup and motor oil. Her and her friend Sherri. I can't imagine how much that must have hurt, stinging its way into his burns, his open wounds.

Paula makes me sick. The kind of sick that makes you want to punch someone and walk away.

Next they light more cigarettes and run them over his body, little burning caterpillars leaving ash trails.

At this point in the story, part of me wants to get up and leave.

So many burns that his body looks disfigured, twisted in discomfort. You can't see his expression in any of these pictures. You can see his face—that there is one—but not enough to tell what he's thinking. Can you ever?

He isn't smiling, and he isn't asleep, even though in some of the pictures his eyes are closed and his head is craned to the right, away from the camera. But his arched body gives away that he is awake with pain.

There are no pictures of the flames. But there are pictures of what he looked like afterward.

Paula and Andrea keep passing the photo back and forth silently.

I begin to cry without meaning to, the way your eyes water when you're really mad.

"Mother Teresa, here," Paula says.

They stole everything they could carry away. They took his microwave and stereo and paintings off the walls. They took his lamps and barware. Sculptures they liked and sculptures they didn't like. They loaded it into Paula's car, and before the lawyer passed out he told them the combination for the safe.

I admire Andrea's thick skin. Her internal fortitude. Paula shows me another photo.

"How much did you guys get?" Andrea says, her eyes beaming.

"*Who cares?*" I say. "Seriously."

"Who cares?" Paula repeats. "What the hell?" She said it like you'd say, *Bird shit? Bird shit on my windshield?*

"Keep your shitty pictures," I say.

"I don't think I could do that," Deb finally speaks, "no matter the money."

Paula beams. "That's why I'm me and you're you." She pauses. "Thank God."

What power does Paula think this gives her over Deb? Part of me understands not wanting to be broken. But if Paula thinks Deb now regards her with awe, she is wrong.

"Did you leave him there?" I ask, changing the subject. I haven't come here to give Paula any glory.

"Yeah, *duh.*"

"Fuckin' barbecue," I say. I want to be hard. I want to be tough.

"God, that's gross," Paula says, like *I'm* the witch.

I swallow. "I guess it takes all kinds," I say. Did I mean him asking for it, or her giving it to him?

"He *wanted* us to."

If someone asked me to set them on fire. To kill them. Let them die. What would I do? "Did you at least call 911?" I say to everyone at the table.

Deb hugs me. The waitress comes to take our orders. Andrea gawks at me as if I'm joking. But some days the world's beauty hurts. You have to let it. Not care who sees. Who hears.

Deb rubs my shoulder.

"We put out the fire, stupid. What do you think? We killed him?"

"Let it out," Deb says. "That's right."

Deb would have called 911. Deb would have waited with him until the ambulance arrived.

"Then, get this," Paula nudges me with her elbow, "he actually says thank you."

All's I know is this. It's been three days since Paula and Sherri did that date. Sherri's still not back at work. Maybe they made so much money she's able to take the time off. Or maybe the experience screwed her up. I don't know which. Do you always give someone exactly what they want? Certain experiences turn us into people we never thought we could be.

"You make love like a woman," Deb says, imitating A.C. again. "So what's that mean? Paula's not a woman?"

I think of the photos. I tell Deb she better watch her back.

PART III

NIGHT VISIONS

THE DEMON OF STEVESTON

BY KRISTI CHARISH

Britannia

I crouched down over the white plastic bag and carefully teased it away from the baby formula bottles, all sealed, still filled with the grayish-beige liquid.

"The formula might be what did it," I said, surveying the cordoned-off docks for the fourth time, trying my best not to look at the body or the open dead eyes, lined with a smattering of heavy, dark eyelashes. "Unnerved them. I can't see why else they'd leave the body here." I stood with a small groan, my rubber shoe taps scuffing against the dew-laced dock. The plastic bags stirred with the morning breeze that buffeted the sea grass flats off the Britannia shipyards. "That or the milk stains."

"Jesus Christ," Murray whispered, more prayer than statement.

I shoved my hands in my pocket to keep Murray from seeing them fidget. I suspected he'd called me out here for charity more than necessity, but still I felt obligated to muster my best. I squinted against the sunlight coming off the water, only now high enough to sting my eyes, and tried remembering the last time I was up at daybreak. I didn't feel the need to apologize for the cigarette I lit, stashed in my pocket months ago for a rainy day.

Or a dead body.

"Runaway, prostitute—or a little of both?" Murray asked.

A long drag did wonders to calm my jitters. I forced myself to scan the woman's meager possessions once again—and then her.

Young Asian woman, hair bleached within an inch of its life, small frame yet I'd guess athletic. Dressed in a vintage-looking cargo jacket, combat boots, and a matching canvas backpack lying off to the side. Her skin only now starting to lose color. Not dead long.

On a hunch I turned her ankle to check the brand of her boot. It took a lot of money to look that disheveled. As I suspected it was expensive. I could see where Murray's mistake had been made; the diaper bag could have been a backpack.

"She isn't a street kid." I indicated the embossed mark on the heel. "Not with these boots."

He swore and stepped out of earshot before pulling out his phone.

"I banked on her being a heroin hippie or a fentanyl elf," he said when he returned. "Figured she was Native." As if that was an explanation in and of itself.

"Chinese. And you're a racist asshole."

Murray had the good grace not to argue. It was an unspoken rule that if a victim were an addict, runaway, prostitute, or combination of the three, no one blinked an eye if you phoned in the investigation. Murray had a full caseload, and with no ID he'd been hopeful—999 times out of 1,000 when a girl was found like this, it was one of the three.

I glanced up at the tall lamps that overhung the docks. Most were still on, even with the morning light. "Those two are out." I nodded at two dead lights overhead. "She probably didn't even notice. Who sounded the alarm?"

"Night guard heard shouting. Stepped out of the shed and swears he saw someone crouched over her. Took off before he got a closer look."

I frowned as something metallic glinted just underneath her jacket, where metal shouldn't have been.

I motioned for Murray to hand me a pair of gloves. "Search the area yet?"

"Mike's bringing the dogs. If she's like you said, chances are there'll already be a report." He added something else about searching social media. I half-listened, gingerly pushing open the lapel of her jacket.

A few feet away on the dock stood an Asian woman, black hair done at the nape of her neck and wearing a calico-print dress that would have been more appropriate on a woman in the twenties or thirties. She was staring straight at me. An exhibitor from the museum here early? I opened my mouth to interrupt Murray but the sunlight flickered with a passing cloud. The woman flickered as well.

Not again.

I shut my eyes tight, willing the woman to disappear. I was lucky to catch it so quickly, especially since cutting my meds in half. They made me so damn sluggish.

"Ricky?" Murray had crouched down beside me. "You having one of your—episodes?" It was impossible not to miss the hidden distaste and suspicion. "I thought the doctors said you were better now."

"They did. I mean I'm—" I stopped my defense. The ghostly woman was back, this time hovering over the tidal flats, the edges of her old-fashioned dress tinged dark with water. She stared sadly, not at the strangled dead girl, but at me.

Best to ignore these slips. They couldn't be helped, and worrying only made them worse. At best they were rabbit holes. At worst?

The woman vanished. I covered the momentary lapse with another drag from my cigarette, feigning concentration directed back on the body. If Murray suspected, he pretended not to. He'd always done that better than the other detectives. It was why I'd taken his call. That and my own curiosity.

I nodded at the strap and refocused the conversation. "Thing is, Murray, you aren't asking the most important question." I pulled the jacket the woman had been wearing aside, exposing the source of the metal glint. A strap, innocuous at first, unless you knew what it was. I glanced up at him. "If she was wearing a baby carrier, where's the baby?"

Murray swore something foul but it was lost in the phone as he retreated to his car. I stole another glance at the tidal flats. The ghostly woman was gone.

I gave the dead girl's possessions one last glance, but I already knew what was there—a mix of baby supplies: wipes, diapers, formula—all strewn across the dock and into the mud below. They held no more clues.

I paid attention to the docks instead, well lit for tourist season. Warm night, the watchman would have been looking for kids sneaking into the park. If it was premeditated, it hadn't been well planned . . .

Opportunity? A chance encounter? Not impossible, but odd considering the remote location and the groceries. As if she was meeting someone.

Back to premeditated. But then why not dump the body in the water? Unless they intended for her to be found? An argument gone wrong? An accident? Or just inexperience.

Not something I was used to seeing. Not for the runaways, drug dealers, and trafficked prostitutes I consulted on. Without knowing who she was and why she was here, I had no motivation. A field full of rabbit holes.

"Ricky, I need you to do your thing," Murray said, back from his call.

I swallowed and resisted the urge to take another drag. "I find teens and women. Missing babies are outside my social circle." Verbalizing what it was I was good at always brought up a familiar ball of guilt.

"I'll pay you the same rate as last time. Off the books."

I bit back a hiss, taking in a mouthful of smoke. Of course off the books. There were some things you just couldn't be forgiven for in the court of public opinion.

"No one finds people like you do, Ricky."

Because I knew where they went.

"Get your forensics to canvas the docks," I told him, avoiding a solid answer. "Then we'll see." I kept my eyes on the mud as I retreated to my car, an antique VW Bug that needed a key to open its dulled yellow doors, the necessity of it ruining whatever ironic fashionable veneer it had once held. I didn't bother searching the lot for the ghostly woman and whatever it was my mind imagined she wanted. Instead, I stared at my hands until the engine in my car turned.

No rabbit holes this time, Ricky.

Cigarette still lit and without saying goodbye to Murray, I peeled out of the parking lot before anyone else arrived to find me at the scene.

An hour and another cigarette later, I arrived home at my condo in a refurbished heritage building on the edge of China and Gastown. My living space clashed with my income and what I alone could afford—or deserved. A peace offering from my father when he'd paid the deposit on an exorbitant North Van home, a wedding gift for my brother. Not wanting to break a streak in fairness, he'd purchased this place for me. The fact that it was now worth well over four times what he'd paid in the nineties just dug the knife in deeper.

I dropped my coat on the wooden stand by the front door and headed straight for my desk. I didn't smoke inside—it was the one concession I'd made to my ex and the only lifestyle improvement I hadn't been able to renege on. The ashtray was still out on the porch with a view into the gated alley–turned-garden two stories below.

I put the coffee pot on, then headed into the shower, something I hadn't had a chance to do before Murray had called. It wasn't until I was dry and had a warm mug in my hands that I checked my phone.

I was relieved not to see a text from Murray. Trafficked babies weren't the same as trafficked girls. I had half a mind to go visit my brother for the weekend in North Van, just to avoid being useless.

The scrape of the metal gate outside distracted me.

Sliding my phone in my pocket, I took my coffee out to the porch, knowing who would be below.

Sitting on the rim of one of the large flowerpots was a woman in her fifties, face framed in a brown bob, with high cheekbones, tanned skin, and a slimness that hid or flattered her age well. I guessed First Nations, but had never gotten up the courage to ask, and she'd never brought it up.

This morning she had the same stroller I'd noticed last night squeaking down the sidewalk. Her other grandchildren had grown well beyond it, so this one must be new. I smiled as I leaned over the rail. "Marnie." She was the only neighbor I knew by name.

"Ricky." She offered me a warm smile and settled the baby on her lap—a girl in a pink outfit with black hair and expressive eyes that searched the courtyard.

The infant gave me a brief glance before fixating once again on her fingers, apparently much more interesting. I noted a darkened birthmark on her leg, exposed by bare feet.

"Haven't seen you in a couple weeks," Marnie said.

She had lived in the building since the eighties, before it was fashionable to live in Gastown. I had no idea what her financial situation was, if she'd been married, widowed. I'd never seen a man or her adult children, though they must have existed as she had three grandchildren. Two boys and now the girl. I had no idea what their story was. Marnie had never once asked me about the tabloid-like stories in the paper. Maybe that was why we were tentative friends—we didn't bother each other with the usual details. Our acquaintance was centered around living proximity. No need to pollute it with the outside world.

"You going to show that coffee up in my face, or get your manners together?"

I headed back into my kitchen and filled a second mug, adding the cream and sugar Marnie preferred. She nodded in thanks as I passed it down.

Marnie and her grandchildren were the only ones who used the garden regularly. The rest seemed either ignorant or uninterested in frequenting an alley in Vancouver, however gentrified. Creatures of our environment. It took someone who knew what a dangerous alley looked like to recognize when there was no danger. Maybe another reason we were friends.

Juggling the infant on one knee, Marnie took a deep sip, savoring the warmth. "How are things?" she asked. "More dead girls?"

That took me aback. Marnie had an unhealthy interest in my obsessions. There was something ironic in that—or comical.

She tsked. "The only thing that gets you out of your bed

before noon is a dead girl." The baby fussed and Marnie jostled her until she stopped. "Well?"

I shouldn't tell her, in theory it was confidential with Murray . . . Screw it, I wasn't even an official consultant anymore.

"False alarm so far—not a prostitute or a runaway." Though that didn't make it more or less tragic. I sipped my coffee. "Missing baby though."

Marnie made a cross sign over her chest and out of reflex held the infant tighter. "That's much worse."

"Depends on whether the baby is still alive."

I inclined my head as my phone buzzed in my pocket. Murray. I excused myself from the balcony and closed the door before answering.

"We found the SUV," Murray said. "Empty car seat, no sign of the baby anywhere."

So much for finding the baby. "Who was she?"

"June Xian. Kitsilano housewife, first kid born five months ago, named Blossom. June was born in Hong Kong, the husband and baby here."

Despite my reluctance, my brain churned through the possibilities. "Suspects?"

"Husband. House and most of the cash is in her name. Her parents used her to invest heavily in real estate."

"Money for motive?"

"According to the neighbors and a slew of noise complaints, the two have been fighting. Apparently she kept threatening to take the baby back to Asia."

Money and children, common enough motives. "Affair?" I asked, completing the trifecta of domestic discourse. Still not in my realm, but closer.

"That's what the husband claims."

Maybe some of my old vice channels would prove useful. More rabbits ducked in and out of their holes. "Whoever killed June might simply have gotten rid of the baby—" I froze. The Asian woman in the old-fashioned dress was standing in my kitchen, her translucence unmistakable in the sunlight. She lifted a finger and jabbed it at me, her face, almost featureless, twisted in anger.

"Shit," I said to myself. No, not here, anywhere but here.

"Ricky?" Murray's voice on the phone.

"Yeah." I squeezed my eyes shut. "Where's forensics at?"

"Waiting on the preliminary."

"In the meantime I could tag my old contacts and dig up dirt on the husband."

"Just—can you be discrete? We, ah, don't need a repeat of last time."

The professional thing would be to assure Murray there wouldn't be a repeat. I decided not to jinx it and risked opening my eyes. She was gone from my kitchen. I stifled a sigh of relief while Murray carried on, as if lack of my response was normal. "I really appreciate it, Ricky."

My goodbye verged on rude. It was almost eight a.m. now. I made my next call.

"You realize I'm Japanese?" said the young, attractive man in his twenties as he slid into the booth across from me. Today he was wearing waxed jeans and an expensively cut leather jacket, tattoos visible under the cuffs. Yoshi was more fashionable than I'd had any chance of being, even a couple decades ago.

"You realize I like the tea?" I said.

He snorted but didn't protest further. It was the same every time. He thought I invited him here because I couldn't tell the difference between Japanese and Chinese. I always insisted it was because I liked the tea—which I did. We agreed to disagree. I wasn't changing the spot, especially if I was the one buying.

"Did you bring my payment?"

"Depends. Do you have what I want?" I silently chided myself. I wouldn't be that snippy if it wasn't for the Asian woman following me. I'd spent the entire walk here searching for her in the faces of passersby.

Yoshi didn't care. He nodded and slid a tablet across the table to me. I slid an envelope to him.

Phone records, bank statements, e-mails, police reports highlighting domestic disputes, dates and times she'd crossed the bridge, locations where she'd opened her social media. All her life in painstaking detail. I glanced up at the preliminary autopsy report. "You're not supposed to be able to access these."

He shrugged. "I was already on their servers. Figured you'd appreciate it. Besides, I was curious. Girls like her don't end up dead often."

Death by strangulation, relatively healthy—I frowned at the mention of marks carved into her bare shoulder. Not a birthmark, not a wound. More like a brand, as if the skin had been filleted out. Three lines, too parallel and straight to be anything but deliberate.

I skimmed through the rest, but the symbol had my attention now. The rabbits didn't want to let it go . . .

Credit cards showed she'd purchased the groceries at eleven thirty p.m., then crossed the toll bridge at eleven fifty p.m. Yoshi also confirmed the husband had been home, according to his phone and the voice-activated alarm system. I found the confirmation I was looking for in her e-mail. "An affair," I said.

Yoshi arched an eyebrow at me. "You should see the texts, and the pictures. I didn't know pregnant ladies—"

I shushed him and he fell silent. Where you had money and marital discord, you usually had the third. Still, it left a dry feeling in my mouth. Couples were assholes to each other all on their own, they didn't need a third-wheel catalyst.

Yoshi of course had included the catalyst's details, his name, Victor Miller, and his work and home addresses. He lived right near the Britannia shipyards. Well, now I knew what she'd been doing in the area. Miller worked downtown as a bartender. I finished my tea and tossed some bills on the table.

"What's your hurry, Ricky?" Yoshi said.

"To find out just what June saw in this guy."

I tapped the bottom of my soda on the bar as I watched Victor restock the bar, it being early in the afternoon and slow.

He eyed me every now and then—in the mirror mostly, discretely. He didn't recognize me but he knew what I was. *Had been,* I corrected myself. Once learned, you never lose the identifying affectations. No one does. Like a permanent scarlet letter—or brand, not unlike what had been carved out of June.

He wasn't my type but I could see why June had chased him—roughly the same age if not younger, attractive in a surfer bum way. The opposite of the husband who looked at home in a three-button suit as he pleaded on TV and in the papers for information on his daughter. Victor didn't strike me as the kind of man a woman like June was serious about, more a tool to get a rise out of her husband.

I held up the empty soda glass and smiled as I figured out the best way to broach June and her baby, how to phrase it just right. It was harder when I wasn't officially on a case.

I could lie, tell him I was one of June's friends, or hired by her friends to find the baby. It was all over the news now. Usually Murray had these conversations, not me.

I'd half decided on lying when his eyes drifted to a spot behind me. Something about the way he frowned made me pause. He called for one of his coworkers to fill in before abandoning the bar.

Not wanting to give myself away, I shifted on the barstool until I got a good glimpse of the doors in the mirror. Between the bottles of Grey Goose I made out two detectives, one of which I recognized, Mike. He'd called me a parasite and worse to Murray on more than one occasion. They flashed their badges at Victor and though I couldn't hear details, I could well imagine the line of questions.

I watched his face carefully as he responded. Great boyfriend he was not, but he wasn't a killer. He didn't have the markers for violence. Those I could spot, my other talent from a previous life.

The other detective started scanning the bar, his eyes in the mirror falling on my back. I left cash under my empty glass and nodded at the bartender who'd replaced Victor, before heading for the washroom to slip out the back.

I was past the kitchen, almost to the back door, when she appeared. Not the Asian woman in the calico-patterned dress, but June, wearing a white T-shirt over simple blue jeans. Her eyes were red, her expression angry. A grotesque welt, red and purple against her graying skin, burst across her cheek in the shape of the carved brand. She bared her teeth at me, like a wild animal.

I shut my eyes and counted to ten before opening them, but she was still there. They always lingered when my mind made them grotesque like that.

No, not now. I ran through her, hitting the door open with a bang. They aren't real, they're never real.

I raced the block back to my car and shoved the key into the lock. *Come on.* The door finally opened before either woman reappeared. I slid behind the wheel and scrambled to open the glove box. It was still there. I swallowed two of the Risperidones, hoping the high dose would drown them out faster. I'd taken too few over these last weeks, trying to strike a hard balance between crazy and vegetative. I shut my eyes and counted until the panic ebbed. The ghosts didn't bother me here, not where I might kill myself driving. The ghosts had their own sense of self-preservation.

Once my heart stopped racing, I opened my eyes. She was gone. I turned the ignition over and headed back home before the Risperidone made me drowsy. As I drove I focused on what I knew: the boyfriend wasn't the killer.

I waited until I was through the front door before checking my e-mail. It had been a half hour drive back, and I'd stopped twice to rest my nerves.

There was a single missed call from Murray. If Mike had recognized me, there would have been a lot more. Returning Murray's call could wait.

The brand carved out of June haunted my thoughts. I searched my shelf for a yellowed plastic binder I hadn't perused in years, one filled with details from a decade-old criminology class. The early West Coast had bred a different kind of criminal, specializing in vice: Shanghaiing unsuspecting travelers to fill crews, trading in Chinese slaves, Gold Rush scams of every which way and flavor.

I found it, and my fingers tripped over the pages until I reached the familiar passage. A group of Chinese shipbuilders and canners at the Britannia docks in the early 1900s had been some of the first victims. Later ones had included fishermen and cannery workers, Native and white. The murders had largely been ignored by the press at the time, only linked in later years by historians who found the circumstances curious. I remembered it vaguely, it having piqued my interest in class when described as one of BC's first modern serial killings. The occult-minded of my classmates had been riveted by the circumstances.

I brushed my fingers along a grainy black-and-white photo. The same three parallel lines carved into June decorated the bodies in the photo.

That's why my mind must have concocted the ghosts, a long-forgotten lecture resurfacing. Murray would have missed it. He hated the occult as much as he hated history. I snapped a picture and texted him: *It's not the boyfriend.*

"That's not what our guys think," Murray said when I answered his call.

"Mike is a bigoted idiot," I responded.

He sighed. "He'd vehemently disagree."

"I know what the brand is." I filled him in on what I'd discovered, omitting June's ghost.

"It's interesting, and I'll be the first to say it's suspicious, but all it points to is that the killer is either into the occult or a history buff."

"Did you see the photo? Those carvings are the same."

"They're 120 years apart. And I didn't hire you to look for a killer. I hired you to tap your old trafficking contacts and see if anyone was offloading a baby." A slight pause. "Ricky, are you taking your meds?"

My meds. The only way Murray would talk about my condition—writing off my insights as an odd, useful quirk of a broken mind, not unlike the brand on the body. My finger paused over one of the pages, over a photo that stared up at me. The woman in the calico-patterned dress, the same brand on her arm still distinguishable in the grainy image.

"Ricky? You still there?"

"I might have found something, just . . . this isn't one of my mad goose chases." I didn't give him the chance to interrupt me before hanging up the phone, hoping my mind hadn't tricked me into lying once again.

I stared at the photo and the caption underneath. A cook who'd worked at the cannery, one of the Chinese shipbuilders' wives—

There was a rap at my balcony window. I turned but there was no one there. I swore and folded the binder back up. I wasn't that high up . . . it could be a burglar.

"Hello?" I called out. No answer. I swallowed. *It's not real.* I searched my drawer for the Risperidone, thinking I never should have quit.

"Ricky?"

Marnie. I breathed a sigh of relief.

She narrowed her eyes at me as I stepped out onto the balcony. "You look like you've seen a ghost."

"Just the case getting to me," I settled on. I told her about the brand on June's shoulder, and the historical connection—more to settle my own thoughts.

The glance she gave me was sharp as I passed her a mug of coffee. "Brands carved into the flesh? Like strips of bacon taken out for a frying pan?"

At the look I gave her she was quick to shake her head. "Just thinking about old stories—stupid ones, but . . ." She shrugged. "Your dead girl with that brand reminds me of one." She jostled the baby, who was also examining me now. "Ever heard of a *wechuge?*" She pronounced it *way-chu-gay.*

I shook my head and her lip twitched as she tsked. "Didn't suppose you had—but you never know. It's like a windigo."

I searched my Risperidone-addled brain. "North American monster. A demon or something, no?"

She half nodded. "A cannibal to be precise, with maybe a little magic thrown in—don't look at me like that, Ricky. It's not some mystical insight. I studied First Nations culture and legends as part of my anthropology course in the nineties. Was interested in the stories my grandfather used to tell me."

Marnie coddled the baby. A bottle appeared from inside her bag, the nib disappearing into the baby's eager mouth. "*Wechuge* is the Western, not so psychotic version of the windigo—if there is such a thing as a nicer, nonpsychotic cannibal."

I gave her a terse smile. "I'm pretty sure Murray won't go for a cannibalistic First Nations monster as a murder suspect."

Marnie shook her head. "Never said it was. One of the stories my grandfather told was about a Ukrainian fellow out in Saskatchewan in the early twenties. According to my grandfather, the Ukrainian fellow made a deal with a *wechuge* spirit to get vengeance on the folks he thought wronged him—farmers, local police, and then a priest, though the priest probably deserved it, even if the others didn't."

I shook my head and braced myself as the Chinese woman in calico appeared behind Marnie. She was a faded visage now, barely perceptible if I angled my head the right way so that the sunlight drowned her out. "Completely different from a dead Chinese woman."

Marnie shrugged. "*Wechuge* or not, the man was real enough. Caught and hanged him for murder—and worse." Marnie tsked again. "The *wechuge's* price was flesh from the victims. He ate a bit of all of them, strips of flesh, fried up like bacon with his breakfast. Farfetched, but still, my grandfather described those same markings. Three strips carved out of the skin. There's even a public record. I found it a few years back. And you're missing my point."

"Which is?" I did my best to ignore the ghost's grotesque pantomime of strangling Marnie. The figments of my imagination no longer satisfied with misbehaving, now acting out. I clenched my teeth and forced a smile as Marnie placed the baby back in the stroller, pocketing the bottle and accessories.

"If a crazy Ukrainian man a hundred years ago figured he'd made a deal with a devil to exact mystical vengeance on a whole town through consuming their flesh, who knows what your killer came up with? That's the thing that doesn't change about people. They always try to justify their craziness." Marnie winced as she stood, from sore joints and stiffness. "And on that morbid note, I hope you find the baby."

"You say that every time."

She waved over her shoulder. "I mean it every time. And try to take care of yourself. You never do."

I focused away from the ghost on the baby fussing in the stroller, her bare foot with the dark birthmark kicking free.

I went back inside and checked through the pictures that both Yoshi and Murray had sent me of June. None of my contacts had given me any inclination they'd heard of a baby being moved. It had been a long shot at best. I stopped the scroll of my screen on one of June's social media images. A birthmark, dark and prominent on the baby's foot. Very much like Marnie's granddaughter's.

My hands shook. It couldn't be. I'd seen the baby with Marnie before . . . starting the night June had died.

Halving my Risperidone had been a mistake.

But what if it wasn't? Marnie would understand if I just went to check.

I ran up the steps to her apartment—308 was what she'd told me. I banged on the door three times. "Marnie? Answer the door, it's important."

The door swung open before I could knock a fourth. The woman who answered was blond, late thirties or early forties, Caucasian. It took a moment for my mouth to recover.

"Ah, is Marnie here?" I asked.

She stared at me as if I were crazy.

"I'm sorry, I live in the building," I stammered. "She must have moved out. I'm sorry." I hated my fluster, I'd had enough practice with this over the years, but when they surprised me . . .

I stumbled back and waved as she closed the door. My heart pounded so hard on the flight of stairs back to my own apartment that I barely noticed turning my lock.

I opened my laptop and entered: *Marnie Wallace 1990s*. That was the decade Marnie had said she'd graduated in. There she was staring back at me from the screen. *Marnie Wallace, Criminology, third year, survived by a daughter. Death, 1997.*

I closed the computer, my mouth dry. My memory had conjured her from a case file I'd read. My mind had fooled me. Worse than last time.

Yet I'd seen the baby before I'd seen June's body, the night before, the stroller creaking down the sidewalk.

It took me two tries to raise the phone to my ear.

"Ricky?" Murray answered on the fourth ring.

"Murray, I'm—" Where to start? I couldn't get the image of the birthmark out of my mind.

"You don't sound so good."

I had to tell him, to say something. "I think I've got a lead. On the baby."

"Won't do much good, Ricky. We found her in the water an hour ago."

"I know this is going to sound crazy—crazier than normal." How to convince him? I wetted my lips. "Have you ever heard of something called a windigo?"

More silence, followed by a sigh. "I knew it was too soon to bring you back in."

He didn't believe me. My heart pooled into a dark pit. "No, I'm *fine*." I ran my hand violently through my hair, longer than I should have let it grow.

"No, you're not." His voice was firm. "Just stay there. I'm coming over."

"Murray, wait. Shit." He'd hung up. I redialed but there was no answer.

"Don't feel so bad, Ricky."

I spun around. Marnie was behind me, holding the infant. This time I could make out their faint translucence.

"You weren't exactly coming into this with a full deck of cards." She smiled at me, a glimpse of teeth that were dark, pointed, menacing. She nodded at the binder and laptop. "Was supposed to have a granddaughter but my daughter wasn't so good with keeping to the straight-and-narrow. Little girl didn't stand a chance. Died a few days after she was born, a poor sick little thing."

I tried to speak but words caught in my mouth, dry from the medication.

"Reality is such a strange, fragile thing, isn't it? And sanity. That's something I suppose you value, though, Ricky, much like I value my grandchildren."

June appeared behind Marnie, wielding a kitchen knife

that she drove into her back, over and over. It made no difference.

"You can't be real," I finally managed.

Marnie arched an eyebrow. "Wouldn't you like to know? That's the problem with the sane nowadays, they never believe what's possible until it's too late."

There was a knock on the door. "Ricky?" Murray called.

"You should get that," Marnie said, but both she and June were standing in my way.

I let the knocking continue. I didn't plead for my life, didn't beg. I still wasn't sure any of it was real.

"You killed them," I whispered.

She inclined her head and tsked. "Think of me less as a cannibal, more of a carrion cleaner. I take people's burdens, the ones festering under their skin. June's unwanted family, this woman's guilt over not raising a child right, the Ukrainian man's vengeance for a murder left unpunished. I take their *despair*." Her eyes glowed with warmth. "Your madness. I'm not just a killer or a cannibal. I'm a release."

"Ricky? Open the door!" The knocking continued but I was fixated on Marnie.

"You want your sanity, Ricky? To be free of the ghosts stalking you at every turn?" She nodded to the counter. Right beside the Risperidone was a plastic bag that hadn't been there before. Something red and raw inside. Three strips of flesh.

"Taken in context, it doesn't seem like such a steep price to pay." She nodded to the door where Murray still pleaded. "And time is running out."

I swallowed. Sanity, something I'd never had, the lack of which had crippled my life. Both June and the calico woman were standing behind Marnie, shaking their fading heads at me.

"Will it hurt?" I asked.

A pointed, toothy smile. "Everything hurts."

I picked up the bag of June's flesh.

The banging continued. Baby on the hip of the younger, stronger body, I answered the door. The madness was still there, but fading into the background of me now.

"I'm still me," Ricky said out loud.

The voice tasted strange on my mouth.

Yes, of course, I whispered. *Now wipe your mouth before you answer the door.*

Murray stood in the hallway, angry. His eyes drifted from my new face to the baby. "What the hell?" Confusion, and fear. That was a familiar smell.

Smile, just smile.

"Come on inside," Ricky said. "I'll explain everything."

STITCHES

BY DON ENGLISH

Crab Park

N o one sees as he wrestles her plastic-wrapped body out of the backseat of his Volvo and carries it down to the beach in Crab Park. He's sat alone in his car every night at this time for two weeks; he's confident no dog walkers or drifters or kids smoking a joint under the stars will be around as he lays her body down gently behind a log. He walks close enough to the ocean that when he kneels in the sand the waves lap his knees. The wind blowing in over the water seasons the air, heightens the smell of the still-warm pavement, the sunburned grass, and the overflowing trash bins.

He'd seen her waiting on the sidewalk on Hastings Street and there was room enough for him to pull over right in front of her, like it was meant to be. He'd leaned over to lower his passenger window and asked her if she did Greek. He'd heard that on TV once and thought it sounded good.

"Nope, I took French in school for a bit but I dropped it. I know a bit of Spanish. *Chinga tu madre.*"

She was trying to be funny and he didn't want her to be funny. He had to deal with enough women trying to be funny whenever he went on the Internet. For a minute he was angry and thought about driving away, but she looked too perfect in the short skirt and the jean shirt tied under her breasts. She leaned into the window looking impatient.

"Are you supposed to be lost? Should I pretend to give you directions or something? No one gives a shit. Thirty bucks and I'll take you where you need to go."

"Thirty is too much. Twenty bucks. For mouth stuff."

"Twenty-five for mouth stuff."

He unlocked the door in a hurry and told her to get in. She was beautiful; he didn't like that she tried to be funny, but she was beautiful. Confident too, she took one look back over her shoulder before she got in the car and then sat with her arms crossed, glaring a hole in his windshield. He decided to break the silence.

"What's your name?"

"Pilot."

"That's a funny name, did your parents want you to fly?"

"You'd have to ask them."

He wanted her to smile a little. He thought the look on her face would be better later if she smiled. "I don't know much French or Spanish. But I learned a lot of Japanese in high school."

"So you didn't need the subtitles on the cartoons, right?"

He blushed a little. "Right! That's exactly right. My favorite was—"

She clicked her tongue against her back teeth. "We're not doing small talk unless you're paying me more, sport."

She looked different to him then, more like the girls at work. Another reality TV watcher. He was looking for a genuine connection with someone who liked substantial things, things out of the ordinary. A girl who lit up when she saw you, listened to you, had a laugh that coated you like butter. Not someone who looked at you funny in an elevator when you told them their hair smelled nice. He nosed his car into an alley between a warehouse loft space and the chain-link fence that separated it from the railway tracks. It was always deserted there. They sat for a minute listening to the engine ticking and he waited for her to reach into her purse for condoms before he grabbed her by the throat.

Pilot Cassidy is lined up to get into a concert at the Astoria and is amusing herself by eavesdropping on the two women behind her in line. The sound from the bar leaking out into the street is brutal, but the women are drunk and loud and Pilot can't help but overhear. One of them had met a guy though Craigslist who was willing to exchange a six-pack of beer for a hand job, any kind of beer, and so she'd done it and would totally do it again.

"Weren't you afraid he was going to murder you or something?"

"Nah, he wanted to meet in Dude Chilling Park, daylight and everything. It took about five minutes, max. Didn't even get any on me. I told him in advance what kind of beer I wanted and he had it right there in the trunk of his car."

"You went with him to the trunk of his car? You are so stupid!"

"Bitch, I shared that beer with you!"

Pilot lies on her mattress after the show, the room lit only by her phone. She makes herself scroll through pictures of the night first—a sea of raised hands obscuring the shitty opening band, a bloody-nosed selfie taken in the bathroom mirror after someone threw an elbow back and hit her, one of her room-mates barfing with scary accuracy into a pint glass—before opening Craigslist and cruising *Men Seeking Women*. She answers the first one that seems weird, offers the most money, and doesn't get specific about what her body looks like.

Rob messages bright and early the next day, tells Pilot

he hasn't had many replies so far, and she blinks through her hangover and tells him that she doesn't imagine vaguely worded ads involving punishment has ladies beating down his door. He seems quiet, rich, and boring, and he likes it when Pilot tells him she isn't scared of anything. He sends Pilot a series of wardrobe ideas, tells her not to wear underwear (followed by a wink emoji that curls Pilot's lip), what corner to stand on, and what he'll be driving.

He struggles to keep the plastic wrapped around her. He wasn't sure if he should buy it all in the same place so he went across the city to multiple dollar stores to buy shower curtains that he stapled together. His hands tremble as he tries to tear off strips of the duct tape.

Pilot walks out of her house and makes it a quarter of the way down East Pender toward Heatley Avenue before her brain starts to pester her about whether she locked the door. She's almost all the way to Hastings when she realizes it's no use arguing with herself and she heads back. Her annoyance dissolves the second she sees the house; she's lived here for a year and her heart still swells to look at it.

When Pilot first came to Vancouver she lived in a shelter, and then a tent, and then a car that wasn't hers. She lived in a house with three pregnant vegan Wiccans where the black mold was so bad the city inspectors Pilot called walked out when they saw it, said their union wouldn't let them be in an environment like that. After that she moved to an unfinished basement where a series of bedsheets on a clothesline separated her "room" from a ska band's rehearsal space.

This new house is a little two-story postwar Special, covered in purple bottle-glass stucco. The front yard of this house is small and ratty with weeds choking everything. Cracks spiderweb the stucco and it looks like a stiff breeze could pull it down in big powdery chunks. The front porch is crowded with a never-ending supply of empties that the homeless binners can't seem to carry away fast enough. Standard exterior of a punk house in Strathcona, but this is just camouflage, something to keep the landlord from venturing in for a closer look.

Over the last year, Pilot and a hurricane of new roommates have salvaged materials and fixed up the busted hardwood floors, painted, put tile in the kitchen, and installed a hardwood bar in one corner of the living room. The backyard is even better, there's a huge vegetable and flower garden, a big plum tree, and a little greenhouse where Pilot grows tomatoes. Benefits of living with some budding carpenters and landscapers.

She won't let herself put the key in the lock because she knows later she'll convince herself she somehow unlocked it by checking like that. She turns the knob and pushes but the door doesn't budge. Her satisfaction evaporates when she turns to leave and sees her landlord's son walk around from the side of the house. Her landlord is a failed hippie who didn't manage to alienate his parents enough in the sixties, so they left him a bunch of properties when they died. He's a wearer of socks with sandals who once told Pilot, straight-faced, that an infestation of raccoons in the attic was a standard feature of a heritage house. His son is the type who asks his dazed-looking girlfriend to hold his shirt before he fights someone outside a nightclub. Pilot used to sell drugs to people like him and he makes the bottom of her stomach drop out.

"What are you doing here, Jimi?"

"The backyard looks amazing. How long have you been working on that?"

"You have to let us know when you're coming by. You know that."

"Just business, huh? That's cool. I came to talk about your rent increase."

He's standing too close to her. His breath smells like those mouthwash strips that dissolve on your tongue. "You can't give us another rent increase, your dad just gave us one."

He smiles like he just silently farted and no one has smelled it yet. "Yeah, see, when you didn't complain, I knew I had to come down here. I'm like, *Dad, that house is a fucking pit, no way will they pay more rent.* So when you just paid up without bitching, I thought for sure you were growing weed or something. And then I saw your backyard. Walked through the house too. Sweet setup you got, but you didn't ask to make all these changes."

"What do you want?"

"Three hundred dollars per month paid to me, and my dad doesn't have to know how I suddenly want to move into this house."

Pilot's block has three houses on it full of dude anarchists. If a car backfires, six of them run into the street, hoping the revolution has started. Of course, none of them are around now to hang Jimi from a lamppost, there's just Pilot's ancient next-door neighbor who's come to her window to make sure she's okay. Pilot gives her a little wave.

"You'd never live in this house or anywhere around here."

"Of course not, my condo is totally the bomb . . . but I could have some great house parties here before I decided it wasn't for me. My dad respects my life journey. Your band could play the parties or something. You're in a band, right? Everyone in East Van dresses like they're on their way to band practice."

"Three hundred dollars is too much. I can't swing that, none of us can."

Jimi's eyes flicker over the new sleeve tattoo that glistens on her arm. "Nice ink."

Pilot fights the urge to tuck her arm behind her back. She saved for months to get the work done, and the artist cut her a break on the price. None of this is Jimi's business. She grinds a thank you between her teeth.

"Hey, I know how hard it is to get by these days; it's a good thing you're so industrious, you'll figure it out. Or you can get kicked out and wander from shack and shack to fix them up before they get torn down. Like a shitty East Van Johnny Appleseed. We got a deal or what?"

She could explain it to her roommates tonight and they'd all be angry for a while, but they'd just move on. She likes her roommates, they're kind people who don't make her feel like she needs to padlock the door of her room. One of them just got a job in a kitchen and has started bringing home Cuban sandwiches for everyone when he gets off work. Pilot will figure something out, anything to get Jimi and his plastic mint breath away from her.

"Deal."

Pilot picks up shifts in four bars along the Hastings strip and one illegal booze can above a closed artisanal butcher shop on Powell. Tonight's shift is at Dumpster Fire, the newest and by far the nicest of them. Dumpster Fire is a gentrification special, once a hot underground club, now home of the third-best burger in Vancouver. Unlike her other workplaces, this bar doesn't smell heavily of bleach and rot, and no fights break out that aren't solved with sarcasm.

Tonight it's only half full, and Pilot is thankful for the quiet.

The soundtrack inside is third-generation alt-country. Drinkers periodically interrupt the flow of conversation and hold their phones up to identify a song. The beer taps are topped with doll heads and the walls are dotted with flat-screens. The TVs play clips of skateboarding injuries, old chat line ads full of women with giant eighties hair, and YouTube stars giving commentary as if they're astonished or angered by everything in the world.

Charlotte, the other bartender working tonight, finishes lashing her dreads into a thigh-width ponytail and frowns as Pilot checks the time again. "You okay?"

"I guess I am. I'm meeting that guy."

"Creeptastic?"

Pilot nods.

"Gross." Charlotte slices bar fruit while Pilot pulls a pint for herself. Charlotte shifts uncomfortably. "Did you get my text?"

Pilot nods and slurps foam off the top of the glass. "Yep. I can cover your shift, no problem."

"Thanks, I wouldn't ask only my mom comes into town tomorrow and she's really freaked out someone is going to, like, abduct her as soon as she gets off the bus, you know? Small-town moms are scared of everything, I guess."

"Yeah, my mom's scared of everything too."

Charlotte is six foot one and wide, with biceps built for crushing. Pilot has seen her lift full kegs one-handed, toss drunk bros out onto the street like they were inflatable dolls. With her hair tied back like that, she looks like a Geiger painting. She is sure to give her mother city confidence.

"You texted me this guy's details, right? Phone number? License plate?"

Pilot nods, takes a drink of the cold and bitter beer, something local named after a cartoon she's never watched, and sets the glass behind the bar. "Watch this for me? I have to change."

Pilot heads to the storage room, waving at the kitchen staff as she walks past. She stowed her backpack full of slut clothes in the corner earlier, behind stacked flats of cheap pilsner. She thinks about her mother, a woman she dearly hopes has a rich interior life, who has said about ninety words to Pilot, ever. Pilot actually thought she saw her dad in the bar at the Balmoral Hotel two nights ago and she nearly fainted, but it was just someone who could have been his twin: long wild gray hair, wiry bordering on skeletal, and dead eyes like a shark.

She hasn't seen either of them in eight years. Last time she'd been crouched in their little kitchen listening to her father explain himself to a poor legal aid lawyer who'd been foolish enough to make a home visit, foolish enough to try and help her dad.

"Let me tell you something right now—these charges against me are bullshit. I picked her up hitchhiking, no panties, and her skirt was so short you could tell she kept it shaved down there. She told me she wanted it, so I pulled off the road and gave her one. Tell you the truth, it was the easiest piece of ass I ever got."

Her mother was sitting next to him staring at her hands gripping her coffee cup. Her husband snapped his fingers and she jumped, coffee spilling a little into the saucer, lit a cigarette for him, and handed it over. Pilot packed a bag that night. She was sixteen, with a fake ID and enough money saved for a bus ticket.

Pilot pushes those thoughts away, hard. She ditches her jeans and a torn Sepultura T-shirt, changes into the slut clothes, and walks back out into the bar. Charlotte has put a beer mat over the top of her glass. Pilot takes another sip, thinking the beer tasted better when she was dressed more like herself.

Charlotte raises her eyebrows at Pilot's wardrobe change, but a big group has come in and they're too slammed for her to comment. Pilot doesn't notice the time pass until she's nearly late.

"Shit, mind if I ditch out a little early?"

Charlotte waves her off. "Yeah, I got this." She takes Pilot's hand. "Be careful, okay? I really need you to cover that shift. Hey!" She's raised her voice and glares at a table sitting close to the bar that's started to get a little rowdy. They turn around, see her, and immediately quiet down.

Pilot heads out the door, pushing past a clot of smokers. She's glad someone like Charlotte has her back.

Pilot hustles down Hastings Street; her slut skirt keeps riding up and she's worried that she'll be late. She pulls out her phone and checks the time. There's a new text from her boss at one of the other bars she works at: *The ceiling over the bar collapsed. And part of the floor. Don't come to work this week.* No point in asking for an advance on her check then.

There's a mailbox on the corner and she wants to knock it over and stomp it flat, or pick it up and throw it through a car window. She counts to twenty instead, spaces the numbers out by muttering *Motherfucker* under her breath. Her footsteps could crack the pavement by the time she reaches the meeting spot, where she lights a cigarette, takes deep, starving drags.

She leans against the shuttered window of a paint store. A white two-seater Porsche convertible with the top down slows in front of her. She's about to yell at the driver to move on when she realizes he isn't looking at her, but at the storefront. Regardless, she gives him the finger and he speeds away. Another property developer wearing sunglasses at night, rolling down Hastings Street, probably touching himself while looking at vacant buildings.

She's just ground out her cigarette when a car pulls up to the curb. The driver lowers the passenger window and asks her if she does Greek. She can't remember what she's supposed to say to him so she opens with a joke.

Now, he's trembling slightly under the full moon, kneeling in water gas-slicked by the tankers floating offshore.

The plastic wraps her up tight, but her face is exposed, head pointed toward the water. Pilot can't resist it anymore and opens her eyes.

She thinks that if he was really going to kill her, he probably would have done it by now, and she unclenches her fists a little. She rolls her eyes back and looks across her forehead at him. A wave hits him with enough force to splash his face; water flies into his open mouth and he chokes a little. Pilot almost laughs and closes her eyes before he catches her. She doesn't mind this location. The sand is more comfortable than being laid out across tree roots in Stanley Park, or against a stinking dumpster in an alley. She can't remember the last time she went to the beach.

Pilot doesn't know if it's some ritual he's actually thought through or it's just a pantomime of what he thinks he should be doing. Whatever it is, it's taking forever. After he grabbed her throat, he ranted at her about how she's just another sheeple. She recognized some of what he was saying from *Fight Club*. Some of it he must have thought of himself, which was only a little bit worse.

Finally, she hears a little splash as he gets up and walks over. Pilot has worked up a sweat under all this plastic. She's starting to feel cold and her tattoo itches like mad. She doesn't fidget—he might get mad if she spoils the fantasy so close to the end. She can hear the jingle of change in his pockets and it sounds like he's messing with his belt. She swears she's going to demand extra if he's standing there jerking off while she's freezing amongst the sand fleas and half-buried cigarette butts.

"You can open your eyes now."

She does, and is relieved to see it's still in his pants.

He tears at the duct tape that's holding her cocoon together. She wriggles free and stands, pulls her skirt down, brushes sand off her knees. She's only wearing one of her stilettos, on her foot that has a razor blade taped to the bottom of it. She's painted one edge of it with rubber cement so she can grip it easily.

He crumples the plastic sheeting, shuffles his feet, avoiding eye contact. All the bravado seems to have spewed out of him. Pilot flamingoes on one leg, slips off her shoe, then tears the razor free and palms it, just in case.

"Can I drive you somewhere?"

"You expect me to call a cab?"

His stammering small talk starts up while she searches through his car and pretends to listen. She finds her other shoe behind the passenger seat along with her purse. Pilot digs her cigarettes out as the car rolls past grain silos, old warehouses, and new microbreweries. The Volvo is spotless and well maintained but old enough to still have a cigarette lighter in the dash. Pilot enjoys the novelty of lighting up that way.

"I'd prefer you didn't smoke in my car."

Pilot rolls the window down. "You should do something that frightens you every day, Rob."

The wind is bringing the scent of rancid chicken fat from the rendering plant toward them and she blows smoke out her nostrils to cover up the smell. Rob turns up the volume on the stereo, the one modern thing in the car. Pilot doesn't know the band but it's statement music, banjos and smugly clever lyrics about an ex-girlfriend. She snaps the volume down.

He turns onto Hastings Street a little too hard and she's pulled a little closer to him. He takes one hand off the steering wheel and she thinks he's reaching toward her. Pilot can still feel his hands around her neck, can still smell him on her. She reaches for the razor blade she's tucked between her thigh and the car seat but grabs the wrong edge and slices open her thumb. She barely feels it cut her, but it's deep and the volume of blood is substantial. Drops splash onto the ugly tan seats.

Rob pulls his hand away when he sees the blood, clears his throat. "Sorry, I was just reaching for the volume! I hope you don't think . . . I mean, I would never have really . . ."

"You owe me three hundred dollars."

He's already got it in the pocket of his coat, wrapped up with a rubber band.

"When can I see you again?" Rob looks at her so earnestly she wants to leave a bloody handprint on his face.

She drops the razor in her purse, grabs a pack of tissues, and wads a few of them around her thumb. She reaches to tamp out her smoke but the ashtray is full of loose change so she drops the butt out the window.

"I'll text you," she says as she gets out.

There's a prowl car approaching and Rob's already rolling before Pilot has the door shut.

She keeps her shoulders back as she walks home. She can feel the bruises forming on her lower back, her arms, her ribs. Jimi has left a cheap cardboard *For Rent* sign leaning against the porch. There's a Post-it note stuck to the front: *Just kidding. Don't forget my rent. xoxo.* Pilot tears the sign into four pieces and stuffs them in the recycling bag next to the front door.

The door is propped open with a skateboard and a fan is blowing the scent of weed out onto the street. Inside they've got the music playing loud—someone else must have gotten paid today because she can hear the beer bottles clinking together over the sound of the stereo. No one hears her come in and walk into her little bedroom at the side of the house.

Pilot texts Charlotte to say she's still alive, and Jimi to tell him she's got his money. Then she texts Rob to set up another date. Outside in the living room the music changes to a song that she likes. Pilot walks toward the noise, debating how many rounds she will let them talk her into.

THE ONE WHO WALKS WITH A LIMP

BY NICK MAMATAS

Greektown

Papou's apartment was on West Broadway in Kitsilano, or at least the door was. Step inside, like Manolis did most every afternoon to check in on his grandparents, and the place was Greece. White walls and fake marble floors, ANT1 news on the TV featuring politicians shouting at one another at jet-engine volume, the smells of *rigani* and lemon and oil wafting out of the kitchen. Instead of books on the shelves, cheap but well-dusted statuettes—*The Discobolus* and the headless but winged *Nike of Samothrace*, next to an old bottle of ouzo in the shape of a white-skirted soldier. And Papou, stationed at the head of the table in the living room, a pair of Greek-language newspapers from Toronto and Montreal spread out in front of him. Manolis bent over and kissed the old man on both cheeks.

"Did you get the money?" Papou asked.

"Sure, Papou, sure I did. Five hundred. I'll give it to Yiayia later," Manolis said. He actually only had a hundred dollars for Yiayia, from his job as a personal trainer. That would keep the lights on. Papou would worry if he thought Manolis wasn't rich, so the boy lied frequently. In the old days, nobody would dare have lied to Papou, especially not about money.

Once, Papou had been the man, and West Broadway had been Greektown. If you owned a restaurant and wanted your windows intact and the soft drink truck to deliver on time, you gave Papou a few dollars and everything would be all right. It wasn't just a racket, either. Papou once punched a Hell's Angel so hard the man started convulsing at Papou's feet, and it was just for saying something dirty to Rhodanthi Kostoulas, who wasn't even a favorite waitress of Papou's. And he kept the Chinese gangs, all the ξένοι gangs, off the block too. Ξένοι, the Greeks called everyone else, as if Greeks weren't foreigners in Canada.

But now there was no more Greektown. Kits was Yuppietown, and there were more vegetarian restaurants than souvlaki joints. Manolis had tried, years ago, as a big and muscular sixteen-year-old, to collect, but at his very first stop the staff just laughed at him. The restaurant was going to be shut down the following week, and the building torn down and replaced with a new condominium complex in six months. Ευχαριστώ, μαλάκας! Some protection!

Yiayia came out into the living room and called Manolis to set the table and bring out the food. There was a knock on the door and Papou shuffled over to answer it—it was his old friend Stelyo, who had a truck and a bread route. Other people trickled in—cousins Nikki and Popi, Vasso and the baby, even Rhodanthi. She came with her face all painted, and had even plucked the hairs on the mole atop her lip, Manolis noticed. She'd always had a crush on Papou, that one.

In the old days, Papou's apartment had been busy like this every night. Three chickens, or a leg of lamb. Guests brought pastries and wine. It had been a long time; Manolis remembered when Stelyo had brown hair, and Popi was thin, when Mikey and Greek Mikey were both in the closet but not the same one. They all still loved Manolis's grandfather, but not enough to come around regularly now that the old man was powerless. Nobody but Manolis lived anywhere near West Broadway anymore. They all passed the baby around—her name was Georgia, after Papou—giggling and tickling her chin, making ritual spitting noises to keep away *vaskania*, the evil eye. Can't admire or love anything too much if you're a Greek, or it'll be taken away. That was the lesson the Turks had taught the family in the nineteenth century, and the German occupiers in the twentieth.

Papou spoke in Greek, which Manolis mostly understood, but Papou was talking about people Manolis didn't know, and places he had never been. Manolis had baby Georgia on his lap, and that occupied him. He'd held all sorts of babies, but never one for so long, and never one without the constant direction and critique of three or four of his aunts.

Stelyo leaned over and said, "Eh, you know how to work this?" He had in his hand an iPod Touch. Vintage 2008. "My boy Vangelis put my old *rebetiko* records on it, but it's all Chinese to me."

"Sure, it's like a phone. It's easy."

"No," Stelyo said. "It's not." He shook his head.

"Like a smartphone. You press the screen. No real buttons."

Manolis found the list of songs and chose, randomly, "Ένας μάγκας στο Βοτανικό." "A Manga in Votaniko." A *manga*—one of those swaggering men who affected limps and wore thick mustaches and pointy shoes, who patronized the hashish dens of Athens. Hustlers and ne'er-do-wells. Papou had told Manolis all about the *manges*, hinted that he had been one of them. "They're like pimps without whores," he'd told an eight-year-old Manolis, "though sometimes their girlfriends are whores," and somehow that conversation had ended with Yiayia slapping Manolis for letting his grandfather's words into his young ears.

The iPod had an internal speaker, and the volume was loud enough for mostly deaf Stelyo to enjoy, but it sent the baby crying, and the family yelling. Then Papou slammed his palm against the table and stood up. He wasn't angry though. He snatched the baby from Manolis's lap and shuffled away from the table, his legs finding some old rhythm. Papou started to dance the *zeibekiko*, his free arm outstretched, fingers snapping, his knees bending like he was a man forty years younger. The women began clapping along to the rhythm of the song. Greek Mikey flung a five-dollar bill at Papou's feet, and the old man bent low and swung to snatch it. Georgia howled, and finally Vasso clambered to her feet and rescued the baby. Papou staggered like a sailor on deck, like a happy drunk, and winked when everyone grew afraid, but then his face turned ashen and he took to one knee. Yiayia got to him first, her meaty hands on his thin shoulders.

"Τέλειωσα," Papou said. *I am finished.*

Yiayia snorted and helped him to his feet. The table cheered.

"Bravo!" Stelyo exclaimed, and like a criminal he snatched the iPod Touch out of Manolis's hand and shoved it back in his pocket.

"Enough playing," Yiayia said. When she spoke, people really listened. Imagine a classically trained contralto dedicated to telling people to be quiet and clean their plates. "George has something important to say."

Papou hadn't had anything important to say in a long while. He read the papers, he walked around the block, he even learned to use Skype and talked to the relatives he wasn't feuding with back in Greece twice a year, on Christmas and Easter. But his world got smaller as Greektown did, and he'd had little to say since Manolis was a kid.

"When I was a boy," Papou started, "I had four first cousins from my mother's favorite brother," and he named them: Manolis, Michalis, Vasso, and Nikos. Names repeat in Greek families. This is how the story went: When the Nazis came, and brought with them violence and hunger, the cousins made their choices. Nikos was a Red and joined the Communist underground, and little George helped by sneaking him food and information. Michalis joined the National Republican Greek League, which kept things in the family reasonably harmonious until the civil war. Only after the Germans left were the brothers at each other's throats. Vasso had a baby while her husband was off in the mountains as part of a Trotskyist guerrilla group. During her pregnancy, when Vasso was questioned by the local Nazi captain, she patted his arm and explained her swollen belly with the words she knew—"*Guter Soldat*"— and a smile missing three teeth from malnutrition.

"But Manolis . . ." Papou did not look at Manolis when he spoke. Big Manolis, Papou's cousin, had decided to provide for the family by joining the Security Batallions, the Nazi collaborators who were mostly just out for whatever they could steal from their neighbors. Vasso turned down the spoils Big Manolis brought to her, spit in his face, and refused his protection. "Manolis became one of them. It's been war between us since then."

"Is that why they're not in the family pictures, Papou?" Manolis asked.

Yiayia held up two fingers and made a clipping motion. "We cut them out."

Rhodanthi spoke up: "Yes, cut them out! What are you going to do about the Nazis we have now, Uncle?" Papou was not her uncle. "The new ones, from Greece?"

"Easy, easy," said Vasso, dangling the baby over her lap. "We just got her to stop crying. Don't shout."

Greek Mikey said something fast in Greek, and Mikey repeated it in English: "Greeks are like dogs sometimes, always seeing each other on the street, sniffing asses, and ignoring everything else. Ever see a dog look at a bus, like he knows how to read the sign on the side? There's a whole world out there, and we have police now, and the college kids will rally or do something. Don't worry about it. Take it easy, Papou."

"Don't worry about Nazis?" Rhodanthi said, still loud. Then to Papou: "Uncle, you have a responsibility."

Popi said, "It's not about Nazis, really. Is it? How could anyone even join the Nazis anymore." She looked to Papou, but he was done for the night, staring at his glass, into the gray fog of ouzo and water. Yiayia had moved on as well, to and from the kitchen with a pair of trays—one of small glasses, the other of bowls of rice pudding.

"They're here," Rhodanthi said. "They're in Parliament in Greece, in the police force, in New York, now they're coming here. Why does Canada even let them come over from Greece, I want to know! Let them starve with everyone else over there. They come to the store, they're looking to recruit . . ."

Papou exhaled deeply. "I read the papers. Χρυσή Αυγή opens a chapter in Montreal, no one cares. Now Vancouver? My own cousin was a Nazi, I . . ." He paused, looked over to Yiayia, then to the baby, then his eyes lost focus. "I never talk to my cousin again. Τέλειωσα."

It had taken a couple of weeks of nightly walks, but the manga was used to the snickering. It was the other Greeks who most often guffawed, pointed at him from across the street, yelled, "Hey, nice hat!" or simply nudged one another and muttered, "Μαλάκας," as he passed.

The normal white people in the neighborhood, with their

tight old-man sweaters, all-weather scarves, and arms covered in tattoos, didn't matter at all. They were just in the neighborhood to raise the rents, and to annoy waiters with obnoxious questions—*Where do you get your beef?* and *Are you people really like that movie about the wedding?* Their women were like titless little boys; like hippies from old TV shows, except that they didn't believe in free love.

The manga knew they didn't matter, because when he walked down West Broadway, normal white people lowered their eyes, suddenly very interested in their smartphones. Occasionally, one would sneak a picture or a quick video of the manga in his big hat, with one sleeve of his long jacket hanging from his shoulder, the practiced limp that ostentatiously suggested a hidden weapon or stamping along to music in a hashish den.

The manga was a modern man, his sartorial choices aside. His thoughts were still his own, even if everything else belonged to the past, to another continent. He even thought of himself as "the manga" when taking his nightly promenade down the streets. The outfit—a costume, really—helped. The fedora, the striped pants and pointed pimp shoes, the mustache he waxed and twirled at either end. Greektown was all but a memory, so it was easy to search West Broadway—Ουέστ Μπροντουέι, as they used to say with their accent—from end to end. The people knew who he was, yet nobody dared snicker at his suit. They stared, but nobody would tell him where the Nazis were, or even if they'd ever shown up for a meal.

Finally, Stelyo's son Vangelis spotted them while eating dinner out, and snuck a picture with his phone. Minutes later the photo showed up in the manga's Twitter feed. Now his walk tonight had a purpose, a destination.

The manga eased his large frame through the door of the

Dionysus Diner. "Diner" was a stretch, really. Dionysus was a lunch counter with three four-tops up against the wall. There weren't even mirrors lining that far wall; the place felt like a furnished alleyway. The daily specials were written on the backs of white paper plates with black markers, for Christ's sake. It wasn't very busy. It had opened after the decline of Papou's business, after Greektown was nothing more than a parade one day each June.

There was a girl behind the counter. Rhodanthi, who worked there, had taken the night off, but the manga had come by often enough even when she wasn't working. The girl's name tag read, Anita. *Too embarrassed to be called "Athena" by the ξένοι*, eh? the manga tsked. This waitress normally frowned and turned her head when he walked into the Dionysus Diner. This time she smiled.

"Hey, Χαλιαμπάλιας," Anita said. The manga had no idea why the last name of an old Greek soccer star was an insult, but it was something their parents used to shout at one another. Usually the girl's eyes were brown and half-dead, like a cow's. Tonight they burned with glee. She was with the Nazis now, happy her family had an edge on Papou after all these years.

From one of the four-tops, a man said, "Haliabalas! Shitty baller. Welcome to the 1970s! Nobody says that no more. Vancouver's like a time warp." The guy's accent was thick. If immigrants still arrived via boat, he'd have been fresh off of one.

He stood up. A young guy—maybe just out of his teens. Muscular, like an underwear model with a broad chest and flat stomach. The manga was simply large—a Volkswagen Beetle with arms and legs. The kid wore a black T-shirt with an odd symbol on it—a white swastika on a blue field, like the canton on the Greek flag. Χρυσή Αυγή. Golden Dawn.

The kid said, in Greek, "Get the fuck out of here, ma-fia. You dress like a *rebetiko* album cover. A Greek preying on Greeks? Who do you think you are?"

The manga laughed. "How much is she paying you?" he said, tilting his head over to the girl. The few customers at the lunch counter looked up from their coffees, interested. The four-top at the back emptied out. Two other young men, both wearing the same black T-shirts, took up positions right behind him.

"You're the one who's going to pay, μαλάκας," said the first one. These men were new in town. They weren't backing down. The manga realized that, and he was afraid.

But he was afraid only inside. The manga was outside, with his coat slung over one arm. There was a reason for that, now and then. The arm is quicker that way. The manga's knife was in his hand and slicing up into the first man's nose before anyone knew what was happening. It was like a blood-filled balloon popped in midair. Everyone started shouting, but the first man's shriek stood out. The manga kicked him in the crotch to make him stop.

The guy on the left flew at the manga and ran face-first into the coat the manga has just shrugged off his shoulder. The third man followed the first to the floor, kneeling and clutching at his comrade. The first man's hands were up at his face, blood pouring out from between his fingers. The manga glanced down and decided to take the third man's ear off, then spun and plunged his knife into the flailing second man, piercing his own long coat. He finished with a kick to the second man's head.

"I'll call the police!" Anita shouted from behind the counter. The manga briefly considered throwing his knife at her, but instead just covered the ground to the countertop in two steps, leaned over it, and smacked her hard across the face.

"Money! Four hundred dollars," he said. "And you owe me a new coat."

As Anita was falling to the floor, he said to her, more calmly, "I see another Nazi in this place, it burns down."

It was a very late night for the manga, and for his Papou. There were calls for the old man to make, and even a two a.m. meeting with a few of the friendlier police officers from the old days. Self-defense, sure. It was three on one. And the fascist with the stomach wound had been carrying a pistol. Not on him, but in a knapsack under the booth. The one with his EU passport in it.

All three of the men were named Nikos. They were being stitched up. The one guy might even be able to use headphones again one day. It would be easy for the police to get them back to YVR, so long as Anita insisted that she had seen nothing at all, not even the manga, and that the bruise from her face came from slipping on a spilled egg in the kitchen earlier during her shift. Another phone call, from Papou to her parents' home, made sure she would.

As the sky lightened Papou slept finally, his snoring audible from the living room. Yiayia came out with a plate of scrambled eggs, made the way Manolis never liked them—with olive oil instead of a pat of butter and a splash of milk. It was the first time in his living memory that his grandmother served food without a smile.

"Why you take Papou's old clothes, eh?" she asked. "Don't you have money for your own?"

"The Nazis, Yiayia."

Yiayia clucked her tongue. "The Nazis."

"Papou hates Nazis. You hate Nazis."

"You don't know what Papou thinks of the Nazis," Yiayia said. "Half his family was Nazis. Papou waves whatever flag someone gives him. Nazi, Communist, Canada. That's what's good for business."

"But he never talked to Big Manolis again," Manolis said. "Because he was a Nazi collaborator. Manolis's sister turned down his food, she—"

"Shut up," Yiayia said. Manolis flinched as if smacked. Yiayia hated *shut up*. She used to scold Manolis when he was young, telling him never to tell Mikey or Popi to shut up. *When you say shut up, your face ends with a frown; it's the devil in you*, she'd say. *When you say, "Be quiet, please," your face ends with a smile.*

"Oh, baby-*mou*," she said. "Yiayia's sorry. Big Manolis wasn't a Nazi; he was just pretending."

"Then why'd you cut him out of the picture? Why did Papou never speak to him again?"

"During the war, he went to his sister's with food and money. She'd just had her baby, little Toula. Beautiful baby. And Manolis gave Toula so many kisses and held her and told her of all the good things he could bring her, and then she died."

"But that wasn't his fault . . ."

"Manolis, he said all these beautiful things, then forgot to spit. Vasso was so angry, she sent him away." Yiayia crossed herself three times. "Then the baby got sick, got sick and died. The devil took Toula away; it was the *vaskania*. Manolis had given her the evil eye and killed a little girl. All he had to do is spit, and he wouldn't. He said it wasn't *modern*. He liked to be modern, not messing with goats and olives like everyone else. It's like he didn't want to be Greek."

"Come on, Yiayia, it was war. She was probably starving, sick and weak. The evil eye?"

"Vasso's husband was a Communist. Everyone in the village knew it. She was too ashamed to go to the priest and have him make the prayers to save Toula."

"You know that's not how it works," Manolis said.

"In Greece, that *is* how it works. Vasso wanted to be modern too." Yiayia looked over Manolis's borrowed clothes again. "It's good you're not modern."

Manolis didn't correct his grandmother. He ate his eggs quietly, and kissed both her cheeks, and shuffled out the door, one foot dragging, and got the hell out of that apartment before sunrise, before his grandfather woke up.

SURVIVORS' PENSION

BY S.G. WONG

Victoria-Fraserview

They're waiting for me as I leave the cemetery.

The hefty one gives a slight bow of the head, then grabs me by the elbow. His friend, tall, slender as a reed, gives our surroundings a quick assessment. My heart races. I know everyone else is gone. The open grave awaits the digger, the massive backhoe parked ten feet away, on the paved path.

"You were a good friend to Mrs. Lin. We saw the happy photos on her phone," says the hefty one, gaze flat. "She pointed you out to us."

"Before she died." The reedy one has a deep voice, like a bass singer.

"I don't know what . . ." I try quavery puzzlement.

"Skip the theatrics." The hefty one twists my fleshy arm in his hold until I hiss. "She told us about your insurance scam."

I bite down on my tongue, taste blood.

"And your ghost." His breath smells like cigarettes and something overly sweet, Coke maybe. "We're gonna take over the scam, then we're gonna take the ghost."

"You can't just—"

He tugs me toward the mausoleum, his companion close behind. I have a hard time keeping up. The reedy one slides past me, opens the door, checks for bystanders. His shoes squeak on the marble floor.

The hefty one shoves my shoulder, rotating me sideways as I stumble over the threshold. My face collides with the doorframe. I feel a splintering pain in my left eye, a vertical line of agony. My sharp cry echoes across two floors of empty, dead space.

I shake my head, wince at the resulting throb from my eye. "Whatever Stella told you, the scam's over. Everyone's gone."

The hefty one flicks his hand. I reel from the slap. "You're not," he says.

His partner looms inches from my face. "Heal it. Show us the goods."

Damn it. Damn Stella and her big mouth to the eighteen hells.

The big one pushes his thumb against the top of my left cheek. I smell earth and copper on his meaty hand. "Do it, old woman, or I break a bone."

No good choices. "Just . . . gimme some air, all right? I can't work with you breathing in my face."

I back up against the wall. The two brace themselves, bouncing on the balls of their feet. I want to laugh. Like I'm going to fight.

I stare across the foyer, at the wall of rectangular brass placards fronting niches full of urns and ashes. I breath in deep, focus my mind on the area around my left eye, sensing its wrongness. I hold that feeling and reach outward, to the ether. Its energy fills the spaces in and around us, invisible and indispensable. I direct a thin band of it inward, to my bruised face, until the wrongness dissipates. Slowly, the pain fades and disappears.

The reedy one's staring at me, avid. "So that's how it works."

Shit. He could see it.

"It's just guesswork far as I've managed." I mask my curiosity. He might be one of the touchy ones, sensitive about a diluted talent. Me, I been called lucky, among other things. I can do the most minor of healing. Others can do inconsequential spells. Some just aren't good for anything but seeing ghosts.

Wait a minute. I say, "You saw it, how it was done? You don't need me then?"

The reedy one crowds me. "Nhuh-uh. Ain't got enough talent for that."

His partner chuckles darkly. "Old woman, you're gonna be a gold mine." He grabs me by the back of the neck, pinching up the loose skin there, between his palm and fingers. "Mrs. Lin said you're the brains of the operation. So tell us how it worked, this scam a yours." He squeezes.

I yelp. Is this how they got Stella to talk?

I lick my chapped lips. "The girls find a good corner, look for morons driving and on their phones. When they judge it right, they pick someone turning the corner. Slow enough not to risk death, but fast enough to startle the driver. Then they step in the way, get clipped." I swallow. "We're old, we have no extra health coverage. We claim against *their* insurance. We use the physio on Victoria and 46th. She's a heavy gambler, needs the extra money. She bills up to three treatments a week, for maybe two months. No one's gonna look too closely 'cause everyone knows seniors take longer to heal. She does the fake paperwork, creates fake appointments. I do my thing. We split the money."

"So," says the reedy one, "you can heal anything?"

I push away thoughts of Stella. "I can't do broken bones, all right? No healer can, without a doctor to reset first, and no way we're involving a doctor too. But cuts, bruising, sprains, strained muscles, those I can do. Just no head injuries."

"What's the split on the take?" The big man twists the hand holding my neck.

I wince. "Seventy-thirty."

"Mrs. Lin said sixty-forty."

"That's how I split the seventy from the physio with her, yeah."

He stares at me. "How much you take in a week?"

"Each girl got maybe a hundred, a hundred and fifty a week." I have a fleeting image of my old friends, hearing me call them *girls*. It hurts.

The reedy one glares. "Chump change."

"It's enough for pin money, okay? We only got old age pensions otherwise, and they don't stretch far. Not in this city."

His partner shakes me by the scruff of my neck. "How many in a day?"

I gasp. "Not every day. The physio can only claim three sessions a week. Per patient. Too suspicious otherwise."

He's scowling. I don't know if it's the math or he's trying to be intimidating.

"Also, I can't heal that many so quickly. Mine's a small talent." The back of my neck's gone numb. "Can you let go now? I'm cooperating, all right?"

The hefty one releases me, with an extra shove to prove his point.

I rub my neck. It stings. Then I rub my nose, hard. Can't get his scent out.

He points a stubby finger at me. "That means you're making up to $450 a week, old woman. That's more than just pocket money."

"Yeah, well, I *was*. It's over now. Like I told you. Mabel and Mary and June, they were the oldest ones. They died over the past six months. Betty and Liza moved away. It was just Stella and me the past two months."

"And you went and got her killed," says the reedy one.

"It was an accident," I counter hotly. "She miscalculated. It was raining too hard and she slipped."

"Got her head bashed in." The hefty one waves a hand. "Yeah, we saw her in the hospital. We know."

"*How?*" I narrow my eyes. "How do you know her anyway?"

"She's my great-aunt," he says. "*Was*, I guess."

I feel sick.

He pokes me on the collarbone. "You're gonna run the scam again. 'Cept this time, *we* get the money."

I scowl, rubbing the sore spot. "Why should I? You gonna hurt me more if I don't? Go ahead. I can heal it. The rest is just pain. You break bones, it takes me time to heal normal, your gold mine's out of commission. You kill me, you get nothing."

"You got a son, a daughter-in-law, grandkids." The reedy one pokes my forehead, his fingernail breaking the skin.

I heal the shallow cut as he watches, lay on the bravado. "No way am I gonna do this for free."

They exchange a look, surprise clear on their hard faces.

I barrel onward: "You find six old women. No men, too whiny. Three accidents a week, they switch off weeks. Different neighborhoods. The physio's split stays the same. We can't afford to squeeze her. We split the 70 percent." I run the calculations. "If you pay your seniors 25 percent, you still get 225 a week."

"Chump change." The reedy one shrugs. "But easy money."

Stella's great-nephew is squinting at me. Clearly the smarter one. I keep my eye on him.

"I deal with the physio," I say. "If she gets wind of you,

she'll fold." I make a face. "Took me months to suss her out. No time to find another."

He gives a short nod. "Got just the place for the money drop. Ming Dynasty on Victoria at 41st. That's, what, five blocks from your son's house?"

I nod, my mouth suddenly dry. "You trust them to hold your money?"

"They know what happens if they don't." He reaches out. I cringe. He taps my forehead. "Soon as it's set up nice and smooth, we get the ghost. Got a spell caster ready to pull it into a nice little containment trap."

I frown. "What are you going to do with him?"

"None of your business."

"But it could kill me." The quavery note's not fake this time. "Or turn me into a vegetable, as good as dead."

"Not our problem."

I narrow my eyes, thinking frantically. "If I come out of it normal, I want a cut of whatever you're gonna do. It must be a decent payoff, right?"

Stella's great-nephew shoves me. "Get this straight, old woman. You may be smart enough to run some penny-ante scam, but I'm out of your league." He pokes a finger into my collarbone, twists it hard. I swear I can feel the bruise forming.

He grabs my purse, finds my phone, thrusts it at me. "Unlock it."

I do, watching my hand shake.

He takes it back, taps the screen. A low buzz from his pocket. "We'll be in touch. You better pick up or text me back, old woman."

The reedy one snatches my purse from his partner, pulls out my wallet, empties it of cash. He drops the wallet and purse onto the floor. They land with a thud, the metal purse clasp clinking against the tiles.

I watch them as they push through the doors, back out into the early-winter drizzle. I crumple against the door as soon as they peel out of the parking lot, in some low, mean-looking muscle car.

I'm spent, panting like a dumb dog. Pain flares in knees, shoulders, elbows, wrists. Of course. What else is new.

I crouch laboriously and gather my belongings, cursing my useless magic. Can't even heal my own damned chronic pain. I stuff things inside my purse, sling it over my head and cross-wise over my chest, brace against the wall to stand.

At least they left me my Compass pass.

I hobble four blocks west to the SkyTrain station. I sweat and sway with the movement of the train, thinking, thinking, thinking. Bus ride's no different. When I get home, Lauren's already there. She gasps when she sees me.

"*Lai-lai*, are you all right? Did you overexert yourself again? You look exhausted. Why didn't you call me to come get you? You know I'm done work by two."

As always, she manages to be accusatory and patronizing even while being solicitous. If she weren't so obviously *gwai*, with her red hair and green eyes, and her atrocious Cantonese, I'd swear she was Chinese.

I wave her off. "I'm fine. Where are the boys?"

"They're playing at Adrian's. I was just leaving to get them. I'll settle you upstairs first, though." She takes a gentle hold on my shoulders.

I stop, twitching her hands off. "No, no. I'm slow. Take too long to go up." I make a shooing motion. "The boys're waiting. I rest in my room. See them soon."

"All right. No rush though, okay? We'll be back in about

an hour." The front door closes with a solid thud as she leaves.

Instead of the stairs, I move to the rec room and stand at the window, just to the side, lifting away the edge of the blinds to peer out. I watch her walk under her gaudy flowered umbrella, those huge masculine strides of hers eating up the sidewalk.

It takes me forever to climb the stairs, clutching the railing, huffing and hissing through the effort. No Chinese designed these old seventies Vancouver Specials, that's for damn sure. They're clearly not for people who live with aging parents. There are stairs everywhere, long ones. I'm out of breath by the top, need a glass of water and a sit to calm my heart.

I worry at my situation some more.

Four hundred and fifty bucks a week is a decent take, sure. Multiply by three and now we're talking a serious game. Three concurrent scams, eighteen girls, 1,300 a week. *That* was worth my time. I could've continued at least another year, but truth is, after Stella's death, urgency's been hammering at me. So I shut down all the scams. If any of the others can find another crooked, half-assed healer, they're welcome to her.

I'm counting on the two thugs not having a stable of larcenous seniors at the ready, but who knows. I suppose they have family too. Still, it's gotta take them at least a couple days to get six old women, still mobile and game enough for our purposes.

Not that I have any intention of going through with it.

But it gives me a few days to sort things out. Damned if I'm letting them get anywhere near my ghost. That dead husband of mine tricked me into this, sure, but I got my own plans to be done with him.

And it's not fear that's keeping me from freedom. It's money—what else. I just needed a few more weeks from

Stella. I have a monk, ready to cut the magical tether to my parasite. All that swindled cash put toward my retirement, budgeted to the cent, and I'm a thousand dollars short of the monk's fee.

I'm *this* close.

I grind my teeth, itching to break something. Damn Stella for getting greedy. She shouldn't have demanded a larger cut. She should've had a handle on her gambling. What was she thinking, arguing with me in broad daylight? Threatening to expose the whole goddamned thing, as if anyone'd believe her. She should never have slapped me. What did she expect? Of course I was gonna push her away.

But I never meant for her to fall into traffic. That was the rain and a slippery curb. That wasn't me.

I rub my gritty eyes. Things are quickly accelerating out of my control. Gotta handle the things I can.

Used to be, when I first came to Vancouver as a young woman, you'd have to actually go to Chinatown to get decent groceries. These days, I'm only a ten-minute walk away. We've our own little community, along Victoria from 41st to 49th. The fishmonger's got as fresh as anyone in Chinatown and he's not a forty-minute bus ride away. The cheapie salon across the street from him cuts my hair for thirteen bucks. There's barbecue on the corner, fresh produce at two different stores, and a musty dollar store rip-off too. We have an apothecary when we want herbal remedies, and a London Drugs when we want the other stuff. It's not glamourous. The sidewalks are always grimy and spotted with crushed gum and wet gobs of spittle; the air smells like bus exhaust; the rain never washes anything clean—but it's home.

Joint pain or no, I make that walk every day. It's something to do with the long hours and it's good to get my grandsons out of the house. They're four years old, twins. Happy and rambunctious, dark of hair and light of eye. They take turns pulling our small, wheeled shopping cart. I'm sure we're adorable. I'm going to miss seeing them and caring for them when I'm out of the house. They start kindergarten in the fall.

"Are we going *yum-cha, Mah-mah?*" Ewan is always hungry.

"After we visit Brother Wing." I hurry them along. "We have a bus to catch first." That gets them running. Austen falls and skins his hands. He brushes himself off, matter-of-fact, not a tear in sight. That's my boy.

Life is pain, I tell them. Best get used to it and move on.

I let Austen beep my Compass pass on the reader as we board. It's a twenty-five-minute bus ride west on 41st, into the leafy streets of Kerrisdale. Wing's house is a half-block from the stop. The twins point at the tree on the corner.

"A monkey puzzle tree," I say. They giggle.

Brother Wing's house is small. I imagine it must be worth millions. I climb the outside steps to the front door, the twins scampering up and down twice before I'm done. Wing welcomes us inside. I'm surprised at how bright and airy it is.

Wing isn't actually a monk. He left the temple years ago, but it's a harmless honorific and it makes him feel better. I need him to feel good.

I settle the twins on the plump sofa in the front room, sharing their old froggy-shaped electronic reader toy.

Wing looks awkward, ushering me across the narrow hall to a smaller reception room. "I wasn't expecting you to bring your grandchildren. I can't perform the dissolution ceremony with them here."

I shake my head. "I'm sorry for the misunderstanding. I had to talk to you, but I care for them while my son and daughter-in-law work." I pause, settle my nerves. "Something's come up. I need to have it done tomorrow."

He looks at me, wary. His bald head gleams palely.

I pull a manila envelope from my bag, fat and crinkling. "I don't have the full six thousand, but I have five, now. This is two thousand if you can do it tomorrow. I'll bring the remaining three when I come back."

Ewan shouts as the frog-reader beeps a saccharine-sweet song. I look over. Austen reaches over and pushes a sequence of buttons. The reader's song cuts out abruptly. Ewan laughs.

I see Wing move in my peripheral vision, reaching for the envelope.

I pull it back. "You're sure you can do it, right?"

Wing raises a brow, calm. "You came to me. I told you the odds."

I realize I'm chewing on my lip. I straighten up, relax my jaw. "I just want to make sure. It's a lot of money for a risky result."

Wing sighs. "I've been up front about that from the start."

I nod. "It's just . . . I don't know how the ether works. I only know how to use it." My face tightens. "Barely."

"Wouldn't matter," he says. "Healing's not spell casting. I'll be cutting the tether to your husband, simple enough. Since you're only the secondary host, you should be all right. As should he." Wing pauses. "That's what you want, correct? You don't want him permanently dispersed? Because that's a different price. Much bigger risk to you and his main host."

I think of her. Winnie. Frank's American mistress. His host. "No, I don't want to be responsible for that. I just want him to stop siphoning life energy from me."

"It's more common than you think." Wing shrugs. "Ghosts are becoming rarer, even in Crescent City. That's where your ghost is, right, and his host?" I nod. "Energy tithes there are costly. All that infrastructure."

I blink at him.

He frowns, takes the money from me. "One thirty, tomorrow."

I'm abruptly light-headed.

We make our goodbyes and I take the boys back eastward on another bus, then *yum-cha* at the corner dim sum shop, as promised. I'm inside before I remember.

Ming Dynasty.

Too late now. The staff greet us with smiles, showing us to a table near the fish tank. Distracted by worry, I let the boys order their favorites. Soon, our table's filled with enough steamers and plates for six full-grown adults. I'm so busy cleaning faces and wiping hands that I don't notice company until he pulls out a chair.

"Hungry little monsters."

I gasp, swiftly cover my terror with a fastidious manner. "Boys, this is *Pau-pau* Stella's great-nephew. Say hello."

Ewan remains silent, staring and suspicious. Austen obeys in a whisper, cringing away, moving closer to his brother.

"We're just finishing up and I'm afraid this table's a mess," I say. "You'll be better off at a different table." My heart's hammering so hard, I think I'm going to vomit.

He's taken the remaining chair, between me and Austen. He ruffles my grandson's hair. Austen scrunches away. Ewan begins to cry.

"That's enough." That damned quavery note again. "You've frightened them. Please leave." I move to Ewan, pull him up, slide onto his chair, and hold him tight in my lap. I draw Austen into my side.

Stella's great-nephew shrugs. "Making sure you understand your priorities." He rises, saunters to a different table, sits with his back to the wall. A waiter places a Coke and a plate of rice and *chah-siew* in front of him, then backs away with a nervous nod.

None of the staff will meet my gaze.

I pay the bill hurriedly and take the twins home, searching the bushes we pass for lurkers, looking over my shoulder, wondering if the reedy one's set up to ambush us. I fumble the key in the door, lock it firmly behind us. I can't stop trembling.

When I'm ready, I put on an old DVD of that strange blue dog the twins like so much and pull out my phone. In the kitchen, I take a long, deep breath, then tap my son's contact.

"Hi, Ma. What's up?"

"Listen, *a-jaiy*, can you take tomorrow off? I have an appointment. I want you to stay with the boys."

"What kind of appointment? What time? Lauren's home by two thirty."

"It's nothing serious, don't worry. I want to see a medium, but she's way out in Coquitlam. It's a long way, but Mrs. Chiu, you know her? She says she's worth it."

"Ma." I picture his boyish face, that half-grin, half-frown when he's exasperated.

I firm my voice: "Christopher, I want it to be you. For the boys. Would it kill you to take a day off for them? You're always checking your phone anyway, even when you *are* here." I huff. "Call it working from home. I don't care."

He laughs. "Okay, okay, don't guilt-trip me."

"Mother's prerogative."

"Fine. I gotta go. Bye, Ma."

I swallow past the thickness in my throat. "Goodbye, *a-jaiy*."

I hang up, go sit between the twins again, pulling them into the circle of my arms. I don't want to let them go.

* * *

My heart sinks soon as I knock on Brother Wing's door—when I abruptly register the scent of cigarettes and Coke. Copper and earth.

The door opens before I even have a chance to turn tail. Not that it would matter.

Wing doesn't even have the decency to look ashamed. He pulls me inside. The thugs are in two armchairs by the window in the front room. They stand when I enter. I doubt it's from manners. Wing ushers me toward the sofa, pushes me to sit. I hiss at the jolt of pain in my knees.

The reedy one kicks the wooden coffee table out at an angle, then sits on top of it.

Wing leans against the archway, half in the hallway, watching.

Stella's great-nephew drags a straight-backed chair from the room across the hall, plants it two feet from my knees.

"How do you know Brother Wing?" I say.

His hand flicks out, quick as a snake. My head snaps back at the impact. I rub the stinging patch on my cheek.

"Cut the shit, lady," says the reedy one. "You tried to fuck us over." That smooth bass voice, so at odds with his words. "You have any idea how much we can sell your ghost for?"

I shake my head. "What's his cut?" I point at Wing.

Stella's great-nephew kicks my foot. "We ain't here to negotiate, old woman."

I grimace at the *zing* shooting through my knee.

The reedy one sits back, smug.

I clench my fists against the urge to slap him. "Haven't you ever wondered why ghosts were banned in Canada?" I say.

"I know my history," replies Wing, bland as you please.

I speak directly to Stella's kin: "Too many people tethered

to dead World War Two soldiers, driven mad by grief and shell shock. When you try to break a tether between ghost and host, the host could die or become separated from their soul. They may as well be a vegetable, then. Not to mention, the ghost usually disappears for good. It's called a *dispersal*, you know. Tethers are serious business.

"My dead husband told me all about it. Crescent City's really the only place left with a strong culture of ghosts. They got the real deal—healers, spell casters, ghost catchers, monks and nuns for reincarnation, all that stuff." I meet his flat stare. "The rest of us out here? We're just making shit up. We don't have any formal training. There's no guarantee this is gonna work."

"Brother Wing explained it." He shrugs. "High reward, high risk."

"Yeah?" I say. "And you trust him, do you? Guy's got zero training in this and you trust him to capture a ghost from thousands of miles away in the ether and keep it for your highest bidder?"

The big man smiles. "He's family."

I gape at him.

"I *have* training, actually," says Wing. "I completed a full conjurer's degree at the temple in Crescent City, as a matter of fact. Lied to cross the border. There're only a few collectors up here, but they all need a decent spell caster to help use up their ill-gotten ghosts. It pays the bills quite nicely."

Damn it. If I weren't so bloody terrified, I'd be laughing my poor head off.

"What's so funny, old lady?" says the reedy one.

"Are you family too, then?" I shake my head, feeling well and truly had. "Stella's really got the last laugh, doesn't she?"

Her great-nephew shrugs again, turns to Wing. "Let's do it."

"Wait, just wait. Can you at least tell me what my death is going to bring you?"

He growls. "Jesus, old woman, cut the melodrama already."

"Six figures, at the low end," Wing says. "Some have fetched a million. Like you said, they're illegal here. Some people want special spells, big ones, and ghosts are the key to those." His face is placid. "Which reminds me." He comes forward, pulls my purse above my head. "Three thousand, you said." The large envelope crinkles as he pulls out the money. The reedy one stands, expression eager.

I sit, numb. I can't believe it never occurred to me to sell my husband's ghost.

They leave me on the sofa. I think over my choices while I watch them move furniture, clearing space around me.

Wing returns from wherever he's squirreled away the cash, face still bland.

I say, "Will you abide by our original deal, at least, Wing?"

"Your wishes, you mean?" He nods. "It's easy enough."

Stella's great-nephew finishes drawing the blinds. The room grows shadowy. "What wishes? There something extra we gotta deal with?"

"No," I respond. "If I die, he said it'll look like a brain aneurysm. If I'm a vegetable or I go crazy, I'd just as soon die the same way."

The reedy one looks impressed. "Fuck. You can do that?"

Wing nods. "It's actually a pretty easy spell." He peers at Stella's great-nephew. "I call 911. I say I was teaching her meditation, to help with her chronic pain. Next thing I know . . ." He mimes shock, then resumes a mild expression. "Her family gets her body, etc. All above board."

The reedy one shrugs. "Fine with me. Don't gotta take care of the body."

The smarter one, though, he considers me for another beat. "What if you're fine?"

I glare. "Don't patronize me. We all know how this ends."

He nods, turns away.

You'd think I'd be frightened or sad—or angry at the thought of dying at the hands of three heartless assholes. But what's the point?

I planned it out as soon as I discovered Brother Wing last year. Started up the health insurance scam. Bought a life insurance policy. Socked away money like a madwoman. Had the will drawn up, nice and proper. Spent as many waking moments as possible with my little monkeys.

I clench my hands, thrust away thoughts of them now.

I let myself smile, just a little, imagining Christopher's bewilderment at the windfall: five figures placed in low-risk bonds, a separate trust fund for the twins—and a million-dollar life insurance payout. Enough for him to buy that ugly house outright.

Oh yes. I knew where I was headed. And why not?

Life is pain. Best to move on.

THE THRESHOLD

BY R.M. Greenaway

Waterfront

Blaine is out before daybreak, shooting the city as it begins to stir. He's up on the curved Main Street overpass, leaning on the rail above the train tracks. A cold, quiet morning.

No, not quiet. The docks are crashing and beeping. There's a howling noise he can't source—omnipresent, the sound of industry, and the ruckus of wind in his ears.

There's the whiff of the strait waters, and no signs of life at this hour, except a wandering methhead down at Crab Park, minding his own business. And of course the pigeons, great flocks of them rising and settling.

He casts the eye of his telephoto at the harbor. Endless good imagery down there. Fuck the beauty of mist, water, and blue-layered mountains—it's the man-made chaos he's after, badly coordinated prime coloration, chipped and rusted, bent and broken, to fill the pages of *City*.

He focuses on the tracks, then sweeps toward the harbor, at mammoth container cranes fouling the North Shore view. Pans down across Canfisco, the sprawling red fisheries plant, to the more immediate moored tugs, blackberry bushes encircling a parking jetty, sleeping tankers. Then, with a jerk, back to the bushes.

He adjust his stance, zooms, switches to manual focus to fight the interference of dumpsters and razor wire. Is that an arm sticking up from the brambles? Or driftwood? Too distant to say, even zoomed in to max. Probably just a trick of the light.

Still . . .

Like any good mystery, this has to be checked out. What would be faster—continuing along the overpass and zigzagging down on foot, or returning to his car on Powell and driving along Waterfront Road?

He chooses the wheels. In minutes he's entering the parking jetty he had seen from above. He doesn't drive right in, but parks near the entrance. If it's a body in there he has to tread lightly, to not mess it up for the cops.

From the safety of his car he studies the area. Nobody down here. Not even a hobo, not even a pigeon. Skies are brightening, but the sun has yet to rise. The arm or stick in the brambles is not visible from where he sits. He's got to leave his car to be sure.

Blaine walks over, clutching his camera bag, and stares down at the man.

Dead. The body lies on its back, spine arched over lumpy ground. Dark clothes, soiled and gored. Face to the sky, eyes open but past caring. Bloodied nose points toward the mountains to the southeast. One leg is on the pavement, the other lost in the arching, tangled nastiness of blackberry stems. The arm that flagged Blaine's attention is sticking up, wedged in the thicket, and the hand dangles at the wrist.

Must call 911. Blaine snaps to life, digs in his pocket for his phone, can't find it, and realizes it's in his camera bag. He swings the bag off his shoulder and kneels to unzip it.

Glancing at the dead guy again, it occurs to him, this is the epilogue he's been looking for! The final shot. He squints at the sky. The lighting is intense but fragile, filtered by mist, in peril of sliding into mediocrity once the sun pops over the mountains and the rays lose their dramatic slant.

He switches lenses, chooses the 50mm, no zoom but great for low light conditions, and amazing depth of field. Something large is moving at his back and he glances around, but it's just the dawn creeping over the tarmac as the planet rolls. The rays pierce the clouds, and Blaine moves with anxious speed, worried more about the light than the assailant who could be still lurking about, knife in hand.

But unlikely. This is the morning after. The dead guy is leftovers from the night's fun, and the knifer is long gone. He's a gang guy, by the looks of him, sparkle of bling at his throat. It's a drug deal gone wrong, or turf wars, or he got jumped for his wallet. Happens.

Telephoto packed away, 50mm out, along with a brief pause: what if Blaine is caught here and accused of the crime? He shakes his head, standing now, attaching the new lens. It clicks in place, and he checks the glass for specks. He's still thinking about consequences. He's still thinking about 911. But not before he gets his prize shot.

So long as he doesn't touch anything, no blame, no sweat. He steps back to get the whole body in the viewfinder, but decides a close-up would be cleaner, more dynamic. He shifts the ISO down far as he dares—doesn't want grain—and inches in closer. The body is a white male about his own age, early thirties, in expensive black jeans and pricy Nikes, leather jacket awkwardly shoved up to the waist, gray T-shirt underneath steeped in blood. Hair is buzzed short except for a fashionable bit of forelock that lifts in the breeze.

The dead man twitches, and Blaine gasps aloud.

Not dead, but dying. Blood still creeks from the nostrils. The head tilts so the open eyes are taking in a sort of upside-down view of the exquisite skies, a gathering bank of clouds.

It's the dying man's hyper-awareness that fascinates Blaine. The open eyes, the rising sun, death, a fabulous convergence. He edges around so he can see the face directly. Within arm's reach, fingertips on pavement, he says, "Mister? Can you hear me?"

The irises swim, and though the pupils don't shift to focus on Blaine, they seem to search and sharpen. The mouth moves, just a feathering attempt.

"Don't worry, bud," Blaine whispers, "I'll get help."

He squints up. The light is blurry but evolving, about to spill. Two minutes, three max, before the rays slice over the ridge.

Blaine fumbles with the Nikon, checking settings. His heart is thudding. The air is salty and brisk, warm in the sun and cold in the shadows. Gulls circle with thin cries. He crouches and takes three fast setup shots, bracketing the exposure.

He checks the tiny images on the monitor, imagining them enlarged and cropped. It's an interesting angle, with restless water for a backdrop, wobbly splashes of red and blue bleeding off boats and cranes, the dying man angling into the foreground and tapering away to an out-of-focus thigh. Even if he's overestimated the end result, even if the visuals stink, the concept remains dynamite, and Photoshop will do the rest.

Sun rakes across the water. It touches the dying man's hand. It spreads its gold down the arm clad in leather, seeking the face. Safe now, prepped, another minute to wait, Blaine calls 911. He gives directions. The operator wants to keep him on the line, but that precious moment has arrived, and Blaine needs both hands. He's done his duty. He interrupts the questioning, promises he'll wait right here, and closes the call.

Then squats, camera supported on knee, molding his body into a tripod. He's got the man's face in the viewfinder. He shifts closer till he's framed those eyes, waits till they're soaked in amber, brilliant and pure.

"What are you seeing?" he whispers. *Snick.*

The sunlight spreads and dulls, a stone-cold stillness comes over the man, and from a distance the shrill rise and fall of sirens approach, one, two, three, like a chorus of angels coming to take him away.

What a morning. Minutes after the call, the police and paramedics noisily arrive in fleets of strobing light. Shunted to the sidelines, Blaine catches a few more action shots before he's told to cut it out. A uniform tells him to hang tight—Detective Dixon will talk with him shortly.

Dixon turns out to be a bulky woman with messy brown curls, tired eyes, and mannish clothes that look hastily chosen, like she's been flipped out of bed without warning. She leads the way down the road, into the chilly interior of the Canfisco building, the only nearby shelter from the threat of pending rain.

Inside, fishery staff are being questioned in various locations. Dixon and Blaine go upstairs to escape the noisy machinery of the fish plant, into a large lunchroom. The swing doors wheeze shut behind them. In one corner, a woman who might be a janitor is being questioned, struggling with her English. Dixon and Blaine take a table at the far side of the room.

The detective unbuttons her coat, then flips through a small notebook. She searches her pockets, finds a phone, and a pen, places both on the table in front of her, then tucks the phone away again. Finally says, "So." She looks at Blaine with distant interest. She studies her notes again, appears to hold her breath, exhales, and out it comes in a blurt of indifference: "Your name is Blaine Burrows and you're an artist and you live on Union Street, is that correct?"

Blaine agrees it's correct.

Dixon says, "What kind of artist are you?"

He doesn't like the way she flattens the noun. "Visual."

Dixon seems to doodle in her notebook. Seems to be etching triangles, over and over, triangles within triangles, and doesn't ask for elaboration.

Blaine says, "Digital photography, collage, cyber-manipulation. Cold kind of art, my dad called it. His name was Stan Burrows, maybe you've heard of him?"

Dixon shakes her head.

"One of yesterday's celebs. Big in the photographic world, mostly landscapes. The old silver halide dynasty, black-and-white, chemical trays, red lights. Amazing how far we've come, hey? Too bad Stan didn't live to see that my *cold* art is being published too. This fall. The collection is called *City*. That's all. *City*. Lot of structure, not a lot of people shots, 'cause that's been done to death. But they're in there, like puzzle pieces, just part of the chain-link, right? Or the asphalt, or the puddles. Except for on the cover I've got an old guy. I met him on Alexander. He was sitting on the curb, mad as a hatter. Fabulous cover, 'cause it's man *as* city, right? Bang, centered, all face, like this." He crops his own face with his hands to show the detective his focus. "Pale-blue irises, shiny like moonstone, shocking against dark dust and wrinkles. Symmetric wrinkles, like a network of streets and alleys. Super super high-res with just a small glitch over one pupil. Titled the shot *Pixelize*. Play on words, right? Pixel . . . eyes."

Dixon says nothing. Blaine watches her, but his mind is

elsewhere, moving between the book launch and the shot he's going to load tonight, highlights and shadows tweaked. His heart still hammers like he's won the lotto. He'll call it *Threshold*, back of the book, the visual he's been looking for, the perfect exclamation point to end his five-year collection of urban blowdown. *Threshold*. A lead-in to Book II?

Dixon says, "So what brought you to this particular parking lot?"

"Chance," Blaine says. "Was out at dawn, taking shots. Up on the overpass, scanning the harbor and tracks. Viewfinder caught what I thought was a body. An arm, anyway. Zoomed in, went, *Oh my god*. Drove right over and checked. Called 911."

He smiles at her, wanting her to smile back. Even women of her age are taken by him, and flush pink when he turns it on. He's a good-looking guy, and he knows it. But cold shoulders make him nervous, and he doesn't like being nervous.

"What time did you first spot the guy with your zoom?"

Blaine blinks. He places his hand on his camera, as if to shield it from flying debris. "Just about sunrise. Sorry, I never thought to check."

"Sure. Well, let's do it this way. Your call came in at 5:54. That help?"

Blaine shifts in his chair. So he hadn't called 911 as soon as he might have, and it hits him, the proof is time-stamped on the chip. But a minute here or there wouldn't change the end result. The only difference was that he had seized the chance to immortalize a nobody. If anything, he should be thanked.

He says, "Took awhile to drive over, then to find him. I guess five, six minutes from the time I spotted him to making the call."

Dixon makes a note. And then, oddly, she seems to drift.

Big woman, yet light as a bubble. She's watching him, but seems abstracted. Her face is more interesting than Blaine had first thought. He imagines her on the cover of Book II. Stark, artificial light coming in from the side. Maybe even backlit to shadow. *The Soul of Authority.*

But back to his immediate problem, he decides to protect himself with a little white lie: "The guy was dead when I got here."

Her brows hitch without interest, like she doesn't get it and doesn't really want to. She's jaded beyond care. She sits here, half-asleep on the job, thick as mud. He mentally throws a frame around her jowls and brows, cutting out the extraneous, keeping to the theme of face as metaphor. He's nailing down the brand. He'll run it by his editor when he's done here today. Meanwhile, get on this lady's good side, ask if she'll sit for him.

She says, "You see anybody at or around the scene? From the overpass, say, or as you were driving in?"

"No ma'am. I only wish." He slouches, hooking bicep over chairback, showing off his hard-earned muscles.

She almost smiles, finally thawing. He's got her.

He says, "Detective, I know I'm being nosy, but any idea what his story is? Drug deal gone wrong?"

Dixon surprises him with a fairly concise answer: "Drugs, oh, for sure." She closes her notebook, rubs her nose, and says in the casual way of shutting down, "Get any good sunrise shots?"

Just being polite, but the question galls Blaine, pulling him out of his reverie. He straightens. "No *sunrise* shots, no. They're kind of *done.*"

"Done to death," Dixon murmurs.

It's an echo of his own words and it startles him. Now

she's the one doing the flirting, a twinkle in her eye. She says, "Take any pictures of the dead man?"

Blaine hesitates.

"It's just, I see you don't have your telephoto on." She's pointing at the Nikon. "Not much distance with those 50 mils, is there? I take it you switched lenses, sometime between the overpass and now."

Her stare is piercing into him, and for the first time he's afraid.

"You got me," he admits with a boyish shrug. "While I was waiting, I got a shot or two. Hope that's okay."

He won't tell her it's going in a book. He doesn't know the legalities at this point, and doesn't want her to shut him down before he can talk it over with his copyright people. He's also having second thoughts about putting her on the second book's cover. Sometimes ugliness reaches a certain bar . . .

She has extended a palm, and at first he thinks she wants to shake, but it's a demand. "I'll need to take the card."

He stares. "What? No. Why?"

"You'll get it back safe and sound, Mr. Burrows. You want to give it to me now, or do I get a warrant?"

Scowling, Blaine hands over the SD card from his camera, with its shots of the golden God-seeking eyes. "I get to keep the images, right? There's a whole week of work on there."

"Long as there's nothing incriminating on it." She gestures impatiently. "Let me see the camera too."

He hands over the Nikon, still sulking about the chip. Of course there's nothing incriminating on it. Ghoulish, maybe the cops would think—they wouldn't recognize art if it waltzed up and spat in their faces—but hardly criminal. And disrespectful, but respect for what? As un-PC as it might be, cops have their priorities. They know what's what and care accordingly.

This dead man's true name to them is One Less Drug-Dealing Shithead.

Dixon has studied the camera's settings and made a note, and she hands it back. She deals with the paperwork of the seized chip, then both she and Blaine are on their feet. She's so tall that they're eye to eye. She says, "Got anything else you want to tell me, Mr. Burrows? Now's the time."

He doesn't. He hoists camera bag to shoulder and stalks out.

Dixon stands looking at the blackberry bushes and the dead man. He has been eased free from his cradle of prickles and laid out on a stretcher, eyes now closed. The coroner has told Dixon how skin-of-the-teeth close they were, that the Lang kid just missed the train. Lost too much blood. "Betcha five minutes sooner, we'd have kept him here in this mortal coil."

Five minutes.

Dixon bows her head, studying the area around the body. No weapon found, that would be too obvious, but all the proof she'll need is here somewhere. Between trace evidence and autopsy table, the evidence will point unerringly to the killer: Harrison, a fifty-three-year-old hard-nosed pile of shit, known to police for his temper. His weapon of choice is the butterfly knife, fairly rare in Canada, being illegal, and therefore the perfect signature. It'll be found on or near him, crudded with the dead man's DNA. Harrison, Dixon knows, is somewhere in the city. His body will surface in a day or so, stuffed in some back-alley grotto, and both cases will be neatly shut.

Or will they? She grimaces at the unexpected complication. Five minutes. *Who the fuck recruited Harrison, who for all his talk couldn't leave a man properly dispatched? Those murders he'd claimed ownership of, were they nothing but hot air? Had he ever actually* used *that fancy knife for anything besides yo-yo tricks to impress his drinking buddies?*

The team continues at their tasks, mostly silent now. Clouds have blotted out the sun and a light rain is starting to fall.

"Okay, Dix?" someone asks.

She waves her fingers like the pope. She watches as the body is enclosed in poly, zipped up, hoisted into the back of the removal van. The vehicle's doors bang shut, and she reflects that the dead man, Andy Lang, is—was—a windbag just like Blaine Burrows. Burrows's fixation is art, while Andy's—when he wasn't busy blowing whistles and ratting out his partners—was forensics. Infrared-this or 3D-that, technology as investigative tool. Trouble is, distracted by magic, young Detective Lang forgot that he's only human, and that like any human, he bleeds.

"Didn't I say so," Dixon tells him as the van begins to roll. "All the high-tech foofaraw in the world won't be worth a nickel if you come face to face with a real-life bullet." Or blade, in this case.

The ambulance is gone. Another VPD SUV rolls in and idles. Inside are colleagues, Detectives Khan and Purley. Dixon heads over and stands by the lowered driver's window. She doesn't speak right away, but her shrug says it all—things are not good.

Khan in the passenger seat looks like he's been crying. Purley is grim. Both men are staring at her. Purley says, "What's happened?"

The SD card in its small exhibit bag, not signed, sealed, or logged, is clutched in Dixon's fist, fist jammed in pocket. She's thinking about Andy Lang lying there, possibly alive, while Burrows pulls off his artsy shots. The chip's time stamps—

she's already confirmed them on her laptop—establish opportunity. The photos themselves—not bad, actually—have told her Lang was indeed alive. She could see it in his eyes. Cognition. And he was looking right at the photographer, like they were engaged in conversation. About what? The weather?

Probably nothing, but it left enough of a doubt to foul her day.

If Burrows wasn't such a fuckhole, she wouldn't worry. But he's complicated, his mind ticking away behind weasel eyes as he babbles about his dead father or some scrapbook project he's working on. It's a nervous babble, like verbal thumb-twiddling. What was he thinking about, staring at her, smiling like a third-rate actor? Whatever he had to say, he kept it close to his chest.

Why not share the victim's last words with the cop who's questioning him? Because those last words had spelled out loud and clear to Mr. Burrows that not every cop can be trusted, that's why.

The day is in full swing around Dixon, the port noisy with commerce. Trucks roar by under darkening skies, and the cranes are shifting containers like there's no tomorrow. She imagines the happy snapper back in his apartment, looking at his phone, wondering, *If you can't trust the law, who can you trust?* Sooner or later he'll make a decision.

Meaning time is of the essence.

She hands Purley a piece of paper, name and address. Blaine Burrows.

"Soon as fucking possible," she tells him.

Purley takes the piece of paper, looks at Khan, looks at Detective Dixon. The window rolls up and the SUV pulls out. Dixon gets a final glimpse of Khan in the passenger seat. He's staring back at her, and he looks scared shitless.

And so he should. He's here on the threshold, after all.

ABOUT THE CONTRIBUTORS

CARLEIGH BAKER is a Cree-Métis/Icelandic writer who lives as a guest on the traditional, ancestral, unceded territories of the Musqueam, Squamish, and Tsleil-Waututh peoples. Her work has appeared in *Best Canadian Essays* and *The Journey Prize Anthology*. Her debut story collection, *Bad Endings*, was published in 2017.

KRISTI CHARISH is a scientist and writer from Vancouver. She is the author of *Owl and the Japanese Circus*, about a modern-day "Indiana Jane" who reluctantly navigates the hidden supernatural world; and *The Voodoo Killings*, about a voodoo practitioner living in Seattle with the ghost of a deceased grunge rocker. Kristi writes about what she loves—adventure-heavy stories featuring strong, savvy female protagonists, pop culture, with the occasional RPG fantasy game thrown in the mix.

DON ENGLISH'S stories and essays have appeared in *Medium*, *Poetry Is Dead*, and the *Vancouver Courier*. Born and raised in Vancouver, he has spent his life under dark clouds and on rain-slicked streets.

R.M. GREENAWAY lives in Nelson, British Columbia. *Cold Girl*, the first in her BC Blues crime series, won the 2014 Unhanged Arthur Ellis Award (Best Unpublished), and went on to be released by Dundurn Press in March 2016. *Undertow* followed in 2017, *Creep* in 2018, and *Flights & Falls* is up next. The series, a character-driven police procedural set in North Vancouver, is ongoing.

DIETRICH KALTEIS is the award-winning author of *Ride the Lightning*, *The Deadbeat Club*, *Triggerfish*, *House of Blazes*, and *Zero Avenue*. Nearly fifty of his short stories have been published internationally, and he lives with his family in West Vancouver.

Malcolm Tweedy

SHEENA KAMAL holds an HBA in political science from the University of Toronto, and was awarded a TD Canada Trust scholarship for community leadership and activism around the issue of homelessness. Kamal has also worked as a crime and investigative journalism researcher for the film and television industry—academic knowledge and experience that inspired her debut novel, *The Lost Ones*. She lives in Vancouver.

Tristan Crane

NICK MAMATAS is the author of several novels, including *I Am Providence* and *Hexen Sabbath*. His short fiction has appeared in *Best American Mystery Stories*, *Hard Sentences: Crime Fiction Inspired by Alcatraz*, *Long Island Noir*, and many fantasy, horror, and literary venues. He coedited the Locus Award–nominated Japanese mystery/science-fiction anthology *Hanzai Japan* with Masumi Washington, and the hybrid cocktail recipe/flash fiction anthology *Mixed Up* with Molly Tanzer.

LINDA L. RICHARDS is the award-winning author of fifteen books, including three series of novels featuring strong female protagonists. She is the former publisher of Self-Counsel Press and the founder and publisher of *January Magazine*. Richards divides her time between Vancouver, Phoenix, and Paso Robles, California.

NATHAN RIPLEY is the pseudonym of Naben Ruthnum. Ripley's first novel, *Find You in the Dark*, was published in March 2018. Ruthnum writes fiction and criticism, and Ripley is almost finished with his next thriller.

ROBIN SPANO lives in Lions Bay, British Columbia, with her husband and daughter. She writes the Clare Vengel mystery series, serves on the board of the Lions Bay Arts Council, and spends as much time outdoors as possible. She's a member of the Green Party and a peaceful activist against climate change.

TIMOTHY TAYLOR is a Vancouver writer whose first novel was *Stanley Park*. He's since published a collection of short fiction, *Silent Cruise*, and two other novels: *Story House* and *The Blue Light Project*, which won the CBC Bookie Award. His latest book, *Foodville*, is a memoir about his life as a food critic, and his newest novel is *The Rule of Stephens*.

YASUKO THANH is the author of the novel *Mysterious Fragrance of the Yellow Mountains*, which won the 2016 Rogers Writers' Trust Fiction Prize; and the collection *Floating Like the Dead*, winner of the Journey Prize. In 2013 the CBC hailed her as a "writer to watch." Her work has been translated into three languages. She lives in Victoria with her two children and plays in a punk band in her spare time.

SAM WIEBE is the author of the Vancouver crime novels *Last of the Independents, Invisible Dead,* and *Cut You Down.* His work has won an Arthur Ellis Award and the Kobo Emerging Writers Prize, and he was the 2016 Vancouver Public Library Writer in Residence. His short fiction has appeared in *Thug-Lit, Spinetingler,* and *subTerrain,* among other places.

S.G. WONG, an Arthur Ellis Award finalist and Whistler Independent Book Award nominee, writes the Lola Starke series and Crescent City short stories: hard-boiled detective tales set in an alternate-history 1930s-era "Chinese LA," replete with ghosts and magic. She speaks four languages, usually only curses in one of them, and can often be found staring out the window in between frenzied bouts of typing.

Acknowledgments

To the contributors—thanks for your artistry and professionalism. To Ibrahim Ahmad and Johnny Temple at Akashic Books, for the chance to put this collection together. And to Eden Robinson, Emmet Matheson, John McFetridge, Hiromi Goto, Ivan E. Coyote, Jim Christy, Mercedes Eng, Steffi Grey, Shay Wilson, Lisa Jean Helps, Carly Reemeyer, the Wiebe family, Mel Yap, Peter Rozovsky, Charles Demers, Aaron Chapman, Naben Ruthnum, William Deverell, and my agent Chris Bucci at the McDermid Agency. It would have been impossible to put this together without your help, and a lot less fun.

Also available in the Akashic Books Noir Series

MONTREAL NOIR
edited by Jacques Filippi & John McFetridge
288 pages, trade paperback original, $15.95

BRAND-NEW STORIES BY: Patrick Senécal, Tess Fragoulis, Howard Shrier, Michel Basilières, Robert Pobi, Samuel Archibald, Geneviève Lefebvre, Ian Truman, Johanne Seymour, Arjun Basu, Martin Michaud, Melissa Yi, Catherine McKenzie, Peter Kirby, and Brad Smith.

"Montreal solidifies its reputation as the epicentre for Canadian noir in a strong new anthology."
—*Quill & Quire*, selected as Editor's Choice

"The best reason for reading short-story anthologies is to discover new writers. That means searching for talented editors to select the goods and, in this case, John McFetridge and Jacques Filippi have definitely delivered in this elegant collection for the wonderful Akashic city *noir* series. There are no bad stories here, but there are many standouts." —*Globe and Mail*

TORONTO NOIR
edited by Janine Armin & Nathaniel G. Moore
334 pages, trade paperback original, $15.95

BRAND-NEW STORIES BY: RM Vaughan, Nathan Sellyn, Ibi Kaslik, Peter Robinson, Heather Birrell, Sean Dixon, Raywat Deonandan, Christine Murray, Gail Bowen, Emily Schultz, Andrew Pyper, Kim Moritsugu, Mark Sinnett, George Elliott Clarke, Pasha Malla, and Michael Redhill..

"*Toronto Noir* gathers 16 tales of site-specific urban misbehaviour and despair that suggest a whole new spin on Toronto as a 'world class' city . . . It's a tour not likely to be offered to tourists anytime soon." —*Toronto Star*

"Armin and Moore assemble a collection of Toronto tales that will delight readers anywhere. Whether you love Toronto or hate it, this smart, stylish collection will suit you. Those who love the city can wallow in the fine writing about local icons; haters can feast on the city's Toronto-centricism." —*Globe and Mail*